It's Written

It's Written

BALRAJ SIDHU

PARTRIDGE
A Penguin Random House Company

To order additional copies of this book, contact
Partridge India
000 800 10062 62
orders.india@partridgepublishing.com

www.partridgepublishing.com/india

Contents

for all the ladies

who have made me

what i am today

CHAPTER 1

"Monday"

He was able to see that man's back only. That man was sitting on a green plastic chair and that made him a bit restless. Like a kid becomes, when he sees his toy in someone else's hands. He wanted to snatch that chair from him. But then his focus got shifted on a big blue drum which was placed on a table in front of that man. Perhaps it got ignored from him in the first instance. Did his curiosity about that man and an edgy feeling because of his possession on that chair, hold his whole attention that he was unable to notice it? At that point of time it was an difficult question to find answer of. He took couple of steps forward and found out that there was a tap attached at the bottom of the drum and that man was pouring some liquor in a jug. When watched carefully it was like water but the smell was pungent. He quietly took one step further. A sudden arrival of gust took his focus from that liquid and put it on the surroundings; which he earlier believed that were white walls but it was a courtyard. Much like the courtyard of his own home. It was dark night and the place was lit with yellowish light of a bulb.

"Is it possible?" He thought. He was getting very uncomfortable because of these strange transformations. He was unable to understand any of these things. "How is this possible that my consciousness get stuck with something so deeply that it can't even notice its surroundings?" It was enough to have doubt on himself. He inspected his hands and feet with his eyes. A took a long deep breath and after gaining a little faith he started looking at that man again. It seemed like he was eating meat and throwing the leftovers near a kitten sitting beside him. That kitten; he was inadequate at that point in memorizing the reason but he certainly didn't like it. That kitten suddenly looked at him while chewing bones and he felt like it was laughing at him; making fun of him. He felt quite awkward and right before he gets stuck in this feeling, the leaves of tree in courtyard started producing noise as if strong wind was blowing. While looking at the tree he found out that couple of tyres were bound with the top most branch of it. It seemed like they were of a bicycle. Which made him very uncomfortable as well as it scared him a bit. He turned back quickly and smacked his forehead with a wall. With one hand on his forehead he turned back and a sound of weak cry from his left side grabbed his attention. "This bed was not here before!" He thought but then he left-off all the questions rising on strangeness of the presence of things. He started moving towards the bed. The voice was of a woman. She had covered herself from head to feet with a sheet. He went a bit closer and she started sobbing. He moved his hand towards the sheet to pull it off but instantly there was heavy noise of utensils falling on the floor and shattering of glass. He turned back immediately but there was no one and suddenly that woman started wailing . . . .

He opened his eyes all of a sudden and got overwhelmed with the light present in the room. He took a pillow and put it on his face. He was trying to understand the circumstances. He was breathing heavily. He could easily hear the sound of his racing heart. He felt pain in his head so he put the pillow aside and laid on his stomach. Indeed, it was a dream but instead of getting relief from this fact, his mind was taking him towards anxiety. Now he was understanding it, things were getting clear. Certainly, this dream was his part; naked face of his feelings and emotions about his circumstances. Circumstances, which he wanted to change completely and forever.

"You know what you have to do. You know about your path; isn't it!" He assured himself and got up from the bed.

"No no no you are not weak. You were never weak. You can change your life. Ok, just tell me, who is stopping you? Circumstances! Finances! Or Government!" and a sudden chuckle came out with the word 'government' as if the vehicle of words went over the speed-breaker of laugh. "Does government is stopping you! Any politician!" and the impulse of word 'government' ended. He took a long deep breath—"That was all just to deceive. Your intelligence in studies, your capabilities in sports was like as if someone or something let a bird, who had just learnt to fly, have a beautiful flight and caged it forever. To let one get aware of its abilities but never let it use them." He placed his left hand on the wall and bent a little towards the mirror—"But now what is your plan? Want to do something or not! Nobody is stopping you, nor they can, isn't it!"

But it was not that easy. He felt like his own eyes were staring him. Last 3-4 years of his life got stuck in front of his eyes. Lips got zipped, perhaps it came to them that they were angry with him. He immediately moved away from the mirror and sat on the corner of the bed. While sitting he started observing his feet, shanks, thighs, which were quite muscular, in good shape and seemed like hard working. Then he started observing his hands after taking them off of his knees. They were just perfect. Their shape, size, skeleton, length of fingers & their flexibilities and depth of palm; everything was just as it should be. He shook his head after feeling weak and helpless. His face was wearing vivid frustration. This was something he always wanted to get rid from. But 'how', was still to find. He wanted to talk to himself, but with the disturbance in mind it was not possible. He wanted to settle down his thoughts; like a teacher wants the class to stay silent. He wanted ultimate peace around him. That was the situation when even the fan's air was disturbing him. He just wanted quietness, an ocean of it. He got up to switch off the fan and before sitting down, just had a glimpse of his facial expression in the mirror. Then suddenly in few minutes his back got tired, so he laid down on the floor. He closed his eyes and started doing efforts to put his mind at rest which was crowded with various thoughts. But after just couple of minutes tic-tok of table clock started knocking at his ear doors. His gradually fading frown got vivid again. He quickly got up and pulled out the battery from the clock's back and went back to his position.

Restlessness was like got mixed in blood and was circulated in the entire body. Because of the fan put at rest in the afternoon of May, a drop of sweat was forced to slip towards ear from the side of the forehead. He felt like the journey of the drop has left an indelible mark which had put his effort of getting calm in vain. Being patient he kept his eyes closed. But because of the dull and soundless noon along with the small size of the house, the tik-tok of wall clock in the corridor didn't take much time in covering the distance. He slapped his forehead approving expected certain failure and sat with back-rest against the side of the bed.

He was trying very hard but was not getting any closer to peace. No thought of anything was capable to pull him out of this disturbance. A good little nap was impractical now; but he had to find a solution. For how long he could let his helplessness & regrets rule over him? He was hauling his t-shirt, tearing his hair and plucking the pillow because of their intimidation. After failing plenty of times in containing himself he went out in balcony and stood in shade. He felt quite unfamiliar to the sight and said, "This definitely is not my home." One, he was struggling with anxiety and second there were not those walls of his home, not that 'Neem' tree and not that ceiling which was injured severely because of the excessive dampness; which were not less than friends to him. All these factors made the situation difficult for him. It was hard to handle but he tried to concentrate on the sight in front of him. After few minutes his mental condition did not but the nature of thoughts was changed a bit. He started thinking—"Such massive crowd of buildings. Tremendous number of people; how much they use to speak on daily basis! . . . . So many emotions must have taken birth with every passing moment and started finding support right away. Their life time must have depended upon the degree of belief of their respective carriers . . . . All of these people must have used to do great amount of work every day. Some people's work nurture their lives and dreams and others just earn enough food to fill the void in their stomach. Some of them will get a status they desire and some will just shatter; but life . . . ." He sighed. "How much all these things depends upon each other! It is like bacteria; they took birth in specific conditions and die when it changes. Like those flies and winged insects which take birth in rainy season, dies the next morning. A sweeper comes in the morning and sweeps their dead bodies to the side of road. These emotions, these words, these lives will get the same treatment from time."

He accidently placed his hands on metallic parapet but couldn't tolerate the heat. He moved back a little and a sudden smile emerged on his face. "Everyone is suffering in these burning times. Touch anyone and you will get nothing but misery, anger & sadness." He said while trying to capture the whole sight. He wiped his badly sweating face with his t-shirt and went in his room. The motive of getting calm was still not achieved, so with this purpose he got up and went into the washroom to brush his teeth. He was all set to try his old tactic of 'keeping himself busy' in order to attain some quietness. After brushing the precious white pearly arsenal for nearly ten minutes, he went into his room and took almost all of his clothes out of his almirah. Spread it over the entire bed and started folding them again. After some time mind got deviated and he stood victorious and got control over his stabbing thoughts.

He put his tired body on a chair and exhausted head against the wall. Then Instantly something came into his mind so he pulled out some pages from his pocket, grabbed a pen and started writing on them.

"What is this mess all about?" Santosh woke up and said it while stretching his arms.

"Aaaa . . . . actually, sometimes the way to peace goes through stupidity." Inder smiled at the end of his answer.

"Oh . . . . I got it", Santosh said it in daze but with smaller eyes and a slight nod. Then he turned to the other way and started shaking Atul in order to wake him up.

"Hey lazy, wake up, it's 3. Sunday had gone away in the midnight for another 6 days", he cried. "What will we do now tell Saturday morning. Atul my dear, wake up. See my phone, that calendar and even your phone; everyone is telling with conviction that its Monday. Come on Atul wake up, we are doomed", Santosh kept acting as if he was crying along with his own way to explain time.

"Aaaah just go to bathroom and do whatever. Just go away from me, you are so infuriating", Atul screamed.

Santosh laughed with his whole heart and Inder enjoyed the show.

"Will you do it next Monday too", Inder asked in jesting tone.

"Contact my secretary", Santosh replied in same manner while grabbing his towel.

"Hey, keep kicking his butt until he don't leave the bed", Santosh said to Inder while getting out of the room.

"Get lost", Atul shouted and a distant laugh came out.

Inder resumed writing on those drab pages. The word 'lazy' from the act of Santosh got stuck somewhere in Inder's mind.

"I never thought that I would fall in love with a slack." Anger burst out right after he picked her call instead of 'hello'. "I am getting ready, just 20 more minutes."

"You said the same 15 minutes ago. If you don't show up within half an hour I'll go home and then don't dare to ask me to meet again."

"Na na na I am coming", he pleaded.

"You take way more time than girls", and she cut the line.

"How many times I have told you to set your priorities right. You always end up doing certain things at wrong time. Get your timing right." He said to himself by standing in front of the mirror while wearing his pullover.

"Hey lazy! Get up and see if tiffins have arrived." Santosh said to Atul while rubbing his towel on his head.

Coming out of the memories Inder took his towel and went into bathroom. He laid down on the floor right after closing the door. How certain burden can make you lay down anywhere was the exclusive thing he learnt that day. For some time he kept lying on the floor and staring at the roof. This really helped him eliminating the unnecessary burden from his mind. After enjoying the bath, he came out and started reading his book but soon his concentration again got shifted to random thoughts.

"Do it quick I am very hungry". Santosh ordered Atul just to tease him when he was going towards bathroom.

Santosh kept surfing internet on his laptop and Inder on the other hand was still trying to clear his mind while just looking at the book.

After having their meals, Atul started studying and Santosh took the driver seat of his laptop.

"Which book are you reading?" Inder asked Atul to feed his curiosity.

"This bright young man will be 'Marketing Head' of Unilever in coming years." Santosh answered before Atul while slapping on Atul's plumpish bicep.

"Ok, M.B.A."

"Private". Atul replied before Santosh made more fun of him.

"Ok." Inder responded.

"Oh Sir, you too!" Santosh reacted when he saw Inder reading his novel. He turned towards Atul and said, "Atul *ji*, meet Inder *ji*, he is future marketing head of Accenture."

Everyone chuckled.

"No Santosh *ji* this is just a novel". Inder responded in the same manner and a giggle arrived again.

Just to push time Inder kept interacting with them. Small conversations kept emerging and vanishing in the air in the room. Because of lack of continuity in conversations Inder's mind was once again lost somewhere in the space of time.

"Yes, I want to do lots of things."

"I know but you have to start from somewhere."

"But I can't do these type of works."

"Even post graduates are working there. What you think about this! I am not asking you to clean the gutters."

"Well off course mom, but I can't do work in grocery stores."

"It's good that your imagination and expectations are high but no matter of its size or status; in physical world things always starts from zero. You can't start from five or eight or something."

Well, this was a fact, no doubt about that, but his mind was not ready to accept it. At that time this thought was very irritating and annoying.

He kept thinking random things while holding his book. His consciousness was moving back and forth in time while his hand was turning the pages of the time. From a distance the view seemed perfectly normal; quite and focused. It was like an unintentional camouflage. When his mind got tired of running here and there; it settled down. He sighed and felt quite relaxed than before. So he turned back the pages of his novel and started reading again.

'Harf' and 'Stephan' arrived right on their usual time.

"Hello-Hello." Harf said while entering in their room.

"Aha! The real MBA and the real MCA", Santosh responded immediately.

"But I was Stephan and he was Harf till yesterday!" Stephan said with a smile while sitting on a chair.

"No-no, no one is Stephan and Harf. The real I.Ds are 'Degrees' and 'Paychecks'." Atul's explanation left smile on everybody's face but it was thought provoking also.

Inder, with his returned presence of mind, said with seriousness, "Damn! What a fool I am, I thought its *Aadhar Card*." And everybody's smile got converted into good loud laugh.

"How was your day?" Santosh asked them both.

"Good."

"It was OK."

Stephan and Harf replied respectively.

Santosh instantly turned towards Atul and said, "Hey, MCA said Good while MBA said Ok; so why don't you switch to MCA?" In everybody's laugh Stephan's stood out.

"And when my day will go bad, you can switch back to MBA again." Stephan said smiling.

"O come on Stephan! Santosh is already more than enough to pull my leg everytime." Atul begged.

"Hey Atul, you are my darling man." Santosh didn't miss the chance again, "Don't say like this."

By interrupting the laugh session. Harf asked Inder, "You are from Punjab no!"

"Yes!" there was smile on Inder's face.

"How did you find Delhi?"

"I need to explore it enough, before answering this question."

"Yes that's obvious but it has been a week now; you must have noticed some clear differences." Santosh interrupted and Harf nodded.

"Yes why not, 'density of people per-square kilometer'." Inder replied in jesting tone. A laugh session started again.

"Nice, nice answer." Stephan appreciated while laughing.

By recognizing the expectation for a serious reply in Harf's eyes, Inder replied, "For now I have to closely observe many aspects of the city. I'll surely answer later."

"Ok, no problem. Actually I was asking because one of my colleague is also from Punjab and he didn't like the city a bit." Harf explained.

"What were his reasons?" Santosh enquired.

"Dense population off course but I think metro cities means large amount of people from different parts of the country. But the real problem is cleanliness I think, moreover more traffic means more pollution which was the another reason of my colleague for not liking the city. He said that he is from *'Patiala'* and he claims that the city is cleaner and better managed."

"Yes Patiala is." Inder confirmed.

"But that is the advantage of smaller city." Harf expressed.

"That can be the case but responsible behavior of residents makes a city better for living; not entirely, but this is one of the main factor." Inder expressed his perspective clearly.

"Ok . . . . enough for today. Let's go and relax a bit." Stephan said to Harf while removing his wrist watch and then they went into their room.

As soon as the hour hand of clock started pointing towards 7, Santosh and Atul's face started projecting sadness; Inder kept smiling by looking at them.

"Dear it's so boring life; this Monday to Friday life. I just hope to have a sight of a beautiful, lovely girl there which may fill some excitement in my weak-day life. It will be much better then and I'll go to work with freshness and joy." They both laughed on Santosh's desire.

"But if this happened then your weak ends will fill with sorrow and emptiness." Inder cautioned him.

"Yes man! I didn't give it a thought. No-no, weekends are my first love. I must have died long ago if these didn't existed." The degree of seriousness with which Santosh said this made both of them laugh.

Inder took his notebook out in balcony and took out about 5 pages and put them in the back pocket of his jeans. He went back in, placed the notebook near his other books and went out of the room while saying, "I am downstairs, come whenever you get ready", as if wanted to save himself from encounter with any question.

He entered in a STD and dialed a number.

"Hello! Dad it's me."

"How are you Inder? Everything is fine? You didn't called yesterday, your mother was worrying?" Eagerness was quite clear.

"I am good I am good. I tried her number but it was not reachable. Are you at home?"

"No I am not yet. Why you left your phone at home? At least give us the number of any of your room mates so that we can contact you." He requested.

"No I will keep calling from STD, don't worry. Tell her to take care of herself." He cleared his throat.

"Give a number so that she can talk to you. I'll tell her not to call frequently. It will be huge relief for her."

"Dad please stop it. I'll call her by myself. It's been just a week. I have to go, its time. I'll call tomorrow."

"Ok take c . . . ."

He hurriedly put the receiver down and came out of it. Everything felt like devastated. The call didn't went the way he thought to be. Something was pinching him in the chest. He wanted to go upstairs to get normal but he saw both of them coming. One could easily read the tension on his face but both of them decided to ignore it for the time being. Perhaps they didn't feel like asking.

"Did you call someone from STD?" Santosh enquired after assuming because he was standing in front of the booth.

"Yes, I called my Dad."

"You can use my phone man, no issues." He assured.

"No, it's not like that. Actually I don't want to give them any of your number yet." Inder explained.

"Did you really called your Dad or it was someone else?" Atul asked in jesting tone.

"It was Dad." He smiled.

"Ah! My another darling." Santosh pointed towards an old chevy SUV.

After wandering on crowded roads for nearly an hour and after taking a ride in 'filled to capacity' lift they entered in a hall full of people and computers. Some were wandering, some were just standing & talking to each other and others were sitting with their head phones on.

"Sometimes it feels like a control room from where we are going to launch a satellite." Inder said it as if he found his own perspective freaky.

"No man, it feels like as if many boys and girls have come together to call their boyfriends and girlfriends without letting their parents to know about it." The uniqueness of the point of view of Santosh and the way he expressed it with funny tone made both of them laugh uncontrollably.

They settled down on their seats & put their head phones on.

Inder still remembers that how certain he was not to get into this profession. His past experience was not that good in this line. Moreover he didn't have any interest in it. Instead of these factors there was pleasing smile on his face, may be because he choose it after realizing the demand of time and not under any pressure or helplessness. One thing was quite sure now that he quit worrying about the path and his entire focus was on his aims only.

He dialed a number from his computer.

"Hello! May I speak with Mr. Moore?"

. . . .

"Good morning Sir, my name is George Smith . . . .

CHAPTER 2

2nd Weekend

*H*e shifted the curtain aside.

"It's white." He looked around for a while as if he was trying to capture the scene in his eyes. She was quite too, as if trying to gulp two simple words, but with *that* sentiment he said them.

"You know it seems like it had simplified the things."

"How is that! It is actually hard to see in its presence. I think, it has made the condition difficult." She knows why he said that but she wanted him to explain it a bit.

He smiled; pulled a chair in front of the window and sat there.

"You know, sometimes a photographer darkens the corners of the photo in order to put even more focus on the subject."

"Yes."

"Same thing is with fog. It covers the less important things with its soothing white particles and puts focus only around your physical presence. Sometimes you don't need to see more than that. It blur the unnecessary things hence simplifying the required sight."

"Alright dear, and you know it's another positive point?" She asked with same seriousness.

"What?" He smiled as if he already knows the nature of her answer.

"It makes tea more enjoyable."

Both laughed.

"Yes it does."

"And do you know one more thing?" Her tone was different now.

"What?" It was not regular, so he was little curious this time.

"Sometimes you boring explanations really help me out."

Both laughed and her was a little loud.

"How is everything at home?" It had become a frequent question from some time from her side.

". . . . its bit smooth", he replied with a sigh.

"OK . . . ."

"But I know its temporary; it always has been. Its temporary nature irritates me."

"I knows it's difficult; it's very difficult. But I've faith on you that you can change it."

"Yes Soma, this faith is the reason that I am still moving. It is continuously protecting my light of hope."

"Inder" she said," sometimes I feel like you need to take some big steps; some important decisions in order . . . ."

"Yes, yes Soma" he interrupted, "I've to and I've some plans for this year."

"Ok, what are the plans then?"

"First I'll go to Chandigarh or Delhi for few months to get back on my legs."

". . . . ok". She was not expecting this, "and work?"

"I'll get the same job there. My motive is not to get more experience in this field; you know I don't like it much. I just wanted to go away from this noise, so that I can gather myself. There are heap of questions and answers of them are inside me. But I can't reach there until I get some peace."

"I don't know Inder, but my heart is beating fast as if I am afraid of something."

"I know this thought of going far is disturbing but I'll come back after few months. You know even I can't stay away for long."

"Inder . . . ."

"Yes."

"Just make sure that you are going to get better and not just running away from problems."

"I am not running." He smiled, "This is not the way I deal with problems and you know it without any doubt. See Soma, I'll come back with more energy, more confidence and with better effective plans. You know me, just don't worry."

"Yes I do", she said after gathering herself. "But I hate you."

"I love too Soma."

Smiles were exchanged; as they travelled through air to reach their respective destinations, it felt like they have made fog more pleasant for Inder.

"It's Saturday . . . .", this was Santosh's fourth shout of the day.

"What to do with it?" Santosh asked loudly as Atul threw a tape roll towards him.

"On your mouth." Atul chuckled.

"O . . . . so Atul, from where you took crash course on leg pulling?" Santosh asked.

Inder was enjoying.

"You are going good, keep it up 'hamburger'". Santosh kept his winning streak on.

"Atul laughed with folded hands and returned to kept turning pages of his magazine.

"Hey! When will we go out?" Santosh asked to Harf& Stephan while entering in their room.

"We'll leave around 7 till then hold your horses, we know it's Saturday." Harf smiled.

"Ok I'll try", he laughed, "but you know! I don't have to because I'm gonna eat 'hamburger's' head", he said the latter part a little loud.

"Santosh may I use your laptop? I need to check my facebook." Inder asked.

"O! You have a facebook account! A quite unusual thing for a man like you. A man who don't like to keep a mobile phone but has a facebook account. Ladies & Gentlemen, we present to you 'Inderjeet Singh'."

Everyone laughed.

"Come on!" Atul said, "You are acting like as if he is a caveman."

Santosh chuckled and gave the laptop to Inder.

Their reaction was obvious as Inder use to stay reserved and away from technological gadgets.

He logged In, Santosh went intoHarf's room and Atul kept reading his magazine and using his phone every now & then.

Someone was eagerly waiting for Inder on the other side.

"I've been waiting for last four hours."

"Hello Soma, I'm sorry for the late. How are you?"

"It's getting worse with every passing week. Everything feels dull."

"Soma you have to deal with it somehow." "I'm sorry that I made it difficult for you but trust me it is for better change."

"I can understand Inder but sometimes during weekdays it becomes so difficult. I wanted to hear your voice so badly, but I was so helpless."

"I am really sorry Soma but I was so stuck in that city that I wasn't able to move forward with my life; not even a single inch."

"I know Inder; I consoled myself." "I've tried very hard to put every bit of my concentration on exams, in which I almost succeed. But sometimes . . . ."

Inder took a long deep breath.

"Soma help me, support me and we will stand victorious in this hard period of time."

"Yes Inder I'm doing my best."

"Soma we are strong, we really are. Our understanding has enough strength to take us through this."

"Yes yes yes, I can, I'll support you. I can handle this." She said it in determined & promised tone.

"I promise I'll never put you in such difficult phase again."

"Ok Inder, anyways how was your week dear?"

"My Monday was very disturbing but rest of the days were normal and quite."

"Ok! That's good but what happened to Monday?"

"Nothing, my own thoughts and a nightmare."

"Ok . . . .". She said as if she doesn't need to ask anything else.

"There is still so much inside but it is gradually decreasing."

"It's good Inder, come back with the transformation you have promised."

"Yes Soma I'll." "How are your exams going?"

"Lack of concentration may will cost me 20-25 marks in previous exam."

"It's long way Soma. In the end everything will be fine. Just concentrate on the need of time. We'll get our reward for sure."

"Yes Inder don't worry. I'll do better in next one."

"I trust you Soma."

"Anyways, did you call your parents today?"

"No, I'll call them tomorrow."

"It must have been difficult for your mom."

"Yes it is, of course, but she can handle it. She had to."

"We are so stupid."

"Why what happened!"

"Grab someone's earphones. We can make call through facebook."

"Ok-ok one minute."

"I am going to call."

"Ok."

"I can see you!"

"I am glad to see you too."

She touched his face which appeared on the screen from hundreds of kilometers away.

"I love you too Soma."

There were smiles, delighted eyes, desperate desires and calmness.

"I am glad to have you Inder."

His heart started sinking. Heart beat felt like getting deeper and deeper. His heart was getting heavier. It caused burning sensation in his eyes but he controlled it and stopped it from producing any visible effect. He didn't want to convey any weakness.

"I am glad too." His eyes were lost somewhere.

"What happened?" She asked.

"Naaa it's nothing. Concentrate on rest of your exams."

"Yes I'll, don't worry."

"Atul darling, stop reading your boring magazine and get ready." Santosh shouted.

"Who is this?" She asked.

"Ah! He is Santosh; wildly cheerful personality." He smiled.

"My goodness! Someone is having important confidential conversation. I am really sorry for disturbance and one more apology for the person on the other side." Santosh smiled.

"Hey Santosh the other person says 'It's ok'."

"Alright then, I'll disturb you every-time if you liked it." He laughed and others followed.

"Ok Soma, I'll call you tomorrow. We are going out for dinner."

"Have good time my owl."

"Yes I'll. Take care Soma, bye-bye."

"Bye and do call me tomorrow."

"Yes I'll surely do."

"Ok bye."

"Bye."

"Thank you Santosh." Inder said while shutting down the laptop.

"Pleasure is all mine Mr. Smith." He replied in Western accent, "Now please get ready."

"Give me five minutes."

"Let's move soldiers." Stephan said it like an Army officer and pointed towards stairs.

"Hey let's march like soldiers to main road." Santosh said.

Atul hesitated at first but then agreed to the wilder side of Santosh. Harf has always been big supporter of Santosh. Inder just wanted to get blend in the group as he sees his involvement a way to deviate his mind from regular thoughts.

So everyone acted accordingly. They marched through stairs and street until they reached at main road. They even saluted to the people around. Some watched them with confusion, weird for some and some smiled & saluted back. They grabbed almost everyone's attention.

"It was fun." Inder said and everyone's laugh approved that.

After witnessing the struggle of everything on road for moving forward before others, they reached at desired market. Because of their experimental nature they visited a new restaurant.

"Hey Atul, my dear," Santosh said sadly, "I don't know if you have noticed or not," he put his hand on Atul's shoulder, "but you can't have '*DaalMakhni*' here." He turned towards others and said, "Everyone, please console my dearest friend."

Harf put his hand on Atul's shoulder and Stephan hold his another hand.

"Hey Atul, don't worry man, everything will be fine." Harf said.

"Just have faith on Almighty." Stephan added. While Atul just sat there trying to keep blank expression, waiting for them to stop.

"Stop it guys, others may think that we are group of 'gays'." Inder said while controlling his laughter.

"This gay culture has spoiled brotherhood man." Santosh said it with fake anger.

And a good loud laugh helped warming up the empty spaces between them.

". . . . it's all luck man." Harf said while having a bite of pizza. "I was average in studies. I was a medical student in high school but then I opt commerce in graduation even I didn't give any serious thought. After doing job in a bank for a year, which I somewhere deep inside accepted to do for number of years; an ordinary pamphlet in a daily newspaper changed my whole plan and I suddenly started to realize the need of M.B.A. The strange thing was," he swallowed, "that even funds were arranged, which seemed like a difficult task after my elder sis's marriage in the same year." Harf said it with conviction and everyone accepted except Inder. "I see myself in a better & safer place now which I didn't picture for myself when I was in that bank."

"I can feel how much satisfaction your explanation has given to Atul," Inder smiled, "now you will see more determined side of him."

"I already told you, he is going to be the face of unilever." Santosh said it in jesting tone grabbing the opportunity.

On the other side Inder was trying to ignore what Harf has said about 'luck'.

"Really man, we are destined to be what we are." Harf added; pushing Inder to lost somewhere in space of time.

He wanted to tell his point of view but words were not coming out of his mouth. "Coincidence . . . ." Inder tried but managed only one word, which got lost in clacking sound of knives and forks.

"Choices are very powerful Soma but you must have clarity about yourself, about your life and about your aims."

"Inder but luck . . ."

"Hey where are you lost?" Atul asked.

"Nowhere . . . ." He replied as if he woke up from sleep.

"You are such a slow eater." Santosh said.

"I don't know . . ." Inder said.

"Hey what about a movie after this?" Harf asked as if the idea suddenly popped up in his head.

"Yes!" Santosh was first.

No one raised any objection as there was not any reason.

"Let me check the timings first." Harf said while grabbing his phone. "We can reach there on time; ask for the bill."

Another thirty-five minutes of commuting left Inder with plenty of new facial expressions of different people about whom his mind kept calculating the stories behind. After reaching at a multiplex they hurriedly went to the ticket counter and purchased the tickets.

The hall was nearly full and they got their seats on fifth row.

Right from the logo animation of the production house, Inder's whole attention was grabbed by the glowing 'Exit' sign on his right. Now the only reasons behind the disturbance in the connection of him with the sign were sudden loud laugh of people and Santosh's comments every now & then. He had tried to concentrate on the movie for number of times, for what he was there, but failed badly in every single effort. He felt like that sign was trying to talk back to him. The rich color of that sign was making itself deeper & deeper for him. The more he stares it, more he feels like sinking in it. The meaning of word 'Exit' was revolving around his head. He felt like as if it was motivating him to get up from his chair and to grab the opportunity to get out from the darkness. "What is it?" He thought but the sign kept glowing in the same manner. To deviate his focus from that sign he tried to give reactions on Santosh's comments, but failed. As a result, after an hour or so, it became unbearable for him to ignore the call from 'Exit'.

"I'll come back in a minute." He said and then hurriedly went towards it without giving any answer to Santosh's query.

He went into the bathroom, closed the door, put the flap down of the toilet seat and sat on it. He pulled out some pages from his pocket and started writing on them, hastily. He spent about fifteen minutes there.

"I was in washroom. I think that Italian didn't treat me in the right way." He whispered in Santosh's ear and smiled.

Then he sat straight, eyes on the movie, felt quite comfortable, smiled and peeped at that 'Exit' sign. It was not bothering him as if he has done some sort of agreement with it. Though his consciousness still was not with the movie but he was feeling relaxed. He kept smiling on Santosh's comments and even sometimes laughed with them.

After interval he kept himself busy with popcorns. Finally 'The End' emerged on the screen and people started leaving the theater. They came out of the audi and Inder got some free air to inhale.

On their way back to home, Inder saw that Delhi started puking homeless on its streets and yellow light bulbs as slum suns have made their strong presence. All of these things were leaving abstract marks on his mind. Sometimes he really feels the need to know different things of every kind but then again at the same time he just wants to close his eyes and ignore the surroundings. But curiosity for reality and truth had easily ruined his intentions of getting calm and empty-minded many times. Tonight was not much different. He was observing the surroundings and then again was trying to ignore them by placing his one hand at the side of his face. This struggle came to an end when they reached home. Harf and Stephan went in their room according to their routine but these three owls knew they need to do something special to sleep at this time of the night.

"Atul, do your boring talks man, which you read from your business magazine today." Santosh said, "I want to fall asleep."

Inder chuckled.

"Once there was a crow Santosh." Atul started with a smile.

"Is this from business magazine!" Santosh said.

"Just listen if you want to fall asleep." Atul said.

"Ok-ok continue." Santosh said it while changing his side. "I am into more comfortable position now, let's continue."

"Once there was a crow." Atul started again, "He was from a village but had always wanted to go in a big city and settle down there; to become a part of something big, something happening. He really wanted to get out of the boring green village. He wanted to sit on buildings taller than trees and wanted to enjoy doing shit from up there."

Everyone chuckled. Inder somehow got engaged with the story.

"He wanted to eat city food because he was fed up from crops for all these years."

"Don't you think it should be 'It' instead of 'He', when talking about a crow." Inder intentionally raised the point on grammar as he knows Santosh always gets irritated when it comes about rules of anything.

"Ah! Really! Inder, at this point of time. You are so boring and infuriating." Santosh said and Atul&Inder laughed loudly as if it was a secret mission to irritate Santosh.

"So," Atul said, "he flew & flew & flew, over clouds, without compass and got lost. So he asked for the directions from other birds." He smiled. "After tiring flight of 8 hours including a stop for refilling of tummy for about 30 minutes, he landed successfully in a big city. But . . . ."

"What?" Santosh asked.

"But to his extreme surprise, he saw a group of female crows, whose each member was of very fair complexion; kind of brown in color. He went near them and asked about their body color in a rather sad face. 'He is from village. I bet you.' One of the female crow said. Then other female crow came forward, observed him and then pulled out a pouch from a pocket near her shit hole."

"What pouch?" Santosh asked. "And you said 'shit-hole'! She is a girl man, show some respect."

"Wait, what!" Atul said, "I said 'from a pocket near shit hole' and not 'from shit hole'."

"Ok-ok, let it be 'from under one of the wings' to keep things simple and decent." Inder said.

"Ok, so she pulled out a pouch from a pocket, beneath her wing."

"A pouch?" Santosh asked again.

"Can't you wait. I am the storyteller. Be quite and listen."

Both laughed.

"Ok, so now that crow looked at the pouch and asked 'what is it lady?' And she said, 'villager this thing is *fair & lovely*'."

And a loud laugh burst out from all of them.

"That crow said, '*Fair & lovely*? What is that? An infected grain? Ladies you need to eat something healthy.' Then the leader of that group came forward and said, 'Ah villager! You are such a villager; because only a villager like you can talk such villagish things. See villager, this is a cream for our body. A *cream* villager. You know what is a cream villager?' And the crow said, 'No!' He was completely lost at that time. 'See villager, this isn't just a mixture of soil and water, because soil and water can't beautify us. So to enhance our beauty we need this cream.' She explained. 'Enhance the beauty! But I think that we all are beautiful in our own way.' 'Girls, see what I told you earlier, he is a villager. We need to explain this thing in our own way.' And then all the female crows pointed towards, came in line and started singing—

> 'O villager! O villager!
> You are so villagish!
> So villagish.'"

Santosh and Inder started laughing while looking at each other.

"Wait-wait and just after that, about 50 other female crows emerged from somewhere and started dancing behind them while the three incharge kept singing—

> 'Villager . . . . you villager . . . .
> you are one stupid crow
> but don't you worry
> don't worry . . . .
> you will get the ways of city
> of city . . . .'"

"Wait, let's sing together." Santosh said.
"O villager." Inder initiated right away.
Then they started singing all together—

> "O villager . . . . you villager
> you are one stupid crow
> stupid crow . . . .
> but don't you worry
> don't worry . . . ."

Their tired bodies didn't let them talk for long. They were lying on the bed as if they have fell on it. No one was moving even a bit as if ultimate comfort was being found. Inder kept looking at the fan for long while laying straight. It's uniform circles, constant speed held his hand and took him in the past.

"I am so fed up of my routine; of my life." There was a hidden helpless cry in Inder's voice when he said it to Samar.

"Inder these days are not going to last for long." Samar said.

Inder said nothing in response. Instead frustration got mixed up in his already present sadness.

"What happened?" Samar asked though he was having a clear idea about the answer.

"Nothing . . . ." It was Inder's usual reply in frustration.

Samar kept looking at him while staying as clam & patient as he could.

Inder took off his arms from the table and put his rather weak back against chair's. He turned his face aside. He just wanted to cry instead of talking and explain the situation clearly. But then what was the fun of sharing the problem with Samar. This thought made him do the talking.

"I don't know," he said, "I see nothing in front of me. My circumstance are so concrete in nature that I see no hope. I don't know which path . . . ."

"Time changes." Samar interrupted just to break his continuous negative eruptions.

Inder took his eyes away from Samar as if concentrating on the fight between his negativity & sadness with the fact that 'time changes'.

"What happened?" Samar asked.

Inder just nodded.

Samar understood it.

"I am going home. I just need to do more work." Inder said it while gathering himself.

"Yes, that's it. Moreover you are not alone now. An another life, an another responsibility is waiting for you to prove yourself & to succeed." Samar tried to take his focus on Somaya.

"I know, I know." Inder said it in a determined voice.

"Ah! Thank God it didn't took much time." Samar smiled.

"I know I can't afford to be negative but circumstances sometimes do their best to crush you." Inder explained.

"I know, I can feel, but don't worry. Keep doing your work and we'll keep looking for any type of opportunity abroad too." Samar knew that Inder didn't really celebrate the idea of going abroad but he just wanted him to be aware of it and to consider it as a backup plan. He feels that in difficult time the oppotunity of going abroad can act as a ray of hope.

Inder nodded.

"Should we order something now?" Samar said.

"Ok."

"Off course, who will wake up on Sunday before eleven." Inder looked at both of them and then started wearing shoes and went out. It was 8 in the morning and was getting ready for his job to dehydrate everything. He went out of the house just to wander around. Instead of going to the main road, he decided to go further in narrower streets. There were very few people out. He kept going from one to another street and all of them were equally wide and the density of houses was almost same too. Shops were not open yet for obvious reason but some vegetable vendors were arranging fresh vegetables on their beds. A woman was brushing her teeth while standing on the balcony and was spitting on the road. While he was observing her, suddenly that crow from Atul's story came in his mind, who wanted to come to the city to enjoy doing shit from buildings taller than trees. He chuckled and kept moving. His eyes were looking for something which can provoke his thoughts. He was there in the field, ready to deal with anything which comes in his way. But those streets were somehow holding the concrete on both ends so that people can hide themselves behind them. But he was not there to assume something, but to watch, to witness the things going on. The air in those streets was like as if it still has not refreshed entirely. He kept walking through from one to another street continuously as there was not any reason to stop and go back.

About forty minutes of walk took him to another locality where living standard went down further. Small dense houses made up from less concrete and more clay. The streets became narrower. There were very few water connections but streets were made up of concrete beds; plain & without any pot-holes. "May be someone has recognized the locality as voter bank and not as 'people of India'." He thought. Many families were preparing their food in open areas of their homes. Clearly there were no L.P.G. connections.

While peeping around his eyes captured a hen. It was in extremely weak condition and its body was almost naked because of the absence of feathers. He went a little closer and saw a man sitting on his feet, staring continuously at the hen. "Either he is pain or just waiting it to die. Either there are memories of that hen & of the eggs he enjoyed or there is a picture of a bowl full of its flesh. Or there can be both. They must have knew how to move on to survive in these type of conditions." He thought, "A feeling overtaking another one in order to keep living without agony." Then suddenly his attention got deviated from that hen to murmur coming from a home besides that one. He went towards it and a weak cry gave him the idea of what must have been going there. By moving further towards that home, he saw a body of a man which was lying on the ground and was nothing more than a skeleton. A woman was sitting close to him; crying while holding her head. A naked kid sitting beside the man's head and was pushing his face with his little fist. Inder overheard the word 'Aids' from someone sitting near that dead body. The picture was clear. He witnessed more than he expected. A poor death on a day which is synonym with fun & laziness for others. "Is there anything worse than this?" He thought. There was poverty all around him and all were living its side effects; which even he had experienced to a significant extent. He got annoyed, annoyed because of the things which has effected humanity so wickedly that it had eradicated life from humans. He walked away from there. He was trying to figure out the direction which can take him to some open place. A jog of about twenty minutes took him to the main road. He started looking for a bench or something where he can sit for some time. He saw a bus stop at some distance to his

"Moreover he is kind of reserve. He likes to keep things to himself." Atul said.

"Yes." Santosh approved.

"I didn't observe him that closely so can't say anything." Stephan expressed.

"But he is a nice guy anyway." Santosh declared, "Ok change the topic now."

They kept talking about random things over breakfast and Inder didn't express any opinion regarding anything. He was trying to place the things in some corner of his mind which he witnessed earlier that morning.

"You are really such a slow eater." Santosh said to Inder.

"I don't know man I just can't eat quickly, no matter how hard I try. I am slowest in my family too." Inder smiled.

After their meal they engaged themselves in their own interests.

Stephan's phone rang. "Ok guys, see you later."

"Say hi from my side also." Santosh chuckled.

"Yeah sure." Stephan smiled.

Inder kept reading his novel and writing on some pages after regular intervals of time. Atul stick to his M.B.A. and the pair of Harf and Santosh to their laptops.

When hour hand was wandering somewhere between 1 & 2, "I am going to take a nap." Harf said while yawning.

After he left the room Inder got up and said, "I am going to make some calls."

"Hey Inder you will pay at booth, so why don't you call from my phone and you can pay the expenses to me, I've no issues." Santosh smiled.

"Thank you so much Santosh, but I can't. Please don't take it in a wrong way but I don't want to send anyone's number to them or they will start calling frequently. I don't want that yet. I'll tell you the reasons later. Actually; I am just trying to live in silent mode, nothing else." Inder said and left the room without waiting for his reaction.

He entered the booth and dialed a number.

"Hello." A weak but curious voice addressed him.

"Hello mom."

"Inder! My son, how are you? I've been waiting for your call. Don't you miss me? The home is not the same without you."

"Maa, wait-wait", he smiled, "Hold your horses. First I am fine and I miss you too. Please take care of yourself too. It's just going to take some months. I'll be back."

"I know you don't work on Saturdays so why don't you come on some weekend?"

"Maa just some months. If I came back, then it'll be difficult for me leave again."

"If this is the thing then you must come." She smiled.

"I'll-I'll." He smiled.

"This home is wasteland without you."

"Maa please don't feel sad. I'll come back soon, you just take good care of yourself and stay happy. I'll call you every Saturday & Sunday."

"Bribe! I don't need it. Actually I am not able to call you anytime of the week. You must have took your phone along."

"Maa I promise I'll call you every Saturday and Sunday and sorry for not calling you yesterday."

"Ok, anyways, how is your work?"

"It's going good."

"Thank God! I wish everything good and smooth for you."

"I know Maa, that is why I've strength to live far away from you. I think I should start praying for you too. May be you'll get the strength to live far from me too." He smiled.

"I know you and your talks."

"It was actually my heart and my tongue." He laughed.

"I know," she smiled, "but you are so stubborn some times."

"Maa, one needs to be if he wants to bring bigger & better change."

"Ok-ok, I know this. I've heard this before. Now give me promise that it'll be just two-three months."

"Yes, around three months."

"See, I don't trust you. Why around three months? If you didn't came in the third month then I'll come to Delhi to bring you back."

"I promise, around three months," he laughed, "no more than that. You know I can't stay away for long."

"Alright. Did you called your father?"

"No I didn't. I'll call him next weekend."

"No just call him and talk to him just for couple of minutes or else he will say so many things against me after drinking the shit."

"Ok," he sighed, "I'll call him after this."

"Ok. Anything new at work? Hey, tell me about the boys at p.g."

"Ah! They are good. They are really nice and very helping & kind."

"From where are they?"

"Two of them are from Haryana, who work with me. One is from West Bengal and other is from U.P."

"How cruel is the time which has snatched sons from their mothers."

"Maa, don't overreact please. People here are very ambitious. They are here for better future and they really work hard."

"Don't fool me they also do drugs, smoke cigarettes and drinks . . ."

"Look at the fingers of your hand."

"What to do with fingers."

"Just tell me are they of same length?"

"I got it you wise-man."

"Just don't worry I am with the good ones."

"Have you travelled the city?"

"Not much, there is never that much time. I prefer to stay at p.g. We use to go out only on weekends."

. . . .

"Ok Maa, you take care of yourself. I'll call you on Saturday now."

"Ok bye and take care of your meals."

"Yes I'll. Bye." He smiled.

He cut the line and then dialed an another number.

"Hello Dad."

"Hello Inder how are you son?"

"I am good. What about you?"

"I am fine like before."

"Ok, good, anything new?"

"Nothing son. Did you called your mother?"

"Yes I did."

"Ok, good."

"Are you in the market, because there is so much noice?"

"Yes, actually I am. Don't worry, cut the call."

"Ok. I'll call you later. Take care."

"Take care."

He finally dialed the third and last number.

"Hello Soma."

"Hello! How are you dear?"

"I am good. How was your day?"

"It was good as Sundays used to be; lazy and relaxing."

"Ok and preparations for the exams?"

"Don't worry it is going good. Now you tell me how was your outing last night?"

"Ah! It was fun till we went to watch a movie."

"Why what happened?" she smiled.

"You know my taste of movies. But last night I watched the genre I hated the most."

"My Gosh! Comedy drama." She laughed.

"Yes, and you know, no one asked no one about which movie one wants to watch. It was like they already have decided or their choice is incredibly the same." He laughed.

"It must have been a torture for you."

"Naa, I've learnt to tolerate things beyond my capabilities. And you know you are the one finest example of that." He teased.

"O . . . . no Inder sir, I've tolerated you for all these years."

"Ok, no issues." He smiled.

"Ok-ok tell me what you guys did before movie?"

"We had very nice dinner at an Italian restaurant. And you know, the funniest thing was that we marched like soldiers from our p.g. to the main road and also saluted to the people around."

"O my gosh! How was their reaction?"

"There were dumb faces, weird expressions, smiles and some salutes too."

Both laughed.

"And you know when we were running towards the ticket counter as we were getting late for the movie, I felt like I am a stupid running for unknown movie. And when we were inside an item number was about to kill me, so I hurriedly went out of the theater."

Both laughed loudly.

"Ok you had good time, I can feel it." She teased.

"Yes off course, you were so many miles away from me." He smiled.

"No problem, you are not going to stay in Delhi forever. We'll see."

Inder laughed. "Ok tell me what have you been doing since morning?"

. . . .

CHAPTER 3

3ʳᵈ Weekend

It could not get any more typical morning of June than it already was. Inder was sitting on damp floor which was getting dry with every passing moment. Fan was on its full speed but was never enough to beat the heat. His old t-shirt was doing its best to clean the floor under his mother's command. It seemed like everything was burning with grief. His mother's hands were moving quickly and harshly on the rough cemented floor. Her heart was filled with way much sorrow than her face was telling.

"My heart sinks when anyone asks me about your work." Her voice was filled with resentment. "Why can't you see the conditions. If you think that you can take long strides to quickly achieve your aim, your desired salary, then let me tell you, it is absolutely impractical. No one is going to give you 20,000 from starting. Go and see how highly qualified are working on 6,000 per month. I am unable to understand the way you think." The whole environment was filled with her continuous harsh and direct words as if she was filled with resentment upto her throat. "First you stopped giving tuitions to the kids. Even if the earnings were not much but still it was better than nothing. Then you quit the job from call centers twice. Neither you are continuing your studies nor you are doing any work. That was much better offer to work at courier company; you just had to sit there and work on the computer, but you didn't even accepted that. I have not any single idea about how you want to stand yourself. I don't know how can you fix these problems." She said the latter part while pointing at the rough floor which alone was enough to tell most of the truth. The more she sweeps it the more it gets louder and louder for Inder. The more it screams and blames him for not taking care of it; for not taking care of the family; for not taking care of the house; for not earning. She had never taken so much of time to sweep that little veranda than she had taken on that morning.

Inder was just sitting still on the floor wearing a white pajama whose threads were just about to leave each other to make his inner parts visible. He just kept listening to her with his head held between his knees. His consciousness was having nothing which can explain his previous actions. There was just one thing though that he needs huge amount of money as soon as possible. He just wanted to do something which can fetch some good amount of money as well as can satisfy his inner-self, which always has been a problem behind not letting him do any other job, which he feels that doesn't match his intellectual level. But because of this thought he always had paid a huge price in the form of crying heart and worried mind of his mother.

Now as she has reached at the end of the veranda she broke into tears while saying, "Your dad is not going to do anything. He has lived his life. One cannot expect anything from him now. My all hopes are with you only." She tried to contain herself. "But I don't know . . . . just don't become like your father. Do something." And she cried & cried; so many tears were coming out of her eyes, mixing with sweat and were falling on Inder's old t-shirt.

She just stopped sweeping, sat on the floor and she held the bucket with both of her hands, lowered down her head and stopped making any sound. It was difficult to tell if she was still crying or not as drops of sweat kept falling from her face on her *salwaar*.

Normally in these type of situations Inder used to hug her tightly and try to calm her down or cries along with her. But this time he just tightened his arms around his legs to hold his head more tightly in between his knees as if trying to crush it. From that point it can't be said if he was crying or not but he was so still as if was frozen in time.

"For how long you can pretend Atul?" Santosh said after observing him texting from his phone worriedly.

"What!"

"What 'what'? I've observed you for the whole week. To whom you are chatting with?" Santosh showed his concern.

"Nothing it's just an old friend." Atul said.

"Come on, you think you can hide? Ok if it is so then tell me the name of your friend. I know all of your friends." Santosh said it with bit of rudeness.

"Nothing . . . . wait . . . . I'll tell you but wait please." Atul tried to convince him.

"When?" Santosh was hard to handle.

"Just within few minutes. Can't you wait?" Atul said it in an annoyed tone, trying hard not to speak loudly.

Santosh went near him and sat beside him. "See I've observed you even at work. You have been texting for the whole week. If it is something in the family then why are you hiding it from me?" Santosh was rather polite this time.

"Wait, letInder go in the washroom." Atul said in a very low pitch while checking his phone.

"Actually it's about Roohi." Atul started sharing.

Santosh got worried as Roohi was not less than a sweet little sister to him too.

Atul took a long deep breath.

"You look exhausted." Santosh said.

"It's a very difficult situation actually. You know my Dad."

"Yes!" Santosh was feeling very uncomfortable at the moment.

"He is not that conservative but very strict."

"I know God damn it; tell me what is going on with Roohi?" Santosh cried.

"Easy-easy," Atul signaled him to lower down his voice, "actually Mom-Dad were thinking about her marriage and she came to know about it."

"What! Why uncle is in so much of hurry. She is just 22 or, 21; how old she is exactly?"

"She will be 22 in July."

"At least let her complete her post-graduation."

"Actually she is not worried about her studies." He sighed, "Even when she was talking to me about this matter, she was not telling the exact reason but," he paused, "do you remember, on Thursday she called me, when I went downstairs to talk to her, she told me that she likes someone. He was her class-mate right from graduation and even right now they are in the same class pursuing M.Com together." Atul started slowly but then picked up pace to explain it quick as if trying to put the burden aside.

Santosh was numb. At first he felt like his mind has stopped working. He couldn't speak anything as this news was not less than a shock for him. After gaining his senses he wished to beat that boy badly. Was that possessiveness? He was not sure at that point of time.

"She said that the boy is really nice and she likes him very much." Atul said it with a blank face.

This filled Santosh with even more anger. Instead of trust of Roohi on that boy which must have given him some ease, he started assuming that boy as a very clever & selfish person.

"I wish that boy stood in front of me so that I could crush his bones." Santosh said it with anger.

"He will be, tomorrow." Atul said.

"What! What do you mean?"

"Roohi was scared a lot and she asked me to meet her. So I requested Dad to let her come to Delhi this weekend & he agreed. She will be here around 5:30 & then she will go to *Maasi's* home for night stay."

"And that boy?"

"She also requested me to meet that boy once. So with a rather cool and calm mind I agreed. That boy will be here tomorrow morning. We'll meet both of them at café."

Now Roohi's face was wandering in front of Santosh's eyes and he became eager to meet her today.

"I want to meet her today. I want to talk to her or tomorrow I'll lose temper in front of that boy." Santosh said.

"Santosh I want to understand the situation completely and yes we'll definitely meet her today. I've already told her to come at that cafe." Atul said, "We'll meet her around six and then we'll drop her at *Maasi's* place."

"Ok . . . ."

"Hey, what to tell these guys about where are we going?" Atul asked.

"Don't worry about it." Santosh said it while getting up.

In the meantime Inder came out of the bathroom with his towel wrapped around his hip. He quickly started writing on some pages.

"Hey what is this you keep writing about?" Santosh asked.

"Aaa . . . it's just, actually I've bad habit of writing random thoughts." Inder said.

"But why don't you keep a diary instead of these pages?" Santosh said while pointing towards pages.

"These are super easy to carry." Inder smiled.

"I've seen you writing in the break time at work." Atul said.

"Yeah, sometimes any old memories came out of nowhere, so I've to write down the feelings about them." Inder said.

"Can we read it?" Atul said with a smile as he already knows the answer.

"Not yet," Inder smiled, "but someday for sure."

"No problem." Atul said.

"Hey Inder some of our old college friends are coming to Delhi. So we'll go around six to meet them and will be late in the night." Santosh said.

"No problem dear. Should we wait for you to have dinner?" Inder said.

"No you have it. We'll do it with them." Atul said the latter while looking at Santosh.

"Ok, no problem."

Sitting in that room for a while, restlessly, pretending to be doing some work which everyone use to do; everyone was lost somewhere in their own thoughts.

May be Inder felt the unease filled in the room or maybe he was eager to make regular weekend calls that made him go downstairs after quickly winding up his ongoing work of reading and writing. He made aware both of them about his wish and then he proceeded along with his unsettled mind towards the stairs.

He entered into the S.T.D. and dialed a number.

"Sat Shri Akal Soma!" Inder smiled.

"Sat Shri Akal *ji.*" Somaya said the 'ji' word as wives use to say.

There was pleasant smile on both of their faces.

"Done with exams?"

"Yes, finally and I did concentrate on them like I promised."

"Good, very good." Inder felt the satisfaction in her voice.

"Inder you know, when life just comes at a point to almost leave my body then your phone comes, at the end of the week." Somaya said it in rather light mood with a jesting tone instead of mourning over the issue.

"My dear, not for long." Inder smiled.

"I wonder how your Mom has been dealing with this. Phone call from her son, only on weekends and that too when her son wants."

"Don't say like this, please. It feels like I am giving her some sort of punishment."

"Ah! Don't take in that way. I don't want you to feel negative again."

He smiled but some part of his consciousness got lost in that feeling.

"Hey what happened?" Somaya said.

"Nothing, I was thinking, for a girl like you, who is loving, caring and liked to have fun, has dealt with my bad moods, negative phases with so much patience and lots of hope." There was a big 'thank-you' in Inder's heart for her.

"What else I could do? I was stuck with you and I loved you." Somaya teased.

"Thanks to that blind fold on your eyes when you accepted my propose." Inder laughed.

"No there was nothing like that." She laughed, "It was because of your genuineness & simplicity."

"I was simple because, I was not having enough money to be complex."

Inder smiled.

"Oh please, you would have not been any different even if you had lot of money."

"I don't know. Maybe I've become what I am today because of the absence of it; the thing which have put strong influence on my thought process and belief system."

"Ok-ok, what that matter is," she paused, "that you were a good person when I accepted your proposal and now with time you have become even better." She kind of put the full stop to the conversation.

"Alright. O! Somaya."

"Yes!"

"I forgot to tell you that I've asked for some money from Amar last week. I had left a message on his facebook and he assured to wire the money today. So I'll go to 'money gram' after this call."

"Good-good loot your cousin. Take advantage of the dollars." She chuckled, "By the way what was the need?"

"FYI you can't travel the city without having enough money, moreover I didn't get the salary yet."

"Ahm . . . ahm . . . . full on style. From where did you learnt this 'FYI'?"

He laughed.

"Tell me my owl?" She smiled.

"From Hollywood flicks darling."

"Aahaan . . . ."

Both laughed.

"Ok listen I am sweating badly in this tiny little booth. I'll go now to get the money. After that I'll call to Mom and then I'll call you again in the night."

"Ok Inder, see you. Take care."

"Yes I'll and come on cheer up. I'll call you around 10."

"Ok no problem. I am fine, see you."

"Bye dear, lots of love."

"Love to you too."

Inder left the booth and went to find out any franchise of 'money gram'. He asked from few people and then finally a person made him aware about the one in a nearby market. The place was about 25 minutes of walk for him. But he was walking slower than his normal pace. Perhaps because of the lighter mood and less crowded mind, which has been a rare thing for him for the past few years.

"She has reached and has rented an auto for the café." Atul said while disconnecting the phone.

Santosh started wearing shoes and then they left for the market. They took a rickshaw to reach there as they were not getting any auto and on the other hand both were pretty restless and eager to meet Roohi.

Inder was enjoying his little walk while observing lots of people around. That walk was really 'little' for the one who used to walk for hours with the tremendous weight of numerous thoughts. But at that point he was feeling the lightness of his heart in his chest. He was pleased to have some beautiful and precious people in his life who understands him. Then his Mom's face came in front of his eyes. He adored her image. Suddenly the smile on the face of her Mom fainted and his palms get closed tightly automatically.

"You will change, you will, you must keep going, stay on the track." He kept repeating these words in his mind for a while.

Finally he reached in that market and started looking for the shop with 'Money Gram' label on its forehead. After couple of minutes he found out the shop and went into it.

After five minute process he came out of the shop and the sight in front of him across the street made him rub his eyes to see it again. That was Atul hugging a girl and Santosh was standing beside her looking full of worries. No sign of smile or excitement was there on his face. That was very unusual. Right before entering into the café, Santosh accidently made an eye contact with Inder. Inder instantly took off his eyes and started walking to his left towards p.g. Santosh watched him going and then went inside.

There was smile on Inder's face, the smile which always use to emerge on his face right after these type of situations. That was not difficult for him to understand that they had lied to him. But it did not disturbed him, in fact he started looking for the reason behind Santosh's worry. He kept thinking about it for the whole way back to his p.g. he went upstairs, had couple of glasses of water and then quits thinking about it.

He went into the room of Harf& Stephan. Stephan was on phone with someone and Harf was just surfing the internet on his laptop. Harf signaled him to come and sit beside him.

"You all are back so soon?" He asked.

"No actually we didn't go together. I went to get some money wired by my cousin and they went to meet their old college friends over some café." Inder said.

"Oh yes, Santosh has told me about this before leaving; it just skipped from my mind." Harf said.

"What are your plans for tonight." Inder said.

"We are actually going for movie with some of our colleagues."

"Together?"

"No actually he is going with his and I'm going with mine." Harf smiled.

"Ok."

They kept talking on random things and little about past of theirs.

"Do you any girlfriend?" This question from Harf was sudden and beyond Inder's expectations.

A sudden burst of laugh came out of Inder.

"What happened!" Harf said.

"Nothing actually the question is funny for me."

"What's funny about it?" Harf was quite confused now.

"Actually the question should be like this: 'Do you have a girlfriend?' Instead of 'any girlfriend'."

"Oh I understand." He smiled.

Inder signaled him to wait. "And then if we go for precision, in much correct form it should be like: 'Do you love someone?' or something like that. The word 'any' in your question makes a girl as a commodity & label."

"My goodness I didn't know this side of yours." Harf was trying to understand the newly discovered side of Inder. "You feel like very sensitive about this issue."

"First of all this is not an issue, instead it's is an integral part of one's life and secondly the term 'sensitive' you used here is completely inappropriate here. I just have good hold on the truth behind this relation and I've just stood by it."

"My God! It seems like whatever I say or believe about this, is wrong according to your perspective." Harf said with strange un-comfort inside.

"It's not your fault and don't say that it is your belief. Actually it is just what in the air around us. So everybody feels almost the same about certain topic or subject."

"Man I am blown now. You have been way deeper than you feel." Harf said it while sitting in a more attentive posture.

"Hey what are you talking about?" Stephan said while coming towards them after disconnecting the phone.

"Now it's going to be fun." Inder smiled.

"Do you have any girlfriend Stephan?" Harf asked intentionally.

"Yes . . . but you already know about it." Stephan said it with strangeness.

Harf andInder laughed.

"What happened?" Stephan got confused because of their reaction.

"My God!" Harf smiled, "About couple of minutes ago Inder had explained me about the non-serious and disrespectful nature of this question because of the word 'any' present in it, when I asked the same to him." Harf explained.

"What? What's wrong with any? I mean people have more than one so it sounds more appropriate." Stephan laughed.

"Exactly." Inder laughed while Harf looked at him with confusion.

"Explain your point." Harf said with curiosity.

"The girlfriend-boyfriend culture has lower down the value of this relation. Honestly speaking, I don't even like the words 'girlfriend' & 'boyfriend'. Actually there is nothing wrong with the words but it's the sentiment of people and meaning associated with these words."

Both were silent, staring at him.

"Ok, now if you ask me in a precise way, as I have told Harf about it, which is, 'do you love someone?' Then I'll say, 'yes'"; he pointed in a direction and said, "she is the one with whom I want to spend my life with."

"Yes, and, that is the feeling of me towards my girlfriend." Stephan said.

"But we don't really care about the words we use to express our relation and our feelings towards them.

Ok tell me do we people convey anything about our girlfriend in the same way we convey anything about our sister? Well this question of mine can pinch people in their hearts but there is significant amount of truth in it. I am not being judgmental or over sentimental about it but I just believe in using the right way to use right words at right time to express my honest feelings about anything or about any relation."

"But that just make you the better user of the language and who doesn't use it in a right way doesn't prove that their love or any other feelings are not true." Stephan said.

"Yes, I agree, but use of language was my concern at the start of this conversation. If we use right words to express our feelings then it adds value to the words as well as you & your feelings get respect in the eyes of the listener." Inder said.

"The thing is getting complex now." Harf said. "First the concern was the usage of words and now it is shifting towards true feelings."

"See both of the things are interlinked. Both of them go side by side. The absence of any one of the two can makes one a hypocrite. But I think our discussion has already filled with enough confusion because the subject is quite subjective so we can put the word 'hypocrite' at rest for now." Inder paused, "Let me go back in the discussion. When you asked me if I am having any girlfriend; I didn't reacted to tell you that this is how you take this relation but my concern was how this expression is becoming general." Inder tried his best. "Ok let's talk about it some other day. Maybe I can explain it in a more clear way then." Inder smiled.

"No-no I am getting your point." Stephan said.

"Ok then, let me try for one more time then." He smiled. "It absolutely does matter how you take this relation in your heart but how you express it to others is also important. Because it can put influence on others. It can be misleading also, especially for those who don't have strong opinions about it. In worse state this thing can become a belief for certain age group and the morality of this relation can get hurt." Inder knew that this topic needs more explanation & more discussion to bring more clarity but the way they have travelled this far had made it more difficult to discuss it further. "I think we should leave this topic here." He smiled.

Whatever the degree of effectiveness of this conversation was, but it did clear many things about the personality of Inder.

"Anyways I'll go now I need to make some calls." Inder said.

Harf and Stephan just nodded.

He was gradually getting attached to the STD booth. He has been in it for a number of times now. The congested wooden booth painted blue, which had come down from some places, revealing the layer of primer and from some places even the plywood. There was black glass on the door of the booth on which 'STD' was painted vertically with red paint and with yellow boundary. There was an age old little wooden stool to sit, which with every little movement makes creaky sounds. On the left hand side rests the telephone set and above that a calendar, with an image of Ganesha was fixed with broad brown tape. People have written many phone numbers on that calendar.

He picked up the receiver and started dialing a number.

"Maa . . . ." He smiled.

"My son!" she said as if an excessively dry land gets fondled by cool breeze.

"How are you?"

"I am ok. What about you? How is your work going? Are you eating properly?" Something grasped her excitement.

"Yes everything is fine," he smiled, "and I am taking good care of myself, don't worry at all."

"And job is going good?"

"You sound very tired." Inder said.

"No . . . . I am perfectly fine. Actually I was washing clothes before your call came, so that's why."

"No. Dad is drinking regularly again, isn't it?"

She didn't give any reply.

"Maa . . . ."

"Yes-yes I am here."

"Tell me, he is doing the same again?" Inder asked politely.

"He irritates me." She finally broke out. "He made me feel distressed." There was roughness and anger in her tone. "I have tried to ignore him in the best way I could but his alcoholic face fills me with agony. When he gets drunk he forgets every single responsibility. I kept waiting for him like a fool in the evening. He comes home very late and I have not slept properly for the entire week. It has made me very uncomfortable at work."

Inder knows all these things. This was not happening for the first time. But he let his mother to finish it so that she can feel a little relaxed.

"It will pass Maa, It will pass."

She didn't speak a word.

He knows about what is going on inside her. He knows that she has waited for so long to be happy and that now to keep faith alive seems difficult and worthless.

"Leave it." She said. "Tell me how was your week?"

"Ah! It was regular. Just like the last one."

"Ok . . . . I just want that if you have chosen this then give your best to this job."

"Yes Mom do not worry. I am going good." Inder said confidently.

"And Samar called me too today. He said he will come tomorrow." She said.

"That is good. Tell me the time I'll try to call during that."

"He didn't give me any specific time."

"Ok . . . . so anything new?"

"Inder do you have enough money with you?"

"Yes, I do have enough. Don't worry at all."

"You have really, no!"

"Yes I have Maa, don't worry." He smiled.

"Ok."

"So I'll call you tomorrow now. Take care of yourself."

"Ok bye. You too take care and have your dinner on time."

"Yes I'll. Bye." He smiled.

There were tears in his eyes when he put the receiver down. It felt like they have came without giving him any single clue. It was strange for him. He pressed his eyes tightly for once and then wiped his eyes with respective shoulders of his t-shirt.

"What will you do in Delhi?" Samar said with surprise.

"Call center." Inder sounded determined.

"So you really think you can go? What about your mother and Somaya?"

"I have made a tough choice Samar. I feel stuck here. I want to save myself for the future. It's suffocating here. I can't even fall asleep at nights. I need to go somewhere to heal my mind where nobody knows me. There a long way to go; even you know that." He said, "Tell me, do you feel that I can win this war in this condition?" Inder was prepared for the questions of Samar so he said exactly what he knew that will be effective & what can satisfy Samar's confused mind.

Samar sat quite for some time. Inder knew that he understood his condition and has agreed even if he don't say anything.

"So how long you are planning to stay there?" Samar asked.

"Atleast five months. But I've not tell this to Somaya and Mom. I just told them that I'll be back after some months. Even both of them knew that I can't stay away for long so they didn't ask about the exact number of months.

Samar nodded. "The war." Samar chuckled.

"This is how it is." Inder laughed.

"Ok then, enjoy the new type of difficulties."

Both laughed.

"Haaaaa . . . . shit." Inder said.

"You came!" Inder smiled while entering in the room.

Santosh smiled back. "Yes we got free early."

Harf was already present in the room. Atul was sitting on the corner of the bed trying to project a rather casual posture.

"Hey Inder come sit." Harf said.

Inder sat with a smile trying to open his ear doors for Harf by putting the recent conversation with his Mom aside.

"Hey man, your words kept occupied my mind ever since. I just want to say that I have liked the way you think." Harf said, "Actually your words also disturbed me as if something has shook my whole body. It was like as if something was pointing that ugly 'blame' finger towards me, you know."

"Yes I can understand." Inder smiled.

"Actually I take this relation seriously and I have certain respect for this too. I, myself am not that casual relationship types. But even I wonder how I asked you about that?"

"That's why I told you that don't say that it is your belief."

"Yes exactly." Harf said, "But to my surprise that was unintentional but kind of automatic or you can say by default way to ask about this relation. It was not me but you were right about that 'we should watch the way we are conveying'." Harf took a sigh of relief.

"And I was thinking that I've expressed my views in a rather random or let's say 'messy' way." He smiled. "Because I was just in a 'burst out' mode and even look in which direction the whole conversation was going. But I am glad that you took in a right way."

Santosh was sitting near them all the time but didn't get the courage to sneak in. He was still stuck with that eye contact and was unable to find the way to start talking to him.

"Ok so please excuse me now. I need to go to washroom." Inder said while getting up.

"Hey what was it all about?" Santosh askedHarf.

"Nothing man, but let me tell you that this man is very sensitive, sensible and deep."

Santosh said nothing but just took his eyes off from Harf.

"Let's go Harf." Stephan said while standing on the door.

"They went out?" Inder asked Santosh.

"Yes they will come late night." Santosh said.

"Ok." Inder didn't ask him anything about their meet with their friends. He wanted to know the reason behind the worry of Santosh but at the same time he don't want to make him uncomfortable.

Santosh looked at Atul for once and then asked Inder to go to the balcony with him.

"What is this?" Inder said.

"I know you have watched me at the café. Inder actually that girl was Atul's sister Roohi. She was tensed so we had to meet her. The nature of issue didn't made us tell you guys the truth about it."

"Hey, it's perfectly fine. I was just worried because I didn't see that usual smile on that face of yours." Inder smiled. "If there is anything with which I can provide my help then don't hesitate."

"Thanks man, we'll surely ask."

They went inside and Inder said the same to Atul too.

"Ok I'll catch you guys in some time." Inder said and went downstairs.

"What did he say?" Atul asked Santosh.

"Just what he has told you. Nothing else." Santosh said. "Hey when he will come back I am going to discuss the issue with him. I just feel like sharing it with him."

"I don't know." Atul was confused.

"He is very understanding. I really feel he can give us better advice."

Atul nodded.

"What's up!" Inder said.

"Nothing just about to have dinner." Somaya said.

"Good I'll also have it after this call."

"Ok. So, you got the money?"

"Yes, more than I expected; nine thousand."

"Nice, lovely cousin you have got." She smiled.

"Yes." He smiled. "Hey I need to share something with you."

"Yes, what is it." She said in a serious tone.

"You know Santosh and Atul na!"

"Yes what happened?"

"There is some problem going on with Atul's sister regarding her marriage. And that's all I know. I want to know the entire matter and want my best to help them. But I can't ask them to tell me about everything because they are little uncomfortable about sharing it with me."

"Ok. What you think it is? Does she loves someone? How old is she?"

"I know nothing about these."

"Ok, so why don't you ask them to tell you the matter."

"I don't feel like. I hope they tell me when I go upstairs. Actually they both are very worried so I really want to help them out."

"You know, ask them. I know you will find some way."

"Ok I'll try."

"You tell me anything new?"

"Nothing. Hey Inder Mom is calling. I have to go."

"No problem, tata, take care. I'll call tomorrow."

"You have to or I'll come there to take you back."
She smiled, "and you too take care."

"Ok," he smiled, "bye."

"Bye."

"Hey did you guys have dinner?" Inder asked.

"No we will have with you." Santosh said.

"Should we do it. I am feeling hungry." Inder smiled.

"Yes why not." Santosh said.

They were barely talking to each other while eating. Inder was looking for the way to start talking to Atul.

"Atul, I know I must not ask this but," he paused, "you guys are really very much worried so please tell me what is going on. I can't bear this."

"Ok I'll explain." Santosh said. "Actually Inder, Atul's sis, she is the same for me too, she likes someone."

"And parents are not in the favor." Inder interrupted.

"Parents don't even know about this yet. Actually they are looking for a boy for her and she don't want to get married."

"How old is she?" Inder asked.

"She is going to be 22 in July." Atul spoke for the first time.

"Why they are in so much of hurry?" Inder said.

"You know it has been always like this. But the thing is that, first she doesn't want to get marry and secondly she wants to get marry with the boy she likes. They are together for the last 5 years and even we were not aware about this. But she got scared so much this time that she shared the entire situation with Atul." Santosh explained.

"I understand, so you met her today; did you find out any solution?"

"We are going to meet her tomorrow morning and that boy will also come. She wants us to meet him." Atul said in a rather comfortable tone.

"If the boy is earning or is from financially sound family, you know, then it can get simple. Does he belongs to the same Religion. I almost forgot the most important part." Inder said.

"The Religion is same but he is not working yet. He is pursuing M.Com, they are in the same class." Santosh said, "And he belongs to a middle class family. Not much different than ours."

"Ok, so, have you decided anything yet; about how to solve this situation."

"Let's see, first we want to meet that boy." Santosh said.

"See Santosh, if she is in love with him and they are together for 5 years now then she must have been clear about him and their future together. Moreover there are lots of promises in the relationships and if they have decided to stood by them then you can't stop them. Instead you must understand their situation and must find out a solution." Inder said.

Both of them kept quiet for a while.

"Atul, if you and your sister feels comfortable then can I come with you guys tomorrow morning?" It was definitely difficult for them to answer. Something inside of Santosh wants to agree on this but he can't say anything before Atul.

"Ok," Atul said, "come with us. I'll talk about this to her."

This was the first weekend when they were not pulling each other's leg or making noise. After having their dinner they went for sleep. But off course no one was sleeping. They were all wandering in & around their thoughts. There was complete silence in their room but all of them can feel the noise. Atul's phone kept blinking every now & then in that dark room.

Inder has faced this situation in his life before so he was well aware of all the things associated with this type of issue. His mind projected all the images from his past in front of his eyes. He barely even felt any darkness in the room.

Next morning after having their breakfast they left for the café around 12 in the noon.

"Is he with her?" Inder asked Atul when they were on the way to café.

"Yes both of them are about to reach at the café." Atul said.

That boy folded his hands in *Namaste* and then they sat down. Inder dragged a chair and sat on it.

"*Bhaiya* this is Sameer." She said hesitantly.

Atul just nodded. He didn't know from where to start.

"Roohi what you guys have thought about the future, do you have any plans?" Santosh asked her to ease the environment a little.

"*Bhaiya* we both are preparing for the exams in hope to get recruited in some bank."

"The important thing is how much time you guys need to reach at a comfortable state and how to stop Mom & Dad till then?"

"We need at least two years." She said.

"*Bhaiya* I need to get a promising job before telling our parents anything about our relation." Sameer interrupted.

Atul just nodded.

Inder kept listening to their conversation without saying anything. All these things about which they were discussing were secondary for him. He wanted to talk to Roohi to know her passion and determination level about her relation with Sameer and their future.

"You know Dad, if he find any boy he will go for it." Atul said.

"No *Bhaiya* please don't say that." She was about to cry.

"No, he just want to say, that you guys need a solid plan to make your Dad's mind to go against the idea of your marriage for the next couple of years." Inder jumped in the conversation with a try to handle the situation.

She nodded.

"But what can she say? She only can say that she wants to complete her post-graduation and wants to do a job and after that she will go for marriage. But you know our parents, they take marriage as the most important thing for their daughters. Even the idea of job is not going to survive if they got any suitable proposal." Santosh said in order to make things clear in a single effort.

"The same idea of studies and job can save them. She just need to express it in the best way. She has to show them that she has some dreams which she will never compromise with just because of marriage." Inder said. "And she must not try to prove them wrong instead she just needs to express her determination towards her dreams to them."

"But *Bhaiya* people keep coming to our home with proposals of marriage and some of them are our relatives. So at that time my Dad starts believing that it's the right time for marriage." She said.

"So if there are many factors against you then why don't you quit?" Inder said it intentionally so that he can make her realize that if she wanted to be successful in this then she has to focus on right things.

There was quietness and stillness for a while as if Inder's statement was slowly entering in each of their mind and was deviating them from their ongoing thoughts.

"Atul if you don't mind can I talk to her in private?" Inder asked.

Atul signaled her to go with him. They sat on the other table.

"Roohi, even this is for the first time we are meeting but trust me I'll not give you any poor advice. Now, if you are calling me *Bhaiya* then please consider me the same."

"Yes *Bhaiya*." She said.

"Ok good. Now listen to me patiently and give me some answers."

"Ok."

"What do you think a brother wish for her lovely sister?"

"Her happiness & well-being."

"Yes, now, I don't how much Atul has asked you about Sameer; but I want to ask you some questions."

"I've told him everything about Sameer but if you ask me anything I'll tell you everything."

"Ok, so Roohi after five years of relation, if I ask, what I am going to ask can sound little stupid but you have to tell me that do you really feel that Sameer is really worth it?"

She was not expecting this type of question but then she somehow contained herself and said, "Yes *Bhaiya* he really is a very nice and honest guy. If you ask me that from all his qualities which particular thing I admire the most then I would say that his honesty and courage to obey his responsibilities."

This was exactly what he wanted to hear at this point of time. "Ok I am satisfied about him. Now Roohi if you really want to survive through this time you need to get positive about yourself and you have to believe that getting a good job is your dream and that you will do anything for it."

She kept silent.

"Now what this thing will do is that it will convey to your parents that their daughter is not going to accept any marriage proposal at this time and they will start telling people not to suggest them any marriage proposals for Roohi." He waited for her to consume his idea. "The more you will believe on this idea the easier it will get for you."

"Ok *Bhaiya* I'll start expressing this thing in front of them." She didn't sound much confident about this but Inder was ok with the response.

"Good, now there must be plan B also. Is he brave enough to take bold step if needed?"

"He is not a soldier type of personality but when time comes he does good always."

69

"Ok, because if circumstances goes exactly against you then he must tell his parents about your relation as well as must convince them to talk to your parents."

"Ok. I will discuss this thing with him."

"Good, this can be your plan B." He sighed. "You know, the philosophy of people behind relationships and marriages have become less moral. The things which must count are considered as stupidity now a days." She seemed clear and wise enough to understand things, so he just wanted to tell her the truth about relations which he believes and which he realized from his own experiences. "If he cares for you and respects you from his whole heart then fight for him. I know both of you must have made promises to each other and have also pictured the future together; but sometimes you have to put these things aside so that you can have a look on the behavioral aspects of the next person because those are the things with which you have to deal with rest of your life." He was talking to her in a very slow pace to make sure everything sticks in her head. "Now whenever you need any kind of advice at any point, you can talk to me on Atul's number."

"Ok *Bhaiya*."

"Now let's go & sit with them."

Inder sat with them for another half an hour and then he left from there. After that he kept wandering in posh localities of Delhi for about couple of hours and then he returned home.No one was at home when he reached there. He was exhausted; mentally & physically. It didn't took him more than 5 minutes to get to the door of deep sleep.

"Hey, when did you guys come?" Inder said while rubbing his eyes.

"About an hour ago." Santosh said.

"Hour! What is the time now?"

"It's 8."

"My God! You must have woke me up."

"We tried." Atul smiled.

"Ah! Anyways how is Roohi?" Inder asked.

"She is fine and thanks for your help." Atul said.

"Come on man, don't say it."

"No actually Roohi said it."

"It's ok." Inder said. "I need to make a call. I'll see you guys in some time."

He went to the STD; his second home other than his p.g.

"Hello!"

"Look at the time first." She said.

"Sorry Soma; I was very tired and I have no idea when I fall asleep. I woke up just 5 minutes ago."

"It's ok." She said. "Anyways how was the day?"

"I went with Atul & Santosh to meet her sister Roohi and that guy whom she loves." He smiled.

"Good, so you talked about it last night. So the situation was not much different than ours, huh?"

"Yes. That's why I asked Atul last night if I can go with them; after they clarify the whole situation."

"So, how worse it was?"

"Not much it was in initial stages. So I told her to convince her parents that she wants to do job before anything big happens in her life."

"Ok," she smiled, "you know, before meeting you I was not knowing that marriage can be so hectic. I have always seen my cousins getting married happily, without any tension."

Both laughed.

"The social norms are getting stupid and stupid with every passing day." He said it in a rather sadistic tone.

"Ah! I don't want to talk about it now; I am not in mood to have *disprin* after." She smiled.

He chuckled.

"Tell me anything other than Roohi's issue." She said.

"Ok." He said, "After I left them I went to roam a little in posh localities of Delhi and if you 'minus' few of the elements from the road sides, then it feels like as if you are reading a 'lifestyle' magazine or something like that."

"What!" She giggled.

"Yes, it was like everyone has come out from the pages of a magazines. Riding expensive bikes, Bentleys, Beemers and even Ferraris. A completely different Delhi. With no relation to slum part."

"Ok! You visited slum part too?"

"Not today but last weekend. But yes I didn't tell you about that. Actually I was not in mood to talk about that, I was not in condition to . . ."

"What happened Inder?"

"Nothing; actually I didn't go to exact slum, but the lifestyle of even those people was not any better than that of slum one's. And on my way back to home I witnessed a family living in a big sewer."

"What!"

"Yes and they made me feel good. I kept watching those kids playing with their mother for some time. I wanted to help them with couple of hundreds. That was nothing in front of their condition but that must have eased their life for one day at least."

"Okay, then?"

"I didn't because someone might think I am asking her for sexual favor."

"What?"

"Why not."

"And that is how it becomes more difficult." She said.

"Yes. Helplessness rules."

They both went silent for some time.

"Leave it Soma. Tell me how was your day?"

. . . .

CHAPTER 4

4ᵗʰ Weekend

He kept finding the cool spots on the bed sheet to put his feet, hands, shoulder blades and lower back on them, in order to find some ease in the hot morning of Delhi. The sheet served him with some spots which were not warmed up because of his body heat. But the cotton wool mattress beneath the sheet did not let him enjoy the spots for more than a minute. Actually he was never the one who cannot tolerate the typical heat of summers, instead it was the unknown sadness which had occupied his mind which has caused him the restlessness. He was feeling stuck in something unknown and he was not in the state of mind to recognize the cause of sadness. He slept for just four hours that Saturday and was awake since 11 a.m. Santosh and Atul were in deep sleep and that was rather comforting for him. He kept staring at the ceiling for some time as sweat kept travelling from his forehead and neck to the pillow. There was nothing in his mind or may be his mind has stopped working for some time. The relief, the calmness was absent from his mind. He didn't even wrote much on those pages this week. There already were many unsolved things in his mind and now this new disturbance has besieged his mind. He took out a medium sized portable mirror from his bag. That was the first time he has took it out since he came to Delhi. He put that mirror against the pillow and laid down in front of it on his stomach. He kept looking at his reflection as if it was conversing with him, silently. "Just notice your heartbeat." He thought. "Isn't it the one which exists only when you let some fear stay in your heart?" He stopped as if was trying to remove the 'question-mark' from his statement. "Yes, you are afraid of something. Those stupid nightmares have scared you. You can't take guarantee of Roohi's success; it is so obvious. Why are you comparing yourself with her, you know I hate comparisons. 'Hate'?" That word got stuck somewhere in his mind. "I don't hate anything anymore." He kept talking to his reflection by just looking at it. "I just simply like something or not. I have left hatred a long way back.""Leave it and tell me more about how I connect Roohi with myself?" "Ok, see, you are afraid about your and Somaya's future. I am not lying. You are in front of me, you can see yourself. Just look at your face." That reflection was making the truth more harsh because of its way of revealing things to him. "No . . . . it is not possible. We already have thought so much about it. Me and Somaya have plans and we are strictly following it. There is no room for any type of fear. We didn't left any." "I know, don't repeat things. Just tell me that where is your confidence then?" "My confidence! It's alive and well." "No, you are lying. You left some room for doubts right from the beginning." He didn't give any reply to his reflection. He put the mirror aside and then again laid straight on his back with his eyes on the ceiling; but he was looking at somewhere else. He felt like Somaya's hand was slipping out of his. His heart started sinking. His heartbeat started getting deeper & deeper. He put his hands on his face. "What are you thinking; after coming this far. Don't be a fool." He put the mirror in that position again. "I am not scared; I am not." "Then what was all the worry about? What were those nightmares? Why you can't sleep?" "Nothing more than genuine worry of Roohi. I have not connected her with my life and even if I did then the connection has been broken now . . ." "You sure?" "Yes, actually look deep within. Look in my heart. You will find that it was not fear but sadness." "You sure?" "Yes, it is sadness. Even if the connection is not there now nor does fear but the sadness is still there." "I want to laugh!" "Why?" "You were afraid of something. May be you forget how your heart was racing when you woke up in the morning." He took his eyes away from the mirror and closed them. "Ok I got scared. But now only sadness has remained. And fear was obvious as she is way too much precious to me. Don't judge me again." "Wait-wait I am your friend. You made me your friend. You forget! Don't talk like as if we are enemies." "I know; I know. You know, we are just prisoners. We are prisoners, P R I S O N E R S, just prisoners." Now was the time when reflection just listened. "These cities, communities, societies, nations are just jails. Ah! We are in trouble my dear. But you know, I am one innocent prisoner. I am not here to surrender you know; I am passionate to break the walls of it. I am not meant to be here. This is fight. This was the reason of sadness or this still is. Roohi has made me realize again that we are prisoners." He smiled, his eyes shone in the reflection. As if he has found something. "Sadness and prisoners. No; rebellious and prisoners."

He put the mirror back into his bag and wiped the sweat off from his forehead with his vest. He laid back again with his eyes on the ceiling. The disturbance and its cause was not something unknown to him anymore. But the thought of 'prisoners' was certainly going to consume his time and emotions until his heart gets quenched.

"Financial condition has always been an important point." He kind of instructed himself.

"But this must not be in the main things." She was rather sad.

"Why not? Imagine If you are going for arrange marriage, would you not wish for good economic condition of the family?"

"I don't know why are you saying this? These things have not any importance in our lives."

"May be I am trying to fit my feet in your Dad's shoes." He was lost somewhere.

They kept silent for some time. She then hold his hand and the words "we must fight" came out of Inder's mouth as if the touch of Somaya transferred them into his mind; as if she wants to hear them from Inder's mouth.

"It is just about money, it's easy, isn't it!" She said just to hear a yes.

"Off course. There is nothing difficult about it." He served her with rather determined voice.

She smiled after getting assured that hope was still alive. There was not complete darkness after all and why should there be; specially in young blood.

"We are prisoners Somaya because it is a jail. But we are not meant to be here." He hold both of her hands. His voice was reflecting determination but their eyes were projecting farewell; as a wife or a mother expresses through her eyes to their husbands and sons before they go to war.

Santosh and Atul were still sleeping. He could hear Harf and Stephan talking to each other in their room. He got up and went into the washroom. After some time he came out of it, drank a glass of water and went downstairs to make a call.

"Hello Soma."

"It seems like you just woke up and came to call me." She smiled. "Hey wake up lazy."

"Hellllo Soma!" He smiled.

"Now that's like a good boy," she smiled, "good afternoon dear."

"Hey how do you manage to pick my call every time without any risk?"

"By staying in my room for most of time during weekends." She smiled.

"Smart girl. Such a rare thing it is that a girl is acting smart." He teased.

"Time makes you everything you needed to survive." She teased back.

He laughed.

"Hey what about that girl?"

"What, Roohi?"

"Yes, Roohi?"

"Yeah she is fine. She called Atul yesterday and he said that she is all ok."

"Good."

"You had your breakfast?"

"Obviously, I am not an owl like you." She smiled.

"That's good. I am glad." He smiled too.

"How was your week?"

"Usual, the only difference was some nightmares."

"What nightmares!"

"Don't worry. Now when I remember them it made me laugh."

"Tell me what were they about?" She said with curiosity.

"Aaaa, actually the matter of Roohi freshened up some of the old memories of ours. When we were at the stage of Roohi."

"Ok."

"So I was having dreams of that kind."

"What were they? Explain them na!"

"I had them for couple of nights and both of them were very similar to each other."

"Ok."

"In the dream, there were many men appointed by your father against your will. Their job was to make an engagement ring for you."

"Really! So many men to make a ring!"

"Listen na."

"Ok."

"So they started making it. And you know the ring was very huge, like 15 feet tall."

"What!" She laughed.

"Yes, and metals like iron, steel, copper, silver, gold were coming from different parts of the country.

You came to me and told me everything about it and requests me to do something quickly. I go to that place where they were making that ring and got really scared by the pace they were making it."

"Ok, then?"

"Then I don't know, I just went to my home and started writing something. I just kept writing and writing and writing. The noise of *second* hand of my wrist watch kept getting louder and louder. All of my clothes were drenched in sweat but I kept writing. It was like with every passing moment you were going far away from me." He paused. "I started crying but then I wiped off my tears and started writing again. Then at the end of it we were talking on phone and you were telling me that the solitaire has arrived and will be installed the next day. You told me that we don't have any chance now and on the other hand I kept crying, writing and asking for some time, a last chance, all at once. Then I woke up and this happened the next day too."

"This was ridiculous and funny." Tears came in her eyes but she didn't let him know. But he got the idea from her tone.

"Yes, that was funny." He tried to change the mood. "We have come this far and now these type of dreams seems stupid."

"Yes these are stupid dreams." Suddenly her pitch was raised by some emotion.

He didn't speak anything for a while. "Yes, exactly." He said to support her feeling about it.

She took a deep breath. "Hey what were you writing?"

"I don't know. May be a letter to your *Baba Ji.*"

She laughed. "That's good." "You know the dream was really funny. Ask your stupid dream that where I was going to wear such a big ring?"

Both laughed.

"Anyways you tell me about your week." He said.

"Enjoying my break. No more studies now. But I am thinking to join some short term course on personality development or may be cooking classes."

"Ah! How strange is that there are courses on personality development."

"Don't start again, don't say anything. Complete sshhh . . ."

"Ok." He smiled, "Ok then will call you in the evening."

She didn't speak a word for a while. "When will you come back?I want to see you." She paused, "It's difficult or don't even call me on weekends too. It makes me more eager to see you."

"I am here, always with you. It is difficult for me too." He ran his tongue on his dry lips. "Just some time."

"Yes."

"Don't be sad Soma please." He pleaded.

"It's ok go now and do call me in the evening." She somehow contained herself.

"Yes for sure."

The words of love were exchanged.

Climbing stairs to go back to his room seemed like more difficult than climbing a mountain. He felt like there was not even a single bit of energy remained in his body. He went in his room, drank a glass of water and fell on his bed.

"Am I anything more than just a prisoner?" He thought while laying down on his bed. "Why these conditions have to be so difficult? Why we have to suffer? Why the things are not simple enough? Why I am away from my Mom?" Something melted inside of him and it came into his eyes. "Why we have to beg?" Suddenly something inside of him laughed at him and said, "How poor are you!" His fists got closed. A frown emerged on his forehead. He grate his teeth and said, "I am anything but poor, you bloody . . .". When his fists got tired he loosened them and said to himself, "Whatever the conditions are, I know them completely and they will change; I'll change them. Only I'll prevail." His hands had grabbed the pillow abruptly. He tried to make himself calm for some time and succeeded.

Tired from all these emotions & thoughts, he fell asleep.

"I've got some from your Aunt. Now you don't have to worry for next couple of months." She said while showing him the money.

It was a matter of worry for him and now that it was solved, but Inder just gave her a faint smile and said, "I am going for a walk."

"Don't be late. Come before 8:30." She kept looking at him until he went out of the door, hoping that he will look back at her with a smile

"Yes I will." He said while going out of the home.

Something inside of him was broken badly. Hopelessness was expanding its roots in his heart. He had stopped expecting anything good for a while now.

"I have made her a beggar. I am not a bit better than my father." He thought and kept walking on the busy streets. There was so much disturbance inside of him that the outer noise didn't exist for him. "What the hell I am studying? What good it will bring?" He just wanted to run far away somewhere, where nothing can make him feel helpless. One side of him had always the hunger to get higher education but the circumstances were poisoning his wish to get it. "Getting the tuition fee by begging, how can I pursue graduation in engineering!" He thought and stood against the wall. He wanted to sit on the ground but he couldn't. He stood there like a dummy, lost in himself, in a crowded road; confused, helpless, defeated.

"Hey are you ok!" Atul finally shook him up and asked when Inder didn't wake up till 4.

"I am ok," he looked towards him and there was not a single sign of sleep in his eyes, "I just don't want to get up, I want to remain like this for the whole day." He smiled.

"Ok." There was pleasing smile on his face.

"Is he awake?" Santosh said while entering in the room.

"I am." Inder responded before Atul.

"Are you trying to break hamburger's record of sleeping for four days straight?" Santosh said while pointing towards Atul.

"If it is so then I failed terribly." Inder laughed.

"Who the hell can sleep for four days continuously?" Atul said.

"The one whose name is *hamburger.*" Santosh chuckled. "It was so obvious Atul, why are you asking such a dumb question?"

"Ok leave it. I can't argue with you as there is no limit to your stupid talks." Atul said.

"There is a saying Atul, it is like this: The grapes are sour."

Everybody laughed.

"Leave it Atul," Inder said, "you are not going to win against him."

Santosh laughed, "She is my darling, isn't Atul!" He said while putting his arm around his neck.

"Let's eat man I am starving." Atul said while pushing Santosh away.

"First say 'I love you' or you will die starving today." Santosh said while acting as demon.

"That is exactly what you are." Atul chuckled.

"Come on Atul even Demons have heart." Inder joined the party.

"Take the side of good Inder, demons will be defeated one day." Atul said.

"Not this one Atul, not this one." Santosh said it again in the same manner.

"Ok let's eat." Inder said in order to rescue Atul.

"Spread as much laziness as you want but be ready around 8. I am in mood to roam around in the city for many hours." Santosh said.

"Ok sure." Inder accepted but from inside he was not at all willing to go anywhere. He just wanted some time with himself to pull himself out from the locked condition, which off course was the result of some emotions which were ruling over him. He has suppressed them many times in his life but had not successfully finished them, not even for a single time.

"Hey-hey I am not going anywhere," Atul said, "salary has not come yet and I am left with quite a small amount. Moreover I have to wash my clothes."

"You are so poor. Not because you don't have money or you cry at the end of every month but you are poor because you never think like a team member. You always think like an individual." He started as if seriously complaining about Atul but finished the statement in a rather funny way. "We are a team. I am having money. We are going out tonight. I am not going to do any type of compromise with the amount of fun we can have during weekends." He was rather serious this time.

Inder and Atul laughed loudly.

"We'll go tomorrow ok?" Atul smiled. "See, I have to wash clothes."

"What clothes! You can wash them tomorrow morning. Why ruin Saturday night?" He emphasized.

"See, even Inder don't want to go tonight." Atul smiled.

"Go to hell both of you." Santosh was annoyed.

"Hey it's okay we will go." Inder can't stop laughing.

"I don't want to go anywhere now." Santosh said.

"Hey Santosh, Atul is just teasing you. He is trying to make full use of the opportunity." Inder smiled while looking at Atul. "Don't get hostile." He said.

"No it's ok. We'll see." Santosh said.

"Ok-ok we'll go. Don't get angry." Atul said.

"Smile man, it's just leg pulling. We do this all the time." Inder tried to calm him down.

"Yes. But I don't want to go now." Santosh said.

Atul looked at Inder and he signaled him to stay quite.

"Relax man, let's have our meal." Inder said.

"What kind of life we are living?" Santosh said as if he was worried of something.

"What happened?" Atul said.

"I mean this call center, this p.g., these tiffin, weekends, this you-tube & facebook, what are we doing? I don't want to look back in my life and regret." Santosh said.

"My goodness!"

"What!"

Inder and Atul said respectively.

"I am doing M.B.A. to get a better job and you are having fun in Delhi before you join your dad in your family business. We were clear about what we are going to do before coming here, aren't we! What happened to you now?" Atul said.

"We are definitely going out tonight." Inder smiled. "This is one terrible side effect of staying home on weekends. I was not aware of this."

Santosh smiled. "I don't know, I am feeling lost." He said.

"Do you want to do something else?" Inder asked.

"I have no idea." Santosh said.

"Now you are making me nervous." Atul said.

"Come on; don't worry. These thoughts are not going to stay till night." Santosh said.

"You must talk to yourself." Inder said.

"What does that supposed to mean?" Santosh said.

Inder didn't expect this reaction. "I mean if you really want to do something else or you don't want to live like this anymore then you better look for something else." Inder explained.

"Naa, there is nothing else. I don't know why I said it. May be I am fed up from this routine. Leave it, this is not going to stay till night." Santosh said.

"Let's go out tonight. You are behaving strangely." Atul said.

"No," Santosh smiled, "I am feeling very tired now."

"No worries, we have time. Relax for couple of hours." Atul said.

"No, I don't really want to go. I am not angry, don't worry." Santosh said.

"Are you sure?" Inder said.

"Yes man, no worries. Let's just stay home." Santosh said.

"Why the lives are nothing more than just compromises with circumstances?" Inder thought with his diary in his hands. Santosh was sitting on the bed playing with his phone. He was rubbing his hands every now & then with his t-shirt to keep them dry. Atul was in the washroom, trying hard to heal the weary clothes. Harf and Stephan were out before they even got up. Inder kept writing in his diary in order to lighten the weight from his mind.

"What should I do?" He thought while sitting on the bed, wrapped in blanket. "I want her to quit her job but how can I?" He kept thinking.

"Yes Inder how can you? You are working so damn hard, isn't it? You are going to make her proud as soon as possible. Come on cheer up. Why are you feeling so sad?"

He hold his head tightly in his arms. "What can I do?" His hold was getting tighter. "I know everything. I know. But from where I should start. Nothing can get me exactly what I needed. Nothing."

"What makes you so sure? You haven't done anything yet. You haven't accomplish anything yet. You know what have you learnt so far? Quitting.Yes you have become a good quitter."

"Nothing which I've quit was going to give me what I needed. I need something solid. I need something promising. Because I can do better than this. I can do better. Did you hear what I just say?"

"Yes I heard it. You need something solid, I agree. But are you looking for that solid thing? Are you really carrying passion inside you?Or you just know to toss & turn on the bed or how to tear your hair or how to tear newspapers or magazines. Look at yourself, you do exactly what losers do best."

"Shut up!" he shouted. "You know nothing about me." His own voice shook him. There was no one to hear what he has to say. He looked all around the room, there was nothing but white walls. There was weird stillness in the room. The curtain, the calendar on the wall, clothes hanging on the door; everything was dead still. Actually the whole house was dead still. No wind in the courtyard, no one in the house to make any movement or sound or reaction. He was alone, alone with a crowd of thoughts and most of them were against him. He couldn't run away from them. He himself has told to himself that talking to one's own self clears the mind and solves the problem. But this time it was not helping. He got up from the bed.

"What do I do? I want her, I want my Mom to be happy.I want her to quit her job." He cried to himself while standing in front of the mirror. "I need money, a whole lot of it. Why don't you tell me how can I get it? I want money . . . ." And the pace of tears coming down increased. He sat down on the floor and cried for a while. Because of the low temperature in December, the coldness of the floor made him uncomfortable. First he thought of getting up from the floor but then something came into his mind and he placed both of his hands on the floor. He put his slippers aside and sat there with naked feet.

"This is fight and I can win this." He pressed his fists against the floor with more pressure than before.

"How can you win this fight? You don't have any degrees. You don't have any skill, if I am not wrong. You don't have any job neither any significant working experience. All you have Inder, is some hobbies and dreams."

"Yes all I have hobbies. I'll show you what can I do with them." He wiped off his tears, "I am going to show you. I have imagination and I'll show you what can I achieve with them."

He got up from the floor, wore his slippers and went in the courtyard to have some natural light.

Inder kept writing on his diary and Santosh kept listening to songs through his headphones. Both of them were taken somewhere else by their respective engagements. This went on for a long time and then Atul came in the room. He meant to talk with them but the entire atmosphere of the room didn't let him to do so. He laid down on the bed and started shuffling the pages of his magazine. That was not exactly that type of day, which let you relax and sleep at any time, but the atmosphere of the room was equally opposite to that of the typical summer evening of Delhi. There was enough noise coming from the street which was trying its best to fill the entire room and it was almost impossible to stop it anyhow. However Atul stood up to close the windows but then left them open so that ventilation don't stop. There were couple of fans hanging down from ceiling, doing their job, but were never enough. Even with all the factors against the tendency to feel asleep Inder and Atul fall asleep, tired from all the thinking and washing of clothes. Santosh was all quite, kept lying with his eyes shut and headphones on. It seemed like he was midway to fell asleep but he was not completely conscious, clearly.

"Hey wake up." Santosh said while shaking Inder's shoulder.

"O my, what time is it?" Inder asked.

"It's 9."

"My goodness! I need to call my Mom." Inder said and hurriedly went out of the room.

He went into the booth and dialed the number.

"Hello Maa!"

"Where have you been? I've been waiting till I got home. Are you all right?"

"Yes Maa I am perfectly fine and really sorry for the late. I don't know when I fell asleep again and now when Santosh woke me up it was 9."

"It's ok." She smiled. "How are you? How was your week?"

"I have been perfectly fine throughout the week." He smiled. "How are you?"

"I am good. How hot it is in Delhi?"

"More than what Amritsar use to be in May. Anyways how is Dad?"

"He is ok."

"Drinking?"

"Yes but not as badly as he did previous week."

"Good. How is your health?"

"It's good, same as before." She paused, "Did you have your dinner?"

"No, not yet; may be around 10 and you."

"I will start preparing after you hang up."

"Dad is home?"

"Yes he is. Should I give it to him?"

"No wait. Is he near you?"

"No I am in the kitchen." She said. "You talk to him then he will go to take bath I guess and then we'll talk." She whispered.

"Ok give it to him."

"Inder." She said while handing over the phone to him.

"Hello Inder."

"Hello Dad. How are you?"

"I am good. How is your work going."

"It's good. How is your health?" He asked as if he was having nothing else to ask.

"I am good. I take too much of my medicine, what could happen to me!" He said it in a jesting tone.

"Yes off course. It must have killed all the bacteria and viruses."

"Yes it did." He laughed. "Even I asked your Mom to have some she always kept complaining about her joint pain and exhaustion."

"Ah! She is never going to recognize the qualities of your medicine." He laughed.

"Anyways, it's been almost a month, isn't it!"

"Yes it is."

"Why don't you come some weekend." There was a hidden request in his voice.

"Dad, I'll but, not now, but I'll."

"Ok, talk to your Mom." He handed over the phone to her without listening to what he was saying.

"Inder."

"Yes mama." He smiled.

"Tell me something new."

"There is nothing much. Same routine every day."

"Do you have enough money till the salary comes?"

"Yes Maa don't worry. Moreover it's the matter of few days and I have enough for that."

"Ok," she paused, "how long it will take?"

"Just few days. Don't worry at all."

"No not the salary; your frustration. How long it'll take?"

He felt like something shook his entire being. "Maa what are you talking?"

"You know what I am talking." She took a deep breath as if preparing herself to hear the truth.

"No Maa, there is nothing like that. You sound like as if it is over and I am never coming back. Please don't lose faith in me."

"Tell me you will come back." She was not able to hold the tears anymore.

"Where I can go! Please do not talk like this. I can't stay far from you."

"I'll never forgive myself."

"Maa please." And tears came down from his eyes in fraction of second. "Even I would not be able to forgive myself in that case. I can never do this."

"Please don't cry, I am so sorry. Every week I try not to do this but; I have no more strength anymore."

"Please Maa stop crying. I am going to come back to you forever. Please don't cry." He was so scared of himself at that point. "Maa I am such a bad child. I have failed you. I am so sorry."

"No . . . . please don't say this. No one can have a better kid than you. I am so sorry." She was trying very hard to talk in a low voice so that his Dad could not hear.

"Maa listen to me, I am no more frustrated. I am all right. Please don't think like this. I will come back to you. Don't worry, please don't worry. In a few months as I have promised."

"Yes, okay, I am ok." She somehow contained herself. "It's ok. I just, I got scared."

"Yes I can feel Maa but you have to help, just one last time. I'll not put you in such difficult situation again." He wiped off his tears.

"Go now have your dinner and let me prepare too." She smiled. A smile which was not any different from the sunlight which tried to reach on earth's surface through dark dense clouds, but never could.

"Yes Maa, please take care of yourself."

"Don't worry and now go."

"Ok I'll call you tomorrow."

"Ok. Bye."

"Bye Maa."

He put the receiver down and took a deep breath, gathered himself and came out of the booth. He put the money on the counter just like every time after reading the cost from the digital meter and went out quickly out of the shop.

He needed someone who knows him well. He wanted to hide himself in someone's embrace. He wanted to hide himself in someone else's matters, in someone else's issues. He just wanted to take his focus off of himself. He wanted to hide himself from himself.

He was feeling stuck at that time. Neither he was able to call Somaya nor we was able to go in his room. He kept wandering here and there for some time but didn't get any relief. There were so many people around with so much noise and he was just looking for a silent corner. After wandering for some time with agony he went back to the booth and dialed a number.

"Hello Soma."

"Hey dear! No plans for tonight!"

"Naa, we are just staying home tonight."

"Ok . . ."

"Soma do you believe in me?"

"What happened Inder?" She got worried.

"Nothing, just tell me, do you believe in me?"

"Yes without any doubt with my whole heart." She said it with confidence.

"I know I have some weaknesses in me but I am fighting here and this is not easy, ok?" He was determined not to shed any single tear.

"Yes," she controlled her worries and said, "you are very strong Inder. You are one of the few who don't compromise with the values and believes in the best."

"I know but Soma I know I am not perfect. I am not. I was not getting any better in Amritsar. I have to leave that place. I needed some solitude so badly. You understand me no!" He pleaded.

"Yes Inder I can feel and I understand fully." She tried her best to pull him out of the misery. "See, I am holding your hand and I am never going to loosen my grip." She said it in a determined tone. "Inder we have lot of work to do. Now go and do something."

"Yes Soma, thank you so much. I love you." His heart was crying but he has promised himself to keep his eyes dry as he didn't want her to worry or cry.

"I love you too Inder. Now smile please."

"Yes I am good." He smiled. "Soma."

"Yes."

"Mama was very sad actually and," he wiped the sweat from his face, "she was really worried about that what if I don't go back, so . . ."

"See Inder it's extremely difficult for her. You have to deal with it. You have to make her feel good instead of taking yourself into misery."

"Yes Soma."

"This was your decision. You had gone away from all of us to get better isn't it!"

"Yes Soma, I got it."

"Don't let anything happen to your focus."

"Yes I'll not, ever."

"Good, now go & take rest and tomorrow when you call me you better be smiling."

"Yes Sir!" He smiled.

"I love you Inder. You are really very strong. Just get better and come back."

"I'll Soma, I'll. I want to see you too."

"I am glad." She smiled. "Now go and have some sleep. Talk to you tomorrow."

"Bye. Good night and lots of love."

"Thank you and good night."

He started climbing the stairs and with each step he was elevating his positivity and determination.

"We have been waiting man. Let's have dinner." Santosh said.

"I don't want to have it yet." Inder said hesitantly.

"That's is what I told him." Atul chuckled.

"You guys have form the team together. I can see that." Santosh said.

"No man there is nothing like that." Inder said.

"No we have formed the team to kick your butt." Atul laughed.

"O! so hamburger, let me tell you one thing, in your dreams may be." Santosh smiled.

"Guys I really don't want to have it yet. I don't feel like, please you have it." Inder said it again.

"It's ok we can wait. Even my darling don't want to have it yet." Santosh said while throwing a magazine towards Atul.

"I want to lie down for some time." Inder said.

"Hey are you ok!" Atul said. "This is all you have done for the entire day." Atul said.

"I am fine. I am just feeling like, nothing else." Inder assured.

"No Dr. Santosh has to check if everything is all right." Santosh said while going towards Inder.

Both of them laughed.

"Cold as hell." Santosh said while touching his forehead. "Everything is all right. Actually he has just fall in love with his bed." He smiled.

"Ah! You are so right." Inder laughed.

After that Inder fell asleep in no time because of the overload of thoughts. Atul tried to wake him up for couple of times but he didn't wake up. They had their dinner and then kept talking for quite some time before falling asleep.

Inder got up at 5 in the morning. After watching the time he tried to sleep again but it didn't happen. He went out of the room to have some fresh air. Then he went to the terrace. He stood with his back rest against the roof boundary. He looked around him and the dense population made him feel as if he is still in the room. He suddenly looked above to the sky. He reminisce the skies of summer nights which has always delighted him during his childhood and for some years of his teenage. He remembered lying on the bed with his father, looking at the sky and finding out the rockets amongst the stars. He remembered how even after his father fall asleep he kept imagining shapes with specific set of stars. Those days he used to sleep with stars. Making shapes even in dreams and the next night verifying if there really is that kind of shape present up there. That was the era of dreams and now it was the era of nightmares. "Skies were much clear at that time." He whispered. "Surroundings were darker and stars were more shiny." He looked around him, he took a good look of the buildings around. "These are not homes." He thought. "These are just structures to protect you from heat and rain and cold. These are not homes." He stood there and felt like to change the surroundings is his responsibility, like a revolutionist may think. "We need to live people." He whispered. "My goodness we are so many in number." He smiled. "But there must be a solution isn't it! We need to work in a right direction," he paused, "but how can we, there are lot of other fake but much necessary works to do. People, our priorities have been corrupted." He raised both of his arms as if addressing a large number of people. "You understand me no!" He took a complete 360 degree turn and then said, "Let's do something."

He went down in his room. He wanted to write something but he could not switch the light on. Then he stood up with his diary and went to the balcony. There was enough brightness due to street lights. So he stood there and started writing on it. Soon the day break out and the colossal significance of street light vanished. After some time he went back to his bed and laid down for some time, doing some calculations in his mind. After some time he switched on the light in the room and kept writing for about an hour.

"We are living with dire necessities." Samar said. "But the thing is that we have accepted it as our truth, as the way of life and covered it as 'modern times'."

"Yes but there are compulsions, obligations which tie our hands, which don't give us any room to think or do anything freely. There are always so many things to do. Never comes a minute of relaxation. Never comes a time when you don't have to worry about anything." Inder expressed. "What I mean to say is, that these dire necessities are like the most important things in our lives."

"Yes that's is what I said that we have accepted them as our truth and so that no one can challenge this truth we have covered it by believing that these are modern times and this is how things work in modern times; so no questions arises in anyone's mind." Samar cleared.

"And if arises, it is laughed upon." Inder was lost somewhere while saying it.

"Anyways but we have some real necessities." Samar smiled.

"I doubt them now." Inder laughed.

"Leave these things. Have you thought about any other job?You have left that call center, like 3 months ago."

"Yes almost 4 months now." Inder said.

"Time is ticking away and we don't have much. Think about Somaya."

"I don't know what should I do." Inder sounded helpless. "I need something big but it is not possible, isn't it!"

"But a good start is possible so as a promising direction."

"But it is not that easy to find out."

"Inder you have to go abroad. Think about Dubai or something."

"And what do I do there, security guard?"

"May be many other things which we can't think of right now."

"Samar it is not much about that how a girl feels but how her father does. You know what I am trying to say."

"Yes . . ." Samar wanted him to be clear.

"I need something which can be looked upon with some respect." He paused, "I need something better than the idea of Dubai or wherever."

"You have a little time to settle yourself. If you can't get the answers now then no one can save you. You have to find out what you really want to do and then you automatically will get support from people like me. But for that you must know what you want to do and must start doing that."

Inder nodded. He knew this, he has repeated the same to himself many times but the real problem was something which don't let him go for the call. Or there was not anything, which according to him sounds promising enough to solve all of his problems. If these have never let him indulge in something unworthy then at the same time, they also prevent him to make any start. So he was always unknown to what was waiting for him at the other side of the mountain.

"What must be the peak of helplessness?" He thought and stopped writing for a while. "I have always cursed this helplessness of mine. But there must be a solution, that I know. Are there more people who have been suffering from it more than I've suffered," he paused, "or maybe still suffering." He put the diary to one side and laid down and turned to one side. "What must be the extreme face of it? What must have been the mental condition of people suffering with its extreme?" He kept thinking. "Oh shit yes! But how can I? Why not! No, not an good idea." "So this your spirit to explore and witnessing the truth!" His other side responded immediately. "Ok wait, why not." He got up from the bed and took up Santosh's laptop. He started the laptop and plugged the headphones in, to kill the start-up tone. He searched for the way to red light district of Delhi. He wrote it on a paper and put that in his jeans pocket. Now the next problem for him to go there without making Atul & Santosh aware of it. "What will I tell them?" He thought. The place was easily an hour away from his p.g. Without thinking much he decided to went there right away. It was around 8 and both of them were asleep so there was no need to make any excuse. He got ready quickly and then went to the main road to catch a bus. He came down from the bus and then started walking towards that place. He reached there in just 35 minutes because of the lesser traffic. After reaching there he was not sure as if it was the exact place but after spending couple of minutes he got assured. This was his first time in a place like this. He kept looking on both sides of the road. The place looked like as if it has witnessed a gang-war. There were walls covered with phone numbers and abusive words. Lights were still on. There were very few people on the street, opposite to what he expected.

"Hey what are you looking for kid?" A man asked him from the stairs of a building to Inder's left.

"Nothing." He replied rudely and tried not to make any eye contact.

"Come in the evening and remember this building." He said loudly while pointing towards the ceiling.

Inder kept walking.

"*Shaaku*, this is what you have to tell them. Tell them that *Shaaku* sent you." He laughed.

He couldn't understand if it was a joke or he was serious. He kept walking further, looking for a face which he has imagined that morning. A face which can convince his curiosity to look into.

After wandering there for about half an hour he decided to go back to p.g.

"Yes, in the evening, *Shaaku*.I was thinking the same." He thought and a smile emerged on his face.

After reaching p.g. he entered his room and placed his tired body on the bed carefully without making much noise. He was surprised with what he just did and was thinking how he can visit that place again. He slept with the thought of those girls and ladies who have been living there; a place not less than a battle field. But again at the very next moment he felt like that the entire city was not less than a battle field.

At the end of Sunday he found himself at the top of heap of buildings, which were filled with people suppressing their emotions, all the time and at the same time didn't know which thoughts were originally there's.

He found himself at the top of the heap of people who didn't know where to put their believes on. Though he didn't know anyone other than his p.g. mates and some of the colleagues of his but this was exactly what his feelings were after spending almost a month in Delhi, as if he knows everyone living in it. Maybe this was his preconception about people or maybe that was what cities meant to him. But somewhere deep down he always believed that life can be better than this and the entire environment of the cities is not humane. He found himself lost somewhere for the entire day expect those times when he talked to his Mother and Somaya. He finished his novel which he had started about four days ago, filled some pages of his diary with his ongoing thoughts. Even when he was out with Atul & Santosh he kept looking for that face. He wanted to visit that place again but couldn't get the time and condition. Now, at the end of Sunday, he found himself, again, at the terrace, having a good look all around himself. At the end of Sunday, he found himself staring at the stars again but they all felt strange to him, as if he was watching them for the first time. They didn't seem to impress him with their charm or may be that was exactly the thing missing in them. "After all these are city skies." He thought.

CHAPTER 5

5th Weekend

Inder has been reading articles on human trafficking & prostitution in India from couple of hours now. He has been moving like pendulum between his thoughts and what he was reading. As usual he woke up early on Saturday but now it was almost 3 and both of them were about to wake up as 3 was their start of the day. Inder's curiosity to witness the extreme of helplessness was at peak. He has been waiting for the weekend desperately. All he needed was courage to make an excuse to both of them so that he can visit that red light area again.

"Good morning." Atul said while stretching his arms.

"Good morning." Inder smiled.

"I thought he will wake up first with excitement for the weekend." Atul chuckled.

"Yeah, even he is having salary now." Inder added.

"Yes it is strange." Atul said. "Let's kick his butt together."

Inder put the laptop aside and got up from the bed.

"*Oye!* You bastards." Santosh shouted as they kicked him hard.

"He is never going to sleep like this now." Atul laughed.

"No, I am not sure of that but I am certainly going to wake up tomorrow before you." Santosh threw a magazine towards Atul.

"Why are you punishing my magazines!" Atul chuckled.

"Don't worry, just wait for next morning."

"Ok, pause, hey Santosh I've been using your laptop." Inder said.

"What! How can you do this to me? You are so cruel!" Santosh cried.

"Okay, I got it," Inder smiled, "save your energy for rest of the day."

"Ok I am going to bathroom." Atul said.

"I don't know how you control it all night. The moment you get up you feel the pressure, isn't it?" Santosh laughed.

Atul ran out of the room in order to save himself from more jokes of Santosh.

"What are you doing?" Santosh asked.

"Nothing just facebook and a blog of mine, which I haven't updated from ages. I was just reading my old posts." Inder didn't want to tell them about what actually he was doing. He never liked telling a lie but he also don't like to share certain things which he feels that people will not understand exactly the way he want them to understand.

"Man I hate facebook."

"Why what happened?" Inder asked.

"The girls I like, never accept my friend requests."

Both of them laughed.

"I think I need to change my profile picture."

"No worries I'll click one for you." Inder smiled.

"I am going downstairs to see if tiffin have arrived." Santosh said while getting up from the bed.

"Okay."

"Everybody up!" Harf said while entering in their room.

"Yes the day just got started." Inder said.

"How was the week?" Harf asked.

"As ususal, nothing special." Inder said. "How was your week?"

"Got the first salary after appraisal." He smiled.

"That's lovely!"

"Yes, that is. Don't have to live stiffly now."

"Yes, off course. Hey where is Stephan anyway."

"He is out with his girl, o, I mean with his love."

Both laughed.

"You remembered!" Inder said.

"Yes, why not, after all that conversation highlighted your presence in this p.g. for me."

"My goodness!"

"Hey-hey how are you?" Santosh said while entering the room with tiffin.

"I am good. What about you?" Harf smiled.

"I am rocking as usual." Santosh laughed.

"And this is what Santosh is all about." Inder said.

Everyone laughed.

"He didn't came out of the bathroom yet?" Santosh said.

"No, not yet." Inder replied.

Santosh went out and started knocking at the door of the bathroom continuously.

"Hey what are you doing? What is taking you so long; dirty boy." Santosh said the later part in jesting tone.

"Shut up!" Atul laughed. "I am coming, wait for couple of minutes."

"Ok no worries, I will be ready with the deo spray."

Everyone laughed as Santosh hurriedly went in the room to have a deodorant spray and stood in front of the bathroom door. And when Atul came out he sprayed the deodorant to his lower body.

"Actually the right spot is this." Atul said while turning backwards.

"Exactly." Santosh said and kicked his butt. "I didn't do anything, actually it is kick-ass deodorant." Santosh said and ran into the room.

"You cannot save yourself from him." Inder laughed loudly.

"Hey, even Inder was with me, kick him too." Atul said while pointing towards Inder.

"You are such a kid." Santosh laughed. "But as we all know that you are my darling, I will fulfill your wish as soon as possible."

"My goodness! I have to save my ass then. It never happened in Amritsar. Delhi has showed her real colors." Inder said in jesting tone.

Everyone laughed loudly.

"Okay so you get freshen up and I'll back in few minutes and we'll have our breakfast." Inder said.

"No problem Mr. Smith but don't be late." Santosh said.

"I won't." Inder smiled and left the room.

He went in his dearest booth and dialed the number.

"Hello Soma!"

"I have been missing you so much."

"I missed you too." He said it in a very polite manner.

"What! How this happened? My God." She smiled.

"Don't say like this. I have missed you so much this week."

"My God, I was feeling so sad that I was about to get angry with you but these words of yours," she took a deep breath, "have fondled my heart."

"I am glad." He smiled.

"So, how was your week dear."

"As usual but I got the salary." He smiled.

"Wow! I am happy."

"This is love, transforming an ordinary thing into something extraordinary." Inder said.

"You keep silent. I am extremely happy."

"I love you too Soma!"

"I love you." She giggled.

"Anyways, how was your week? How are your cooking classes going?"

"They are going good. I am making different types of cakes."

"I always knew that you are the right girl." He said it in a funny way.

"Really!" She laughed.

"Hey how is everybody at home? I haven't asked about them since I came here." Inder said.

"They are very well and do not worry dear. Just keep working on the things and come back with clear and calm mind." She smiled.

"Yes darling and don't stop me while I say that thank you so much for everything and really am glad to have you in my life." He felt like kissing her palms.

"You are so boring." Normally she says this in funny way but this time it was said with rather irritating tone. "Just;", she paused, "nothing, let's talk about something else."

He smiled as he felt the sensation of something divine.

"Hey I told you earlier about that red light area!" He said as if it suddenly came back to his mind.

"Yes . . . ."

"I'll visit that place this evening."

"You must feel shame and you are telling me proudly about this." She smiled.

"I really want to witness someone from that kind of life." Inder put forth his wish.

"I know," she smiled, "I am just kidding. Just take care of yourself."

"Yes." He smiled.

"By the way what are you going to say to your p.g. mates?"

"What about if I say them that my old friend is in Delhi and I have to go to meet him."

"And if they say that they want to meet him too or if they say that call him and ask to come at any specific place so that both of them can also meet him to have fun together or something like that."

"All this is the effect of my company, isn't it!" Inder said.

"What effect?"

"That you are using your mind to greater extent than before." Inder laughed.

"O! Yes off course. Some people live with such big misapprehensions." She said the later part in relatively low voice as if talking to herself.

"And some people are so jealous." Inder said it in the same manner.

Both laughed.

"Okay leave it and think a better excuse." She said.

"What if I say he is here along with his fiancé."

"Better."

"Now all I have to do is to say it in believable manner."

"Yes but tell me one thing, even I wanted to ask it last Sunday when you told me about that place, from where suddenly so much craze for place came from?"

"I . . . . I was just struggling with myself & thinking about society one day when suddenly a thought of people like this came into my mind."

"Okay."

"And after that I got very curious to meet a person from this world."

"I know you Inder. I know you more than anyone."

"Yes, I know Soma."

"And the reason you are telling me is not the prime reason behind this curiosity, isn't it." She said it with confidence.

He kept silent for some time and tried to rummage his heart. "Soma, actually, it's helplessness, I have felt it in my life for so long & for so many times and now I want to feel it someone else's life too."

"What good can come from that?" She said.

"I don't know yet. May be I just want see myself in others." Inder said hesitantly.

Both of them didn't speak for a while.

"I am here just to support you." She said. "I hope it helps you in good way. I wish you get your answers."

"I wish so too and I love you so much."

"That's ok but don't forget that I'm going to take revenge for everything when you come back." She smiled.

"I'll surrender myself right away." He smiled.

"Ok leave it. You had your breakfast?"

"No, not yet. They must have been waiting."

"Now go and do call me in the evening."

"Yes for sure."

"Bye Inder."

"Bye dear."

He went upstairs filled with confused thoughts.

"Let's see what happens." He thought and went into the room.

"Mr.Smith you take so much time man." Santosh said.

"I am really sorry guys. Let's have it." Inder said while sitting with them.

"What are the plans for the evening?" Inder asked.

"Obviously we'll go out." Atul said.

"Why are you asking? I smell something fishy." Santosh said it with smaller eyes.

Inder laughed and said, "Actually one of friend is in Delhi with his fiancé. Somaya told me about him so I called him and he insisted me to meet."

"Come-on man!" Santosh said.

"I'll go with you tomorrow. Please." Inder was feeling uncomfortable in the situation now.

"At what time you'll leave." Atul said.

"Around 7." Inder said.

"How are you going to meet up with them without cell phone?" Santosh said.

"I already told them that I am not having my phone with me so they told me to come at their place and then we'll go out together." Inder said and felt that he has become a skillful liar.

"Okay, that's sensible because people now-a-days cannot stick their butt at one place for more than 5 minutes," Santosh stopped to have a bite, "so it is practically impossible to catch up with them without contacting them on cell phone." He completed the sentence with mouth full of food.

Inder smiled. "Yes, true indeed." And he continued with his meal. The bite was chewed up enough to get through from throat but something came in the way which stopped it from going forward. He pushed it again to save himself from getting caught. Lies have always made him restless even if they were totally harmless to others.

"Lies are lies, big or small." Somaya said, putting all the arguments at rest.

"It's quite conservative philosophy about lies." Inder said while taking a sip of coffee.

"What! Some things are neither conservative nor broad or bold they are just right or wrong." Somaya cleared her point.

"Strictness has always hurt flexibility." Inder said.

"Strict or not but it is my belief and I'll stick to it no matter of what."

"That is why you will never come to know about the depth and variety of lies." Inder said it with a smile.

"Boys are always so comfortable with lies. See how you are defending 'lies'." Somaya was little frustrated. "And what variety!"

Inder laughed. "Every lie has a reason behind it and not all reasons are ethically wrong or sinful." He leaned towards her a little, "Lies are not bad it's the motive behind them. These motives behind them gives variety." He smiled.

"I've never seen a lie doing anything for good." She said.

"Ok firstly I'm not defending lies and secondly It is not about my comfort level or that I like telling lies. My concern is your attitude towards lies." Inder said it while maintaining his composure.

"What attitude?" She said it with a mixture of strangeness, anger and self-confidence.

"Nothing."

"No what?"

"Somaya, dear, you seems like scared of something."

"I am not scared of anything but I'm not comfortable with the way you are justifying lies."

"Okay, now tell me how many people do you expect, which are in your social circle speak the truth all the time?"

"Not too many. I mean I don't expect the truth or I don't know may be even if they are telling me the truth but I don't believe."

"Ok that shows that truth is little precious; no, actually very precious and people don't spread it normally, especially when it is about them."

"Yes it can be said in one sense."

"So whoever tells you the truth about themselves must be very close to you?"

"Yes, actually they are."

"So why you think they tells you the truth?"

"Simply because they trust me."

"And why you think they trust you?"

"What are doing Inder? I am fed up from all this now."

"Just little more patience." He smiled.

"I don't know."

"Simply because you have good mutual understanding." He picked up his cup of coffee and leaned back on his chair.

She kept doing some calculations in her mind while staring at her coffee mug. "So you mean that people lie because of the lack of understanding?"

"No, not exactly, they do so because they are insecure and there is no mutual trust to eliminate insecurity." He paused, "We lie because we believe that the next person will not understand us the way we want to be."

"So this is it! This is why people lie?" She said as if she already knows the answer.

"No, but this is one of main reasons." He paused for a while. He knew exactly what was her mental position at that time and he knew exactly what words can calm her mind down. "Somaya I know you hate lies but . . ."

"Oh shit!" She said while maintaining calmness on her face.

"What happened?" Inder said in a troubled voice.

"That man behind you in my Dad's friend."

Inder turned back to have a look while that man sitting on a chair.

"Let's pay the bill and get out from here." She said.

"Let's take our craziness out of ourselves!" Stephan said while entering in their room with his laptop and speakers, which were throwing beats.

"Hey when did you come!" Santosh said it in joy.

"Just 10 minutes ago." Stephan said while placing laptop and speakers on the bed.

"Is this exactly what I am thinking it is?" Atul said with a smile on his face.

"Yes,", Santosh turned towards Atul and bent a little by his knees with his arms stretched towards him, "my dear darling, time to show your wilder side to me." He ended it with a devilish laugh.

"No!" The word just came subconsciously from Inder's mouth.

Harf went near Inder and pulled him out of his bed.

The bus was filled way more than its capacity. While standing in that squeezing condition, he memorized his childhood when he used to be so afraid of crowded buses. He tends to believe that he'll be suffocate to death because of the crowd. Travelling in that bus he smiled at his thought and closed his eyes to took a deep breath. He could easily smell the presence of weariness present in everyone's body. And that bus seemed like nothing more than 'a worn out carrier of used up bodies' to him. He looked outside the window in front of him and a strange sadness overwhelmed him. After reaching at the destination he left the bus and kept looking at it for some time. It went over a hump and everyone's weary body inside of it suffered its consequence but kept silent; non responsive. He shook his head and took his eyes off from the bus and started walking into the depth of that red light area. A strike by the shoulder of a passerby dragged him out of his thoughts to the present raving. He started trying to adopt the surroundings by focusing on his motive. But there were more men than women; wherever he looks, he gets stares back at him and most of them were from men. He kept walking trying to carry a rather casual yet confident expression. He turned into another lane; a bit more narrow, a bit more crowded. He kept going forward and then sooner he found out that he was not at all looking for any face instead was just busy maintaining his expression. With some courage he looked above and to his sides.

"I smell fresh young blood." Someone from above spoke that and loud laugh followed. Three ladies were laughing, clapping and staring at him. He kept walking and a frown emerged on his forehead to save him from humiliation.

"Hey . . . . you look like a virgin." A distant voice said and this time laughter was as high as sky.

Moving further a strange hand clutched his right forearm and pointed towards stairs of a brothel and women standing on the porch of it started laughing. He rescued himself from his grip and started moving forward. "Come-on! Don't be so rude my darling." Someone from that porch said which killed almost rest of his spirit to look for that face.

He kept wandering in that area, with a little more pace, trying to ignore the comments and struggled to focus on why on the first place he was there. After every few steps he tried to look around him to catch a face, an expression; to follow. There was this weird commotion all around him. Suddenly all the scenes came into his mind from the afternoon, when they all danced madly in their p.g. He felt like everything around him is intentionally acting crazy as if they loved to do so. He thought, "Like I was not getting involved in that initially but then after some time and according to the situation & surroundings I fell in the act, I got mixed up so well in the craziness. It's a big act going on in here and everyone has just got mixed up." He kept wandering there and kept receiving lots of comments. Sooner he found out that instead of looking for a face, he was trying to hide his own.

After circling the streets he was at the boundary of that area, when a women stopped at front of him and after taking the *Bidi* out of her mouth, "Watched heaven?" He quickly moved away from her as she laughed after seeing his reaction. There was a satisfaction floating on her face as if she had crushed the enemy.

He looked at his wrist watch and felt the wave of rush inside his entire body. He was late to call her mother. It was like two way defeat. Once he tried to look for a S.T.D. there but then soon he quitted his search and went to catch something which can transport him to home as soon as possible.

"Hello Maa!" He said hurriedly.

"Hello Inder!" She said with joy.

"How are you?" He has now recovered some breath.

"I am good. Everything is fine. Tell me about yourself?"

"I am perfect, I'm good."

"Good," she smiled, "thanks to God."

He smiled.

"But why are you calling me so late? I've been waiting since I've came home from work."

"Sorry Maa, was just doing fun with them."

"Ok . . . and forgot about me." She said it with smile to hide some other sentiment.

"No Maa, I can never." He cried.

"Ok-ok, tell me about your week. How is everything going at work?"

"Everything is going good at work. I do my work and nobody complaints."

"Is it this simple?" She smiled.

"I just don't let it get complex." He smiled too.

"Your father wants to talk to . . ."

"Hello Inder."

"Hello Dad. How are you?"

"I am good. What could happen to me. Tell me about yourself."

"I am good too."

"How is your job going?"

"It is good."

"Your Mother is asking if you have got the salary."

"Yes I've in-fact, I forgot to tell her."

"Good, is it enough for you?"

"Yes, it is just enough for me. But it can rise with time." He smiled.

"Yes that's obvious. But are you going to stay there till the rise?" He asked in a weird way.

"No . . . . actually, I don't know it yet."

"Then why did you go there if you don't have long term plan."

Right before he could say something his Mother took the phone from his Father.

"Hello Inder, leave him. Don't listen to his silly questions."

"It's ok Maa. I am fine, don't worry."

"He's been frustrated like this for few days now. Abusing all the relatives, neighbors after drinking at dinner."

"It's ok, nothing new in this." He sighed. "You tell me about your health."

"I am good, having no problem."

He knew there were issues with her health but he also knew that 'having no problem' just meant that the length of the list of problems was unchanged.

"Everything will be alright with time." He said as if reassuring himself.

"Yes, off course, with the grace of God."

"Yes." He said silently.

"You stay safe and sound and everything will be alright."

"Don't worry about me. I am having fun." He said as if reproving himself.

"Do not take any pressure unnecessarily."

"I am not, why you felt that?"

"Nothing, I just casually said that."

"Tell me something new Maa." He said as if he had no control on himself.

"Nothing, everything is in a loop." She didn't want to say that but had no control over her feelings.

He kept silent for some time. He was having nothing to say. How many times he could repeat the same thing. He knew what was needed and that was going to take time. His mother on the other hand want to break the silence but words didn't come out of her mouth. That silence kept growing and ultimately he hung up the phone. He was so depressed at that time that even tears were not able to find their way out. That trauma was powerful. He got out of the booth, paid the bill and started moving towards his p.g. At the first step of stairs his heart started sinking as if sudden feeling about how his mother would be feeling at that time overwhelmed him. He stopped there for few seconds to gather himself and then hurriedly went to the S.T.D. booth.

"Hello Maa!" He cried.

"Inder . . . ." She tried her best to separate her tears from her voice.

"Everything is going to be alright. Soon I'll be there and we'll move towards better life." He said all in single breath.

"Yes Inder it will be. You take care and don't take any burden my dear son."

"Yes Maa, you too take good care of yourself. I love you."

She smiled as if she didn't have to reply to that thing. Her every breath after his birth was proof of her love towards him and he completely knew that.

He wanted to talk to Somaya at that time. He wanted to hear her voice and he knew even she wanted the same too. At first he thought of going out of the booth, want to go upstairs and wanted to have some water as his throat was so dry even normal talking was hurting him. But he also was not in position to face his p.g. mates nor he wanted to. Sooner he felt unable to leave the booth to get water bottle or soft drink to soothe his throat. He just didn't want to leave the phone as it was the only way to connect to his loved once. He knew it was a stupid thought but on the other side not a single muscle of his entire body was supporting him to get up and went to look for some relief for his dry throat. He ran his tongue on his dry lips and tried to swallow saliva to get some nourishment.

"Hello Soma." His voice trembled a little.

"Hello dear." Her voice contained the joy as well as showed the pain of being apart.

"What are you doing?"

"Nothing . . . . just had my dinner; a little earlier, because I was expecting your call. So I came to my room."

"Ok . . . ," he smiled but his heart was racing and he himself was not knowing the reason.

"Tell me how was your experience there, in that area?"

"Area?" That part of that evening was overcome by other sentiments. "O! that was terrible."

"Why what happened?" She was not that excited about this.

"Actually that is totally another world and was not able to adapt that environment even a single percent."

"So, didn't get anyone to talk with?"

"There was no chance of that."

"Don't go there." Her voice was showing her hidden fear but Inder was not in condition to recognize that.

"Don't worry Soma. Moreover I have chose that I'll go for just one more time and I think that will happen on next weekend now."

"Ok . . . . you had your dinner?"

"You sound so low. What happened?"

"Nothing, everything is fine."

"Anything in the family?"

"No! not at all. Everyone is fine. Leave it. Tell me more about that place and what happened there?"

"Aah . . . . from where must I start? . . . ."

. . . .

He went upstairs and drank lot of water. No one was there as he opened the lock with the alternate key which was given to him by Santosh. He lit the tube-light, shifted the curtains aside, wide opened all the windows, changed his clothes and laid down on the floor. Some weird unease was not letting his mind to relax. All the heat from the ceiling was directed towards him by the fan. He got up from there and went out in the balcony. This was the time when he needed the strength of his loved once but he was not ready to accept that. He was not ready to accept that this was his best and now he needed to go back. He tightened his grip on the metallic parapet and a determined frown emerged on his forehead. He felt as if the parapet is the whole problem and he even imagined in the back of his head uprooting it and throwing it away. He went inside and started writing something on his diary. After some time he had his dinner and just like most of the times he flew somewhere away from his physical presence.

"Hey I've reached home I'll call you later."

"Ok bye Inder."

"Bye Soma."

"Maa . . ."

"Where were you?" She was little annoyed.

"I was with Samar."

"Look at the time. Neither your father nor you come on time and I keep waiting for both of you; when you would arrive and when I'll sleep."

He kept silent while standing at the door of the kitchen.

"I am not having proper sleep from the last couple of days and I feel drowsiness at work." She took the lighter and asked, "Should I cook the food or you had it from outside?"

"No I'll just have a glass of milk." He was felling devastated. There was no room for carelessness in their life. There was no room for any flexibility in their routine.

"You will get your milk when your father will come. Must have been drinking with his useless friends." She came out of the kitchen and stood in the veranda. "Every-time he says that he will not drink on daily basis and after couple of days the same thing starts."

Inder was not able to say anything to her ease her frustration as he himself was late and was regretting that while standing near her.

"Sometimes I really get scared by the way he drinks. I am afraid that he is going to kill somebody on road. His driving is already rash and after drinking I can't even imagine how horribly he must have drove the bus." She paused for few seconds and then turned towards Inder and said, "One day he is going to put the school administration in trouble along with us. Sometimes I get so scared thinking what if any kid in the bus got hurt? We'll not even able to have meal for two times." She tittered. "Rest of our lives will revolve around courts."

"Maa . . . . stop it. Don't worry. There is nothing going to happen of this sort." He wanted to hug her but didn't found the courage. "Just go and sleep, I'll open the door for him."

"Hey when did you came home?" Santosh asked while entering the room.

"I . . . . I think about one and half hour ago." Inder said.

"I told him to wait for you." Atul said.

"But we did the toss and it came out that you will be late." Santosh said.

"And I told him that money lies but he didn't believe me." Atul laughed and everyone followed.

They settled after some time and started talking on random things when Harf and Stephan came to wish them 'good night'.

"Hey Inder what is your dream? What you want to become?" Atul asked when the chatter was going on completely different things.

Inder giggled as he was not expecting this sort of question. He thought for a while and then said, "I don't know, I mean what all of us wants? A better life and I think better here means, most of the time 'easy life'."

"Which is a myth." Santosh laughed. "And Atul you, sometimes the way you ask things, you sound like a girl."

Inder and Atul laughed in confusion.

"What you mean?" Atul said.

"Yes, I am saying right." Santosh turned towards Inder, just like Atul did but exaggerated it a bit and said, "So dear what is your dream?" He said it in a feminine voice and acted like a little girl with his constantly blinking eyes.

Everyone laughed loudly.

"I didn't do that!" Atul cried.

"Even I am not saying that you did it." Santosh tried to control his laugh. "I am just saying that you sound like this when asking something, sometimes."

"Stop it now. You took the entire fun off from the question." Atul said.

They kept laughing at the little act of Santosh for a while and then there chatter gradually fainted over time and then they all went to silence; at the door of sleep.

"Who's car is this?" Somaya asked Inder right after she opened the door.

"Someone's." Inder smiled.

"This is a nice surprise." She smiled.

"What? Me or the car."

"You stupid. You told me that you were busy with dad."

"And that was a sheer lie." He smiled.

"Yes I can see that."

Both laughed.

"Let's go somewhere." She said.

"Where? You will get late and your mom will ask 'where were you?' then what will you say?"

"She will not ask because I am a good girl and I have never did anything wrong. So she is never that strict with me and moreover I can say I am out with my friends."

"Yes she should not and even nobody should. We are good kids, isn't it."

"Yes, now let's go somewhere. Let's get out of here."

"Where would you like to go?"

"I would love to go to a place where there will be no one so that I can kiss you with ease, without any stress."

"Ok . . . . and?"

"And where I can touch your face, where I can hold your hands and where I can shut my eyes for some time . . . . on your lap . . . . on your shoulder."

"Ok, so duty is calling. Let's go then."

Both laughed. He started driving and soon they reached highway. They kept going in that box with wheels which had isolated them from rest of the world temporarily.

"It is better that any café and any restaurant, isn't it." She said with a smile.

"Yes it is." He looked at her and asked for her hand.

"I love you." She whispered.

He smiled but said nothing just enjoyed those words playing with his ears and consoling his heart.

"Hey Inder look at that couple walking on the footpath."

"Where?"

"This side." She pointed towards her left side. "Look husband is walking miles ahead of his wife. What type of couple is this?"

"I don't know. May be weak," he slowed down the car, "may be helpless & hopeless or even worst may be wounded."

"Yes even I think the same." She looked towards him. "I wish nothing happen to us of this sort."

"It will never. You remember I once told you about the ingredients of a healthy life?"

"Yes I do but even those things have not developed in our minds, we still can do things which are not good for our relation, isn't it." She said with expectation of an positive answer.

"We are learning and moreover all those true and pure things will take some time to become our never changing character." He said and speed up the car once again and tried to see the face of the lady; she was his mother. He simply took his eyes off from her. That didn't come as a surprise or shock for him. He shifted his focus back on driving.

"Hey the weather is changing!" she said it with joy.

"Yeah! But don't you think it has changing way too quickly, very dramatically?"

"So what. Even in movies this happens. There must be some truth in that."

"Yes it can be." He said in amazement. "Hey if it starts raining now then how great it will be."

"I wish." She said it while watching the sky from the window.

Sooner it started raining and wide smiles stretched their delighted faces. It was raining heavily and everything on the highway became slower. They turned to their left on a small stretch of a unmetalled road and stopped the car near a tree.

They leaned towards each other and embraced the bodies.

"Something filled in my arms." She whispered in his ears.

"Yes but your nose is tickling on my neck."

She smiled. "But I strongly believe that it must be much better than the feeling of harsh beard on the shoulder."

Both laughed.

"I want your lap, my arms have no energy." He said while loosening his grip.

She moved back and cleared the way for him to come and rest on the most pleasant place man's head can have.

"Can you feel the cool breeze through windows?" She said while moving his finger tips in his hair.

"Naa . . . . firstly my eyes are close and secondly windows are too."

"This is so great." She said.

"Yes it is, indeed."

"You know what it is like?" She said while closing her eyes.

"Heaven . . . ."

"No . . . . you are talking like typical poets."

He chuckled.

"This is like *Kheer*."

"What!" He said without any movement of his head as if it was at the ultimate place.

"Yes, it is like *Kheer*. My mom use to make it for us. But occasionally she makes it delicious and most of the time it misses something."

"Um-hmm."

"And whenever she makes it delicious, coincidently she makes it in lesser quantity."

"What a tragedy."

"Don't laugh because I always use to feel bad about it. Because my brother and I always end up fighting for more."

"That must be sweet."

"Yeah, but for the viewer only."

He laughed.

"So what I did; I developed the habit of appreciating the taste of it regardless of its painful quantity."

"Okay . . . . And?"

"What I want to say is that this particular time, is like that delicious *Kheer*. Quantity is painful but it feels great."

"Wait a minute! Your mother is supposed to make better *Kheer* than my mother and my mom makes it good."

"And why you think like this?"

"Because you are a Hindu. Hindus are always good at making *Kheer* than Sikhs."

"This is silly! Who told you this?"

"Our neighbors are Hindu and my mom always praise their *Kheer*."

She laughed loudly and then he started to laugh too. He took his head off from her lap and started looking in her eyes.

"You look so beautiful." He said.

Both of them leaned forward and their lips unite. They were most alive at that point as if they were each other's support; incomplete and imperfect without each other's touch.

"I want you to work hard." Her lips said in the ears of his lips. But the words got stuck somewhere in his mind and it didn't let him feel her lips again in the same way. They were still soft and lovely but he was unable to feel these qualities of them. Soon he stopped kissing her and sat back in his seat. It was raining heavily and both of them were unable to see anything beyond few meters of distance. For the first time he heard the loud noise produced by the rain by hitting on the car's roof and bonnet. Soon that noise occupied his entire mind and he was unable to find the pleasure in her company. He wanted the rain but he didn't want the noise.

"It is making very loud noise, isn't it." he said.

"I don't know."

He leaned towards her and placed his lips on hers. He opened his eyes while kissing her and saw tears coming out of her eyes. He immediately moved back.

"What happened Soma?"

"Nothing!" there was an innocent smile on her face.

"You are crying." He said anxiously.

"No I am not." She said it with confidence.

"But tears are coming out of your eyes." He cried.

"Where are they?" she said after looking in the rear view mirror.

"No! these are not tears, it's blood." He cried. "It's blood coming out of your eyes."

"It's ok Inder. It's perfectly fine."

"No! what I've done to you!" Tears started coming down from his eyes.

"You have done nothing. It's fine." She put her hand on his face. "Why are you so sad?"

"I've dragged you in my miserable life."

"Stop it Inder!" She said annoyingly.

He looked towards her. "See there is blood on your laps. You are bleeding Soma."

"Will you stop crying? It's fine, I'm fine. I am not feeling any pain."

"No!" He placed both of his hands on his face.

"Inder you are infuriating me now. Are you a coward?"

He stopped sobbing immediately and got lost in his thoughts.

"See you have even caused the rain to stop." She said.

He looked outside the window and everybody on the highway was staring at them.

Inder got up as if someone gave him a shock. It was around 12 and the light present in the room overwhelmed him. He punched in the mattress in anger. He was fed up from these sort of nightmares. "What stupid thing that was?" He asked from himself.

He got up from his bed with an intense frown on his forehead along with sweat and gnash. He took that mirror out of his little bag and went towards bathroom. He put the bucket's upside down and put the mirror on its base and sat in front of it.

"Don't you have anything better to think? From where these thoughts come from huh?" He paused. "Can't you stay strong, solid and positive enough to eradicate these from your mind forever?" He kept staring himself but his focus was hardly on his face. "Stay strong." He closed his palm tightly and moved in front of the mirror. "Does this Inder can achieve everything he ever dreamt of?" "So why don't you bloody change!" He turned aside from the mirror and sat in that position for some time. "Bullshit!" "Bloody pathetic." He took the mirror, put it back in his bag and went in the balcony. He took some deep breaths.

"Come-on, don't be angry with yourself." He thought. "That was just a stupid dream. You are doing good and you know that. Don't criticize yourself unnecessarily." He shut his eyes. After some time he went back in his room. He sat on the floor as it was the only thing which was cooler than anything in that room. He kept his eyes shut for some time. "Concentrate." He said to himself.

He took his diary & pen and started writing. But after writing just couple of lines he got bored. As if some gust of boredom came from the window and consumed every drop of his remained excitement on that day. He kept sitting there for some time carrying a facial expression as if someone placed something extremely bitter on his tongue. He took his wallet and went downstairs to call Somaya.

"Hello dear!"

"Hi Somaya."

"My God! Such a fusty 'hi'."

"Yes I am feeling extremely bore."

"So you called me! Ahan! I am not free." She laughed. "Do you have the appointment?" She said it in a formal manner.

"Yes I took it many years ago and you gave it to me by yourself, that too happily."

"I don't remember that." She replied in the same manner.

Both laughed.

"Ok tell me why were you feeling bore."

"Wow!"

"What happened?" She smiled.

"You said 'why were you feeling bore' and not 'why are you feeling bore'. I am really feeling better now."

"Oh goodness! What a compliment!" She laughed. "Actually I am so lively and my voice is so pleasing," she paused, "you know."

"Yes absolutely."

Both laughed.

"But today I am really going to miss the music I love." He said.

"You must have brought your i-pod along." She said in pitiful tone.

"You are so cruel." He smiled.

"But not more than you. Didn't even take your phone along." She paused. "We should stop this topic right here." There was vivid annoyance.

". . . . yes."

"Leave it dear", she took a deep breath, "tell me something beautiful."

"Beautiful? I can tell you something handsome instead of beautiful."

"Ok and what is that." She smiled.

"My photos, in your laptop, somewhere in hidden folder."

She laughed. "That is not handsome. Those are the photos of a monkey and I've watched them for so many times since you have gone." There was a smile on her face while saying the latter part; a smile which is used to hide sadness.

He didn't speak for a while.

"Anyways what are your plans for today?" She said while putting all the other thoughts away.

"We'll go out, surely but I'm not sure where. I wish they don't go for a movie."

She smiled, "I wish they take you to a movie in which there are 20 item numbers and they all torture you so much, so-so much . . ."

"Ok-ok take a break. I got it, I got it how much I've troubled you and you can take revenge when I'll come back."

"That I'll." She interrupted.

"Wait-wait, hold your horses. But your this dream of 20 item songs is not going to turn into reality." He chuckled.

"Ok Soma, I'll call you in the evening."

"Okay."

"Take care and have some fun."

"Yes bye and you too take care."

"Bye."

"Bye."

He was feeling exhausted and the reason was unknown to him. So he decided to talk to his mother later and went back to his room.

He laid down on his bed and had a look on both of them. They were in deep sleep in that heat which was nothing less than amazing for Inder. He smiled and then took his diary and pen. He kept turning pages of the diary and stops somewhere to read some lines and then again starts over. He hold the pen and tried to write something but it felt like climbing Mount Everest for him at that time. He didn't want to do anything. The boredom was ruling over him and it was increasing with every passing moment. There was no any excitement to do anything. It was not new to him. He had experienced it for many times before and he knew the cure for it. But he was not in condition to access that cure. Normally he used to talk with Samar or Somaya over some topic; a long discussion & sometimes argument. He knew that he need to talk to someone but 'with whom' was still unanswered. While his eyes were wandering all over the room, they stopped at Santosh's laptop for a while. He thought of watching a movie but then again he remembered that the type of movies which he had in his laptop were not at all going to help him to deal with his boredom. He thought for once to go in the room of Harf and Stephan but then his body refused to get up from the bed. He heard little grunt of hunger but he ignored it and tried to sleep. "In the month of June, on Sunday afternoon, in Delhi, without an A.C., a boy is trying to sleep. Will he be successful in his mission? Will he get good dreams? Will he sweat? To know all these useless things please stay connected and do watch our next episode tomorrow. Tan-tana . . . ." He said silently while staring at the fan. "What is going on pal!" He thought. Then he shut his eyes and tried to remember his good time spent with Samar, Somaya & cousins. Remembering the good old times has always conditioned him to do day dreaming and he was so fed up from his habit of day dreaming that he has stopped memorizing the past for long from some time now.

Time passed and they both woke up. They had their breakfast and chatter. Inder was feeling better so he decided to talk to his mother.

There was tiny wall fan hanging on the right wall of that wooden booth which was doing its best to provide the caller enough comfort to sit and talk for some time. But it was producing quite a noise also. Though Inder was good at ignoring unnecessary noises.

"Hello Maa . . ."

"Hello my son! How are you?"

"I am good. How are you?"

"I am good. Had a pretty good sleep last night after quite a while."

"Thank God!" He smiled.

"When did you wake up? Have you done your breakfast?"

"Yes-yes just finished it and I woke up just an hour ago."

"Ok and yes, Samar came this morning."

"Ok, good. How is he?"

"You didn't even call him for a single time."

"I'll, next weekend, for sure."

"You are not a good friend. He is such a nice boy. When I asked him that if Inder had called you and he said that you would whenever you feel like and there was not a single sign of anger in-fact a smile."

"That's why he is a nice guy na!"

"You are so bad."

"Ok," he smiled, "I'll call him next weekend for sure. I promise."

"Ok. How are your new friends. With whom you stay busy all the time." She teased.

"Come-on Maa," he laughed, "I'll call him and my new friends are good."

"There is only a month left for you to come back now."

"What! No . . . ."

"You promised."

"I have not. And you are just going to tease me now so I am going to hang up and I'll call you in the evening now." He smiled.

"Alright, even I am busy. But do call me in the evening." She smiled.

"Yes Maa," he said pleasingly, "and you take care."

"You too. Bye."

"Bye."

While going upstairs he heard the laughter of Santosh and of all others along him.

"Ah! This is Inder." Stephan said to a girl sitting beside him while pointing towards him.

"The man with no phone." She smiled.

"Man! You guys have advertised me everywhere." Inder smiled.

Everyone laughed.

"Hey Inder she is Pia," he paused, "my love."

Inder smiled. "Hi Pia."

"She was requesting me to meet all of you guys from couple of weeks now so today I brought her."

"And he didn't even told me about this." Harf said.

"Yeah I told him not to tell any of you guys." She said.

"Actually there was nothing tempting in our group or in our p.g. The thing is that she saw my profile pic on facebook so she couldn't resist." Santosh was in his natural flow.

"Yeah right!" She laughed and everyone followed.

"And this man here," Stephan said to her while pointing towards Inder, "is quite philosophical."

"No . . . . what are saying man." Inder was little embarrassed.

"What 'No'." Harf said. "He is."

"That's good. While everybody's busy studying and doing management, someone, who is philosophical outside an institute is good."

The way she said took Inder attention. He felt the depth in her statement and the room for the elaboration. He just smiled.

"It's quite hot today, isn't it!" Inder said while sitting on a chair.

"Did you say it generally or you are flirting." Santosh said in jesting tone.

"My goodness! Do you!" Harf added in similar tone.

Inder laughed. "Is it my turn today?"

"Don't change the topic." Santosh said in such a way that made everyone laugh loudly and the temperature of the room raised a bit.

"Give him some coke." Stephan said to Atul.

"No worries I'll take it by my own." Inder said while stretching his arm towards Atul. "Pia brought these?"

"Yes and I said if she can do this every-time she can visit us every-day." Atul said.

They all kept talking casually and after finding the good comfort and after adjusting themselves as a part of a group conversation got a direction.

"No . . . . I believe that corporations have made such situations where people from different parts of the country come together and they all mingle up very well." Pia said.

"Actually what I meant to say was that the focus on profit is way too much and it oppresses other things which have direct connection with one's moral values. Like money gets preference while other things must get it." Inder tried to defend his argument.

"Hey both of you. This thing is going on from the last 10 minutes and for your information it is dangerously boring." Santosh said while pointing towards his phone and showed all of them the running stopwatch on it.

"You seriously did it." Harf said and laughed loudly.

"My God! I'll stop right here." Pia said.

"All these boys are boring including your Stephan expect me." Santosh said in a serious tone. "Do talk to me on the phone whenever you feel bore."

"Yes that's true." She laughed.

"You are so bad," Stephan said, "you were totally in that argument with us and now you are saying like only we were doing it. You are equally boring." He said to Pia and looked towards Harf and Inder to get support.

They smiled.

"Any one starts praising these girls they forget everything else." Stephan said in a jesting tone.

"Don't be jealous Stephan." Santosh said and everybody laughed but her stood out.

"Normally people don't get so happy after listening to truth." Harf said.

And a short period of loud laugh came back again.

Atul was not entirely present there and Inder noticed that. "Hey what are you thinking?" Inder asked.

"Nothing!" Atul said while looking at everyone.

"You are doing M.B.A. no." Pia said to Atul.

"Yes." Atul replied.

"He is going to be the face of . . . ." Santosh said.

"Unilever." Inder interrupted and they both laughed.

Atul just gave a smile.

"There is something going on in your mind." Inder said to Atul.

"Is it really?" Santosh said in jesting tone.

"What happened?" Stephan asked Atul.

The more they were asking the more uncomfortable it was becoming for him.

"Ok . . . wait." Atul said, "When I am seeing you both; as a couple, it feels good but," he paused.

"Yes . . ." Pia said.

"I mean the problems in the way to marry each other are bitter, you know." Atul hesitated at the end.

That caused silence for a short while.

". . . . I'm sorry." Atul tried to break the silence.

"Hey it's ok." Pia tried to ease the situation.

"It's a difficult thing to even think of, so discussion on this is . . . ." Stephan said rest of the words with his gesture.

Santosh knew the reason behind Atul's question. An eye contact of Inder with Santosh evoked the image of Roohi in both of their minds.

"But we can explain it in an extremely simple manner." Pia said while looking at Stephan.

"Atul, this is something for which you do everything you can and even more than that. You do your best." She said.

Atul nodded.

Time passed and the environment was again lightened by the monkey-business of Harf and Santosh. Filled with thoughts and perspectives Inder talked with his mother and Somaya. Then they all went out and wandered in the Delhi's night . . . . as something in their own and as nothing in the crowd.

CHAPTER 6

6th Weekend

Inder was sitting on his bed with his back against the wall. He closed his eyes and seemed like as if was frozen in time. A single window on the same wall was open and the curtain was making slight movements because of the occasional puff of air. He turned towards the curtain and watched the increase & decrease of amount of light coming through the window. He felt like the curtain was asking him to go out but he refused to get up as if he already knew what was out there for him. Plenty of thoughts and plenty was there weight. The more he went deep in his thoughts, more the weight increases which put more pressure on him making even hard to make a movement. After some time he started hitting his head softly against the wall. After a while, doing the same, he started imagining as if all the negative aspects of his life were leaving his very body just like dust starts leaving the mat after one starts shaking it. He kept doing that for some time until all the negatives which he didn't want, leave his body. That was nothing more than a day dream, just to free himself from some weight. But with the removal of dust, the picture which he has weaved for himself, became clearer & clearer. When he reached at a point where the picture was exactly how he wanted his life to be; the distance between the reality and dream forced him to open his eyes. That was a long distance and with lots of hurdles. He has quitted using the words 'would that' or 'I wish' a long ago and this has made him believe that things can be within his reach; change is in his hands. He repeated the words 'you can do it' many times to himself. But these words of self-motivation pushed him in the well of frustration instead of getting up from the bed and doing something. He started regretting about the time he has wasted in feeling hopeless & helpless. But even there was no any answer, no any clue about what must have been done to save himself from helpless & hopeless. There was no any answer about where he had taken a wrong turn, where he had made a wrong choice. There was no any escape from regret. He brushed his hands harshly against his head as if trying to shake off all the dust of thoughts. The thoughts which neither were providing any answer nor letting him to do anything to get even fraction of hope that life will be changed. Reality was pinching him and dreams were irritating. There were lots of plans but the execution was missing. Sometimes even plans felt like dreams to him; not going to happen.

"Either do some work or die frustrated." He said to himself. He got up from his bed and stood in front of the mirror. "Why can't you understand simplest of

BALRAJ SIDHU

things." He rebuked himself. A frown dominated his entire expression. He laid down on bed and closed his eyes. "This is the best thing I can do. No one can beat me in this." He whispered.

Someone knocked at the door and so he went out while trying to cover his condition with an another expression. He tried to smile after seeing his mother's face.

"You didn't get ready." His mother asked.

"Yes, I don't want to go today." He said while moving the door back in its original position.

"Are you alright?" She said while placing her hand on his forehead.

"Yes off course." He quickly moved away from him.

She said nothing.

"Sit down for some time." He said while getting a glass of water for her.

She drank it, slowly, while carrying an expression of hiding her eagerness about the reason behind his leave from work.

"So, you just don't want to go for tonight or you don't want to go there anymore?" She finally overcome the unease birthed at that moment and asked him after swallowing the last sip which still was not completely drowned inside her.

"No Maa, I just don't feel like going today." He said.

"This is not the way to do work." She said after evaluating if she really needed to say this.

He said nothing and became more depressed; his morale moved down further. He took the glass from her, placed it near the water-cooler and went in his room.

She sat there for a while and kept staring at the main door of their house. She had gone weak with time and looked more aged than she really was. The wrinkles on her forehead made the lines of worry more prominent. Her hand made a movement proving that her hope got hurt. He kept looking at her from the window from his room. He knew exactly how she was feeling. So he put his feelings away from himself and sat near her.

"Maa . . . ."

She turned towards him.

There was nothing to share with her. In that moment he was just depressed and weak soul; fighting with itself and was not at all in a good position. His face was forecasting tears; even if not in front of her but sometime in the dark; in solitude, they were having their chance to come out.

"Do you want to change this?" She pointed towards the courtyard and said as it was the best she could do to gather herself as well as him.

"Yes Maa, no doubt about that." He said with broken spirit and it sounded more like a fantasy than an aim.

"Can you do it like this?"

He kept silent.

"Now get up and do something." She said. "Did you went to check out if any jobs are open to apply for?"

"Yes but there was not a single one worth to apply for."

"Ok but keep checking that."

"Yes."

She then engaged herself in the daily household work and he went in his room and tried to read a book. The attempt was not that successful but with the presence of his mother in the home his thoughts were not torturing him as they were doing it before. After a while when things were gradually settling down someone knocked at the door. As he was moving towards the door, he got sure that it was his father but with whom he was talking to?

"See he is so grown up!" His father said with a smile to his fellow man.

"Yes a complete adult." That man said in a shaky voice.

"Son he is your uncle; an old friend of mine." His father said while holding that man from his wrist.

"What are you saying?" That man said while shaking his hand from his wrist.

"Why, what happened?" His father asked while laughing.

"On one side you are telling him that I am his uncle and on the other side you are saying that I am your old friend. You have insulted me in front the young boy." There was more of a complaint in that than anger or otherwise as that can't be told with the way he expressed.

His father said nothing and hugged him tightly and then they both laughed.

Inder closed the door behind them and moved in as he was not at all ready to handle his drunk father with his another drunk friend.

"Inder bring that folding bed out here, in open." His father said while standing in the courtyard. "Where is your mother?"

Inder quietly took the bed in the courtyard and they both sat on it. He then went inside; trying his best not to engage with them as it has always resulted in anger and profane words which he hated.

They opened the bottle of whisky and his father checked the rest of the whisky by holding it high than his eye level and said, "Bring some glasses and ice."

Inder obeyed the command and his mother, while washing clothes understood everything about what was happening in the courtyard.

"Bring a plate too." His father said while taking out a packet of salted peanuts from his pocket.

On the way back to kitchen his mother signaled him to stay quite.

"Son, he is very good friend of mine." His father said again when Inder gave him a plate.

"Yes I know." He said trying his best to maintain the composure.

"See he is very intelligent!" His father said to his friend.

"Do you know the name of the Russian President." The friend asked.

"No I don't." Inder said it quickly.

"You must know son." His father said.

"No worries." The friend said and grabbed his glass of whisky.

Inder went back in his room.

"*Sukh* . . . ." He called his wife.

"What is it?" Inder replied from the room. "She is washing clothes." He was irritated.

"What's new in that!" He said.

"*Jass*, why are you troubling *bhabhi ji*." His friend said.

He said nothing. Turned towards his friend and said, "Let's finish it." And raised the glass towards his lips.

"Bring some whatever you have cooked for tonight." His father said loudly from the courtyard.

"She havn't cooked any dish for the dinner yet." Inder replied from his room.

"There must be some left from the previous one."

"No." Inder said in a harsh tone.

"Inder you must learn to cook now. You don't have any sister so you'll get the punishment." He laughed while saying the latter part.

Inder said nothing.

His father was not happy with the responses he was getting from Inder but he was not saying anything.

"I have got free from here. I am going to cook now. Will give you after some time." His mother said after coming out of the washroom. She didn't want Inder to loose his temper.

"Hey Sukh!" His father said. "Come here, do you remember him?" He said while pointing towards his friend.

"*Sass-ri-kaal* bhabhi ji." He said while correcting his *Turban* and then coming back to the traditional folded hands position.

"*Sat Shri Akal bhaji.*" She said and shook her head in no.

"He is the one with whom I started driving the school van for the first time but then he left." He said with sheer joy.

She tried her best to maintain a smile on her face as long as she stood there.

"You didn't cooked anything yet?" He asked again.

"No, not yet." She replied.

"Why don't you start cooking first and then go for clothes and anything else." He said in a low voice.

"It's ok." She said showing little annoyance and then she turned to go in.

"Maa you come inside." Inder said from his room, extremely irritated from his father.

"Both mother-son are alike." He said and started laughing. "You know she was a fish in her previous birth."

His friend kept sitting on his place with no reaction and expression.

"That's why she is so fond of washing clothes, utensils, floors and everything first and later she cooks; if we ask from any wise man, will say that cooking is more important." He said and started pouring some alcohol in both of their glasses.

Inder kept sitting inside his room, trying to calm himself down. This was not first time and both of them have developed some tolerance to his this type of behavior. Inder's mother was trying to divert her mind. Both of them kept drinking until they finished the rest of the whisky.

"Inder take the food for them." His mother said from the kitchen.

"He is very intelligent boy." His father said while Inder was serving them food.

"Son, you see now how me and my brother going to rule the city." He said while patting on his friend's back.

A short burst of laugh came out of Inder. "I'll see." He said with a smile.

"Just keep smiling." His father said.

Inder went back in before he gets irritated again. After they had their dinner, Inder and his mother had it too. She kept saying him not to say anything to him to save themselves from any unnecessary yelling. But soon after his friend went he came in the room started complaining.

"When your son's friends come, do I ever behave like this?" He said loudly.

And that caused the pressure inside of Inder at a breaking point. Then all the complaints were coming from Inder's side and his father was just defending himself. When the complaints gone above his skill of defending himself, he started shouting and abusing both of them. This made his mother to get involved in the stupid quarrel about which all of them knew that the end result will be a zero. But the stored frustration and witnessing him doing the things over and over again which both of them hated, gave that quarrel more fuel. So that was not actually a fight for the solution or for a cause but was just a way to ease the pressure of frustration from inside of them. This fact made that fight completely different from outside in comparison to what was hidden inside of the helpless, poor soldiers; finishing themselves by their own; for the reasons which were out of there control.

Even if that was just a way to ease the pressure of frustration but still it always takes something away from them for always. The one who consumes alcohol sleeps with long and loud snores as if nothing has happened and those who were completely in their senses were forced to stay awake and had to let them eat themselves more by depression. In that condition Inder and his mother fell asleep and he woke up and a frown was still sitting on his forehead as agony. Once he read somewhere in a poem that every-day starts with different sunrise which brings better life, a new start. "The destiny of next morning is already written at the start of the night." He thought. He got up from his bed. It was 7 and his mother was doing the routine work.

His father was still not awake. "What a fudge all of this is! Absurd & dull."

It was 11 in the morning and he started tying up his shoe laces. A little excited along with some unknown tension but he ignored it. It was the best chance for him to go in that red light area without making any excuse. When passing near from booth his pace was broken by the thought of calling Somaya but then he let it go and kept moving. He reached at the place before 12 and started rummaging the streets of that area. This was not the first time so there was a little hidden confidence in him to roam in those streets. He raised the collar of his t-shirt and started walking a little slowly and confidently. From one street to another, from one stare to another, he kept moving with little determined spirit; a last try. He wanted to give his best. He didn't want to think about it in future and feel that he must have tried one more time or something else. He tried his best to make eye contacts with ladies & girls there. None of them made him to go to them as his motive was entirely different and the fact was that nobody was at that place to entertain him according to his motive. Soon he realized the entire context and prepared himself to go to any of the women. When he was busy looking above, a woman grabbed his arm and started taking him towards a building to his left.

"Hey!" He shouted.

She slowed down a bit and said, "Let's go kiddo." There was no sign of smile or any intention to make fun of him.

"What kiddo." He tried to act like an experienced one.

"Come-on! Put a full stop on your acting and let your small man down there live a little."

He was stunned with the use of the words and right before he could react he was in that building at the first step of stairs. So he went with the flow as something told him that this was exactly what he wanted.

She took him in a room and closed the door.

"Is this your bed!" He was shocked with the condition of it and the sheet on it was badly in need of a bath.

"Stop your snobbish behavior prince!" She said in a scornful manner. "This is not your palace. Moreover this is not my bed." She moved towards him and said in relatively slower pitch, "This is the bed of my customer and my bed is my customer." And she freed her hair from the bun form.

He stood still in that moment, trying to swallow the words. She was about to remove his t-shirt when he moved back.

"Don't be afraid. I know you are nervous but I have handled many first timers. So you can believe me." She said while standing there and after that she sat on the bed and signaled him to sit beside her.

"Look . . . ." He said hesitantly, "I have not come here to do this."

"Bullshit." She said and removed her shirt.

"Oh! What are you doing!" He said as if was disgusted.

"What is the problem with you?" She said and snatched him from his collar.

"I told you I am not here for this." He said while sitting on that bed looking away from her.

"If you want to talk to me look at me." She shouted.

He turned his face towards her and looked in her eyes. "Do you treat everyone like this?"

"Don't make me more angry. Already there been no any earning done in the last couple of days."

"If you are in desperate need of money then I can help you." He said in a friendly tone.

"And that's why I grabbed you from the damn street." She replied in entirely opposite manner.

"What is that bruise on your right breast?" He asked in a sympathetic manner.

"Now you are in looking at the right thing." She said and approached towards his belt's buckle.

He got up from the bed and said, "I told you I am not here for this thing."

"You bloody ass! What's the matter with you?" She was completely confused and frustrated from him.

"Ok I don't think you understand." He said. "I am not here for this."

"Then for what you are here?" She said while trying to keep her calm.

"I am here to talk to you." He said quietly.

"What!" She was extremely surprised.

"Yes and please wear your shirt." He said.

"I don't believe you." She said with smaller eyes.

"And why is that?"

"This is happening for the first time in my life."

"And is this the only reason?"

"I think so."

"So no problem. You can believe me. I am here just to have chat with you."

"No I am not available for that. You are wasting my time. I must have grabbed someone else." She said the latter part to herself.

"No . . . no-no don't worry about that. If you just calm down and have chat with me I'll pay you more than one used to pay for that."

"What!" She was more confused than surprised now. "Either you don't have brain or you don't have that thing between your legs."

He laughed loudly. "None of that is true."

"I don't believe you."

"What do you mean?"

"You have to show me the reason to believe you."

"What!"

"Open your pants." She said in a serious manner.

"Wait, that is not going to happen. Just wear your shirt and let's have some chat." He said while putting few notes of hundred on her bed as he find no other way to convince her.

She still was confused but she decided to go with what he was asking for.

"Wear your shirt." He said again. This time there was less of a request and more of an order.

"Yeah-yeah." She started wearing her shirt.

"What is your name?" He said while sitting on the ground.

"Juliya."

"No I mean your real name."

"What was so fake in the previous one?"

"It doesn't sound like an Indian name." He smiled.

"Rajni."

"I don't care if this too is not your real name but at-least it sounds Indian."

"Are you sure you are not going to be my bed?" She said in confusion regardless of what he was saying.

"Hundred percent." He smiled.

"Ok so I am going to change the sheet of the bed." She said while getting up from the bed.

"You have a cleaner sheet!"

"Yeah but that's just for me." She said as she pull out an orange sheet with white printed flowers on it from a polythene.

"Can I sit on that?" He said while pointing towards the bed.

She nodded.

She moved a little away from him and that put a smile on Inder's face.

"What, you are afraid from me now?"

"No but I don't trust you either."

"Well that's fine for now."

None of them spoke a word for some time.

She shook her head in an question.

"You want to ask something from me; about me." He said just to start the conversation and he was running out of ideas about how to start it.

"What is your name?" That was the first thing which came in her mind.

"Inder."

"You real name?"

"Inder." He smiled.

"Where are you from?"

"Amritsar."

"Punjab?"

"Yes, Punjab."

"You work here?"

"Yes."

"What do you work?"

"I do calls in the night, in Canada."

"Call center?"

"Yes! You know call center?"

"Yes I do. I read about it somewhere."

"Good."

"I don't have anything more to ask." She said as if trying to finish the meet.

"How people could do that on the dirty sheets?" He just wanted to keep it going.

"They have nothing to do with the sheets." She was sitting quite still in front of him and was responding like a robot.

"Hmm, I can understand that."

"Stop all this bullshit and tell me why you have spent so much of money just to have a chat with me?" Her curiosity was getting out of her control.

He thought about it for some time and found himself unable to think of a reasonable lie. "I . . . . actually, just wanted to, have a chat."

"That I know, but I asked about the reason."

"Yes and the reason is that I don't have anyone else in this town to chat with." He said hesitantly.

"I can't believe that. You think I am stupid. You think I live here so I knew nothing!" She was little annoyed.

"See first of all I am not here to make a fool out of you and secondly I really just want to have a little conversation with you." He could not let things fall apart, so he gathered himself somehow to convince her.

"I am listening to that shit for the last half an hour. Can you tell me more about that."

"Please listen to me. People out there like me are living in conditions which you can't even imagined or have never witnessed."

"You don't know anything about the way people live in here." She interrupted as if she felt offended. "But we don't go out there to have some chat with you people. So get the hell out of here."

He literally thought about going out from there for once but then for the last time recalled all the wisdom he has gathered in all those years to find some solution.

"You don't go out there because you can't but we people can come here." He paused to think something better than that. "Just think, do you get people like me on daily basis? I am here for just a conversation, just to share some things with you. Just to listen to you and just want to get listened to." He said with a little pace, not considering if she had grasped all that.

She said nothing. Her anger got comforted a little with his words but she still was not entirely satisfied and was still anxious.

"See, I just want to have normal chat. Just consider me as a . . . . friend or even customer, whatever you feel like who comes to you just to have some chat. Just like people come to you for that." He felt satisfied with his explanation but the concern was her approval; her believe.

She kept silent for some time and then said, "Is it just that?" She said in confused manner but there was no any sign of anger.

"Yes, just that."

"But I have never done that with a customer. I don't know how to talk normally." She was troubled. She was not satisfied but just got transferred from one anxiety to another.

"You just need to talk to me as you talk with the one with whom you love to talk." He paused for her. "See it is difficult to talk with a stranger in a perfectly normal & open manner, because we are not familiar with him. But trust me with time, it will get normal."

"My head is aching now. Can't you just go now? I'll return you half of the money." She said while holding her head with her hands.

"We can stop taking for some time, until you get normal." He was not ready to leave at that time.

"Ok wait. So why would I develop this skill of talking normal with a stranger."

"Because this stranger can pay you double and will not even touch you once."

"Why don't we have some fun on this bed. Because from quite some years that thing never caused any pain to me. But with you, my head has become so hot, like a stove top." She was still holding her head with her hands.

"They say first time is always the difficult one."

"Don't you dare to say that again." Within an instant she became so furious. "That dog said the same to me."

He was first shocked from her reaction but then when he absorbed her words, came in perfect control. "Some things never fade away from our minds isn't it!" He said it with a hope to have a nice uniform conversation.

It took a while for her to feel his reaction and then she responded, "Yes." At this point she was little comfortable than before.

He knew he was at the right path.

"So you are know my customer, who just will come, for talking." She said just to assure herself.

"Exactly." He smiled.

"So long we'll talk. Normally I don't spend more than an hour with a single man."

"Don't get so professional, so that you don't have to compare me with those men."

"Don't teach me how to run my business."

"I apologize for that."

"The owner of this brothel will ask so many questions if I spend more time with you."

"Ok . . . . is the owner a lady?"

"Yes and she is better than the previous one. So I don't want to get sell again to another one." She said it in a perfectly normal way.

It was difficult for Inder to digest that. He already knew these type of dealings but he experienced a shock when he heard from the victim itself.

"What if you tell her that I have paid doubled?"

She thought about it for some time and then said, "Yes then she will not bother about the time much."

"So, can we consider it as a solution to this problem?" He smiled.

She nodded.

He felt little comfort there and was ready, to ask some; share some. "How old are you?"

"21." She smiled.

"No way." He smiled. "You seem around 30."

"I don't remember exactly." She said with pleasure. May be that was just because that someone was showing interest in her ordinary things.

He knew right in that moment that he could come to her at every weekend.

"I am 23." He said.

"Really!" She said as if there was something fascinated about his age. But the fact was that it was of someone who showed interest in her. "Do you ever had sex?"

"What!" He laughed loudly.

"Why are you laughing?" She said in confusion.

"Nothing I was just not expecting that." He felt he must have not laughed.

"It is a big thing for the young, isn't it!"

"Yes it is but people have different opinions behind it which makes it less important for some and more for others."

"And for you?"

"Not much important in a relationship."

"Bullshit. A first timer came to me and he said that it was the most important day of his life."

He laughed. "As I told you earlier, people have different opinions."

She kept quiet for a while. "Some people come to me and do it as if they are doing it for the very first time. So they try to squeeze every drop of it. And then they drink it in the dark, in this room, isolated from rest of the world."

He said nothing.

"Then they go. Giving me compliments that I am better than their wives or girlfriends or whatever. They go out from the door and don't even look behind towards the piece of flesh." She paused. "Sometimes even I start considering myself nothing more than a piece of flesh but then something happens which drag me out of this feeling and I feel more than a piece of flesh; way more than a piece of flesh."

He kept listening to her and each & every word was sinking so deep inside of him that might made impossible even for him to pull them out and throw them. Those words were going to put influence on his actions and he was not aware of that, nonetheless not at that point of time.

"Is this what you want to hear?" She said with confidence.

"Way more than that." He said while his eyes were glazing at somewhere else.

She took her eyes away from him and laid down sideways on the bed. "You know for me, the first time sex is like a childhood memory. Foggy & faded."

He was feeling the weight of his own thoughts now. This was the first time when he realized that may be he can't stay for long without this weightage of thoughts.

"That is enough from my side, I suppose." She said. "Now you tell me about your first time."

"It is yet to come." He tried to get out of his thoughts.

"What! Don't other people make fun of you!" She said while laughing.

"They don't know it." He smiled.

"Do you want some lessons?" She said while getting little closer.

"I am not here . . . ."

"Not here for this. I know." She interrupted.

"Moreover I have watched porn. So I don't need any lessons, I think." He shared this thing as he felt like sharing it with her. He felt like he can share anything with her but with time.

"Porn! I hate that."

"Why is that?"

"Bloody asses come here with their mobiles full of that shit and then ask me to do the same as the bitches in those movies do."

"Seriously!" He sat in a more attentive posture.

"Yes, but I tell them that I will do it in my *shtyle, the Delhi shtyle.*" She laughed.

He didn't make any sound as he was feeling ashamed.

"Do you have some in your phone?"

"I don't have a phone." He said with a smile as he already had clue about the reaction.

"What!" She laughed. "You are lying."

"No, see." He put his hands on his pockets.

"You didn't carry it in here or you seriously don't have it?"

"No I don't have it."

"I have two." She laughed. "But the owner has it in her possession."

"Ok."

They kept talking for some more time and then he left the place after saying that he would come again tomorrow at the same time.

He was feeling very hungry so he ran towards the bus stop. All through the way back to his p.g. he kept thinking about her and about the things which she was saying in such a normal manner which made him feel ashamed as well as degraded. When he reached at the p.g. both of them were up. So he told them that he went to call his mother. The face of his mother stuck in front of her eyes and all her sufferings became alive from his memories.

He went in the bathroom and cried. He didn't cry at Rajni's condition nor on his mother's; he cried because of his own sensitivity, because of his own thoughts. He cried on helplessness; of people & of his own.

They had their breakfast and then Inder went downstairs to talk with Somaya. He went in the booth with a broken heart and dialed a number.

"Hello Soma."

"Hello Inder! How are you dear?"

"I am good. How are you?" He tried to forget everything else to talk with freshness & energy.

"I am fine too." There was some curtness in her voice.

"Is everything alright?" He said.

"You tell me? Do you feel like?"

"What happened Soma?" He was clueless.

"Last Sunday you didn't even called." She cleared.

"But I called you for couple of times." He emphasized.

"Yes but you were in hurry to go with your friends in the evening."

"Soma," he took a deep breath, "I had to." He managed only this much of words.

"Similarly you had to talk to me every weekend."

"Please don't say that." He begged.

"I don't want to fight with you but I am done with these weekend calls. I am living on your mercy."

"Please Soma don't say that. You know that's not true." He almost cried.

"So you tell me how's it going, huh? I wait for whole damn week to hear your voice."

"And I do the same too." He interrupted.

"But it doesn't seems like." She paused. "And when you call, you are in hurry." She was in agony.

"That just happened last time." He defended himself, although he knew that she didn't mean whatever she was saying.

"Inder I can't live like this anymore." She broke into tears.

His hand automatically went on his head. He was trying to do good, he was trying to handle his thoughts but the things were getting worse at the moment.

"Please Soma, don't cry."

"Inder I want to see you." She cried.

He kept silent for a while. "Can you come Chandigarh, somehow?" He asked hesitantly.

"How can I?" She wiped off her tears. "What will I say to Mom & Dad?"

"Think about something." He said. "Do one thing, go at Sonali's place and try to make some plan. I'll call you in the evening."

"Ok, I'll go there." Her voice broke at the end.

"Soma please." He begged.

"Yes I am fine. Did you have your breakfast?"

"You remembered that." He smiled.

"Don't laugh or I'll come there and kill you."

"Then you will be a widow."

"Shut up! Don't irritate me."

"Sorry dear."

"Tell me when did you get up?" She asked as if admonishing him.

"Around 11." He was knowing the kind of response.

"And you are calling me now!"

"I went in that red light area."

That made her more annoyed. "That was more important! Why don't start living there."

"Please don't react like this. I want to share something with you."

"What?"

"I met a woman there and had conversation with her."

"What woman?"

"I mean she works there."

"Oh work! You are saying like she was M.D. of some corporation."

"Please Soma, don't be angry. You will regret your rudeness."

She kept silent for a while but that didn't calm her down. "You are calling me after meeting a prostitute and what you want from me; to pat your back."

He knew that all of this anger was just for him and she didn't mean any of the things she was saying for that woman.

"Soma we'll meet next weekend, no matter of what. Ok? We'll sort it out." He paused. "But if you keep reacting in this way then how am I supposed to share the things which I wanted to?"

She kept silent for some time and tried to calm her down. "Inder I am feeling restless." She confessed. "I can't hear at this point of time. I just want to go at Sonali's place and want to make some plan. After that I'll listen to everything you have to say. Ok?"

"Fair." There was a pleasing smile on his face.

"Ok so see you soon. Do call me at night."

"Yes I'll surely do."

He thought of going back to his room but then Samar came to his mind and his fingers moved on the dialer with excitement.

"What is your problem man?" He said right away.

"My goodness!" Samar was delighted.

"How are you Samree?"

"I am good. Living in the same clamor." He laughed. "Tell me how Delhi's clamor different from this one?

"Ah! This too is quite drenching. Tries its best to squeeze you but in a different way."

Both laughed.

"I kept visiting your mother. She told me that you call her every weekend."

"Yes."

"I used to get your information from her."

"Hmm."

"So, any unique thing Delhi presented you so far?"

"Yes, a sex worker." He smiled.

"Oh my! She must already be tensed with her present condition and to increase that a mawkish came in her life." He laughed loudly.

"No . . ." Inder laughed. "I just met her once and that too today."

"O! So this is fresh as morning shit." He laughed.

"Yuck man! What happened to you." He smiled.

"This actually is the excitement of talking with you after so long."

Both laughed.

"So what did you do?" Samar asked in a jesting tone.

"Ah! The most difficult thing was to convince her to wear her shirt back on" he laughed, "and to convince her that I just want to talk and nothing else."

"She must have considered you as a retard."

Both of them kept laughing for long.

"Yea . . . ." Inder said. "Anyways tell me how's everything at home?"

"I told you already, the same clamor." Samar replied.

"Hmm . . . . anyways, you alright?"

"Yes, I don't cry." He smiled.

"But what about frustration?"

"I concentrate on my dog more." He laughed.

"Hmm . . ." He smiled.

"So p.g. is good, huh."

"Yes and the room mates are really nice."

"Good. Time can pass easily."

"Yes, no problems at work or at p.g."

"How is Somaya?"

"Living my pain with dedication."

"Don't worry. Things will get smooth."

"Yes I expect." Inder said with determination.

"That's it." Samar smiled.

"How is your health?"

"I am taking good care of it and it's better than before."

"Taking care!" Inder said as if the word strike somewhere inside of him.

"Hey, everything will be fine. He said. "Leave this, tell me what was the reaction of Somaya about that woman?"

"How do you know I told her about it?"

"Because I know you can't hide it from her." Samar smiled.

"Oh, I thought she told you."

"Naa."

"She was fine with it, a little worried though."

"Fear from the unknown?"

"Yes something like that."

"Anyways, tell me are you feeling better than before?" Samar expressed his main concern.

. . . .

"This was the first time your laugh had come out from that tiny booth." The owner of that booth said to Inder after he gave him the charge of calls.

"Yes, it was an old friend of mine." Inder smiled.

That man smiled back.

He traced his distance from the day he came to Delhi till now, from the things he told Samar, while going upstairs. He was little satisfied with his mental condition and was feeling good with the motivation provided by Samar.

He went in his room and despite the harsh reality of Rajni, anger of Somaya & the memories of sufferings of his mother, he was feeling light hearted. As if things seemed to be in control. A confidence that he can handle things and ultimately can change them too. He involved with all his p.g. mates well, because he was completely present there; physically & mentally; which was rare. He wrote his diary which was a part of his daily routine. Went to call his mother in the evening before going out with Atul & Santosh. Told her that he had called Samar, fulfilled his promise. But his mind was not free. It still was working in multi dimensions. He kept thinking about his mother, Somaya and Rajni.

Mutual understanding was not an issue in his life but the demands of time were completely opposite to his circumstances and he has always smiled at this fact. Time act as a grinder for him, which has put pressure on him to crush him. He has witnessed himself in a jar along with various problems. Then a set of revolving blades come from upside and try to crush everything in the jar, try to mix all the things with each other, to make him a problem itself; for himself, for others. And even at some point he felt that it was happening. He was transforming into a problem. And he got scared after realizing this. From that point he had always stayed disturbed.

He hardly felt complete contentment after he left his school. He was never satisfied from anything in his life; except from couple of relationships which he always had admired and felt blissful about them. Therefore happiness of his loved ones was his only aim now. Just like to win a war one needs resources, he needed his 100 percent. He has been working to get that only, from some years now. He knew from the very beginning that it was not going to be easy but how it will feel, was unknown to him till he lived them; until he lived the consequences of his efforts to change his life.

"Hey Santosh I need to make a call. Can I have your phone?" Inder said.

"Yes Mr. Smith." Santosh said while giving his phone.

Inder smiled.

"Hey Soma!"

"My goodness! I was thinking who's number is this?"

"It's Santosh's."

"Ok. I was waiting for your call."

"Yes, actually we were out and we may get late so I was not sure if that S.T.D. booth will be open at that time."

"Ok . . . ."

"So any plan, you make?"

"No. We don't have any idea how we will come there." She said with extreme sadness.

"Ok. So now."

"Now it is proved that you are a monkey." She started laughing silently.

"You are coming." He smiled.

"Yes, it was way easy and I was in so much tension."

"Ok, good. So what is the plan?"

"Actually she already was planning to go to Chandigarh."

"Why?"

"Her one of the closest friend from school time is getting married in Chandigarh this Friday."

"Your parents will allow you to go with her?"

"They have to." She said with confidence.

"Okay."

"Actually her parents were not in favor to let her go as neither her dad nor brother were free on Friday to go with her."

"So you filled the place perfectly?"

"Yes. It was little difficult to convince them but they finally accepted. Now I'll ask my parents tomorrow."

"I hope they let you go with her."

"They have to, it's certain. I told you."

"Okay my dear, I got it!" He smiled.

"I am counting days now." She said in pleasing voice.

"I love you too." He smiled.

"Go now." She said.

"Yes, I should. They are waiting."

"Do call me tomorrow."

"Off course. Bye."

"Bye."

After reaching home Inder fall asleep rather quickly with the thought of Rajni. He slept with the bruise on her right breast.

I don't know about how many things she had hidden in her heart;

Which she had prevented somehow to come out from her eyes;

But still hope was shining in them & that too was true; in that single moment, one cannot even imagine; how much emotions she had lived . . . .

"It was lovely." She said.

He didn't say anything. Put his diary aside and turned sideways.

"Write more about her."

"Yes I will." He whispered.

"Sleep now. You get only one day to sleep on time." She said.

"Keep talking and I will fall asleep and then cut the phone."

"Ok."

"I want to sleep with your voice."

"Hmm . . . ."

He opened his eyes to check the time and it was 10:30 in the morning. No one was up, obviously and there was no any movement in Harf's room too. He got freshen up real quick and went for that red light area.

When he reached near that building he went upstairs towards her room. But it was closed and he sooner realized the condition. He went back to the street.

"Come in my room today. I'll show you the next level of heaven." Someone said from above but he didn't looked. Suddenly the entire area started haunting him so he started running from there.

He went towards the bus stop to go back to his p.g. While passing near from the booth he thought of calling Somaya but then he decided to go upstairs. Something came into his mind and he started writing on his diary. He kept writing for couple of hours and then gave up when his mind refused to write anymore.

He laid down on his bed and before he knew, he fell asleep.

"Hey get up." Atul said while shaking him.

He got up and fell into the pattern of same routine. Later he went to talk with his mother and Somaya. They fixed the meeting in Chandigarh. That filled him with excitement and joy. Her words, "You have to hug me right after you see me", put a smile on his face which remained with him for quite some time. But rest of the day was like a smooth stream, in which he kept floating and let it take him anywhere it wanted. There was not any restlessness inside him but he felt like as if something took away the charm of the day. He felt like as if the program to go for picnic gets postponed and the kids feel so sad and everything around them seems meaningless. He just felt like those kids. Though the excitement was little different than that of going to picnic but still the spirit of adventure and knowing the unknown was damaged. It was like, as if something took away the food for his curiosity and the void remained unchanged.

CHAPTER 7

7th Weekend

"There are only regrets when I look in past; nervousness in the future as if there is no believe that things will get better and my present just have anger & frustration. Where could I live?" He cried. "I just want to be happy."

"But you don't need to go to away for that. And why are not taking your phone with you?" She was restless.

"Because I want to feel free. Because I want to sit somewhere and think, think, think." He shouted.

His pitch shocked her. He never talked in such manner. "I am scared." She said in very low voice and tears came down from her eyes and ran quickly towards her jaw.

If anything troubles him the most, that were tears, from the eyes of his mother and Somaya. "I am so sorry." He begged. "But I am scared too." He tried to erase the path of those tears from her cheeks. "But I want to save myself. Please help me. This is my home and you people are my life. I cannot stay anywhere away for always."

The SUV stopped near there p.g. and Inder's small nap ceased. They went upstairs, he grabbed some things and then took farewell from both of them and left for the bus stand. He was eager to meet her after almost more than one and half month. The air was fresh which enhanced his mood. He climbed into an auto-rickshaw. There were very few people out and small heaps of garbage were dominating the streets. His head was heavy but he couldn't just close his eyes. The day was way more important than to give rest to his body. After reaching at the bus stand he climbed in the bus and settled down on his seat; as he already had purchased the ticket a day before. He forgot to call Somaya before leaving the p.g. because of hurry and now was wondering if she would be sleeping or not. "She must be tired from the function." He thought. He entertained this thought for some time and enjoyed. All the aspects of her behavior which he had accepted with his whole heart, admired and loved; were in front of his eyes which fixed a smile on his face. The way she talk, all the time they have spent together, all the times when they escaped at the last moment from getting caught by any known, all the times they have fought and survived; everything was coming in front of his eyes effortlessly. He enjoyed every memory of his with her. And with every memory of her, his eyes were getting lighter and the effect of sleepiness kept decreasing. He witnessed the magic of reunion. He never forget her while living in Delhi and how could he? But there was no any eagerness to meet her like this before. May be it was because he never thought he would meet her before going back to Amritsar. Or might be he had always wanted to meet her while living there but didn't want to make any effort or was not thinking to make an effort to meet her and now as she had made the conditions to meet, he felt like some hidden hunger after realizing that the food was there, came forth. Memorizing all those things and spending good time with each of them, he fell asleep; within his memories.

"I can't study now, even if I want to." Inder said while pushing the cup of coffee away from him as if disapproving it.

"That's ok but you have to settle somewhere. You can't just go from one call center to another." Samar said with concern.

"And it's so funny. Every-time I join any call center I say that this thing is not for me and that I will leave it and then never will join another. And soon after a month or two I join another one." He was frustrated.

"Why don't you find some day job. May be there you may stay for some time until we found something permanent for you."

Inder said nothing for some time. "Nothing sound promising to me and I don't feel like joining somewhere just for time-pass."

"But at-least the flow of money exists, isn't it."

Inder nodded.

"And that, I guess takes a lot of burden away from your mom's head."

"Yes." He said. "But I have to do something better for Somaya. We don't have much time."

Samar said nothing.

"You know sometimes it feels like complete darkness and something it seems like complete light. And that light is occasional faith. But the problem is that I can't see nothing in both the conditions."

Samar kept listening.

"I need answers you know. I am stuck in confusion. There is a big damn rock in my path. I don't know if it has made up of my circumstances or my attitude towards them, but I have to remove it from my path in order to move forward." He said trying to explain his condition right.

"What can I say!" Samar said. "I just want you to find a solution or just walk on a path even if doesn't seems promising to you initially."

Inder nodded. "Let's go from here."

The bus reached near the entrance of the bus stand of Chandigarh. He got all alert to locate her near the entrance as she had told him that she would be there. But he didn't found her. The bus stopped and he ran towards the entrance and the heart was pumping fast than it needed. He saw her coming from the entrance and her eyes found him within couple of seconds as he was the only one running towards the entrance; even if he wouldn't be running she would have seen in his direction automatically. Right after Inder found her the entire environment turned into a desert with only one water source in it. She stopped right where she was and bent a little while placing his hands on her knees. He stopped running and his vision got blurred a little. He pressed his eyes with his finger tips and they get wet a little. She moved back and stood with his back against the wall. He reached near her and saw a couple of lakes, full of water just for him. He must have imagined her face with a wide smile while coming to Chandigarh. But they were experiencing a completely different feelings and there was no control over that. He tried to wipe the tears off but was never able to wipe them completely. But he kept doing that for a while and wiped his also with his sleeves simultaneously.

"Enough." She whispered.

He put hands on both of her shoulders and she hid herself between his arms. Her hug tightened as a proof of recovery. She stopped sobbing.

"Let's go." He said.

She loosened her arms after some time and they went to catch a bus.

"No, we are going in bus." She said.

"Ok. So . . ."

"We'll go by an auto."

"Ok, no problem. Have you already decided where to go?"

She nodded and smiled.

He smiled back.

They went out of the bus stand and hired an auto-rickshaw. She named the sector and things started moving.

"Where are we going?" Inder said with excitement.

"Me and Sonali have already booked a table in some restaurant." She smiled.

"Wow." He smiled.

Their hands found each other while sitting in that auto and didn't let any of them go out of each other's sight.

"We can spend some peaceful time there till we leave for Amritsar." She said.

"So you will go back to her friend's house after this?"

"No, sir." She smiled. "You will drop me back at bus stand and she will meet me there."

"Ok." He laughed pleasingly.

They reached at their decided destination and went in.

"I love you Soma." He said it with passion after sitting in the chair.

"I know and I love you so very much." She said in the same manner.

"How was everybody home?"

"They all are good." She smiled.

"When did your classes start?" He asked just to keep speaking.

"They will start at the end of July."

"Ok."

Then there was silence and there effort of keep speaking was not needed. Silence was all they needed. They kept looking at each other for some time and it made them realized that there was no any need of words.

"You have given me so much of pain." That was not a complain nor annoyance but just a emotion to share, to get couple of kind & sweet words of compassion.

"I am," he paused, "not proud of this Soma. I want to give you happiness." He reflected helplessness in his words.

"Don't worry." She said to convey hope. "Everything will be alright." And her eyes got lost somewhere after saying this.

"Yes. It will." He said and his words brought her back.

"You know how difficult it was?" She said.

"Yes I guess so." He said while carrying a sad expression; sad and tired.

"Whole week I tell myself to concentrate on something else and all the things which are rumored as a sign of true love." She laughed at the end.

"What things?" He smiled.

"Things like distance can't affect love; people live in heart and not in front of eyes etc. etc." She smiled.

"I didn't heard the second one before."

"I made it up. That's what distance makes you do."

"Philosophy . . . . nice." He laughed.

"Shut up." She said softly. "There is nothing to laugh about. All these things sounds stupid some times." She paused while he kept listening with a constant smile. "Sometimes it feels like a curse and sometimes it feels like an exam."

"According to mood huh!"

"May be but sometimes you miss the company of that person, you miss the touch. You miss the voice. You miss so much that it becomes unbearable and you cry." She said while looking straight into his eyes.

"I never imagined that distance will do such things." He was amazed at her boldness.

"I really feel that your decision of not taking your phone with you has done it."

"Yes, I think the same."

"You adjusted easily in p.g.?" She said as a try to change the topic.

"I never tried to adjust in that, I was busy staying away from Amritsar and that's all."

"Hmmm . . ."

"When I try to evaluate all the circumstances, which I have done for so many times after you have left, sometimes I feel that this really was the only option and sometimes when I think over & over again it scares me."

"What scares you?" He said with concern.

"That what if you never come back; I mean to live here. Then another thought comes which says that may be our rest of the lives will stay troubled."

He tried to understand her point of view.

"May be I think all these negative things because I lose my focus from you, from us and from our plans." She elaborated.

"We humans tend to lose faith." He said.

"I wonder how ultimate belief on something may feel." She was lost somewhere.

"That is something extremely difficult to attain. Every-time I have tried it, I lack in one respect or another."

"How do you measure that where and by how much you have lacked?" She was focused on the topic in hand as this was the only thing with which she was living for most of her time.

"Whenever I fail attaining something which I believe is quite possible; I start looking for the weak spots of my entire process."

She smiled; but she was not present there. Her smile was not which appears after experiencing something pleasing or funny but this one was because of the realization about the difficulty to handle testing times.

"But we learn most of the new things during difficult times which demands the best of us." He said.

"Faith saves you." She said while looking at him.

He grabbed her hand to show his approval.

She put her another hand on that couple of hands and then they stayed like that for some time.

Their order came on the table and she served him. "I have missed all of these things." She smiled.

"Let's have it." She said with a little excitement. "It looks yummy, isn't it."

"Yes it does." He smiled.

"I have not eaten like the way I use to since you have gone." She said while taking a bite. "Even the things which are your favorites, no longer seems interesting."

"I still am struggling to absorb everything you are saying." He stopped eating. "Soma I was so busy conditioning my mind that I didn't even realized how you must have been living back there." He paused. "I . . . . feel so bad, ashamed that . . . ."

"Stop it." She interrupted. "My motive is to share what I have gone through and I am not complaining. Like I said earlier, when I go stand at your place everything you have done seems correct."

"I should have already finished myself if I never had relations I have." He hold the glass of water but didn't took it up. "I . . . . am here healing myself just because of my relations understand me support me."

She smiled. "Don't feel so grateful. I am just waiting for our marriage." She pointed the fork in her hand towards him. "I am going to take revenge for everything."

Both laughed.

"You are most welcome to do that. On the other hand that will give me satisfaction that I have come to a position where you think I can handle revenges."

She laughed. "Don't worry. Live your life now." She said. "I'll see you after marriage."

Their hearts were drinking the every single moment passed together. The moments which were drenched in honey and blessed by nature itself. Their hands have grabbed each other many times while eating. Whole energy, whole love, whole wishes, whole promises were flowing in each other's bodies through the touch of their hands. There was no need of words and even words sometimes felt like dirt in the mouth. They were in position where they can live like this if they could.

"Soma time was moving forward and I was not." He took a sip of water. "and that was filling me with whole lot of restlessness and I wanted change so bad that I couldn't even was able to think of a solution."

She kept listening with open heart.

"I had become so desperate that I wanted the change in fraction of second. And when you become so eager, you can't think of anything. You can't concentrate on finding solutions. You have to make room in your mind to think for a solution. Because for that you need full potential of your mind. But it was under full control of desperation. You need to get out from the control of one single emotion or else it reflects in your every choice."

"Hmmm . . . . but it so damn difficult." She said.

"Yes but everything should be done to cure this. And I was not getting any solution besides this one."

"I know Inder." She said with complete assent.

"Sometimes it comes to my mind that I have ran from there and it haunts me. But then again I say to myself that you will prove, you will prove; I repeat it many times to gain strength. And it gives ease to my nerves."

"It is so difficult." She said in extreme sadness.

He said nothing. He felt bad on her condition and a slight anger started growing in his heart for himself.

"Do she need my sadness?" He thought.

"Soma, it will pass. I will push it far away from our lives." He said with determination.

"Yes Inder, I believe." She smiled. "I am happy."

"You are great." He smiled.

"I am not." And some moments of silence returned.

"Anyways, leave it. Tell me about how your p.g. mates sees you?"

"Ah! They . . . . i think a serious kind of person, introvert and a one who doesn't like to share much."

"Ok!"

"And the one who doesn't carry a mobile phone must have some issue behind it."

She laughed. "Did they ever asked you about it?"

"Yes they did for the first couple of weeks and then they quit." He chuckled.

"Didn't you told them that you are a monkey that's why you don't carry a phone."

"No I actually told them that I want to stay away from these things and want to concentrate on other things."

"Didn't they found it senseless because I do."

"Yes they found it weird but then I told them that I want to live a simple life."

"Still senseless."

"Yes even they were not satisfied with my reasons." He laughed.

"So, they quit asking me that."

"Ok. They must be thinking you are secretive."

"I don't know but when they realized that I don't carry a phone but I have a girl in my life, they went all curious, especially Santosh."

"Ok, what happened then?"

"Then finally I told them that I am not here to make any career but just having a distance from my life back in Amritsar." He paused. "But then they stopped asking me any sort of questions and their attitude also changed towards."

"What change?"

"No-no nothing to worry about, actually they became more friendly and more caring. They never question anything I do. First they were not even comfortable with the time I spend with my diary and books but then gradually they never said anything to me regarding this."

"That's good. But you are not."

"I know. But that's why I keep telling you over the phone that there are no problems in p.g. or with p.g. mates. Sometimes if I see from another perspective I find that everything has helped me in fighting with my own self."

"Hmm . . . ."

"Soma, you know, I became so eager for change that I don't even slept many times while in Amritsar."

"What! And you didn't even tell me."

"Please don't get angry."

"No I am not but this is little . . ."

"I know but I want the answers, direction; which can promise me to give solutions to everything. I have spent many nights on the terrace just to feel the air gets all fresh while moving towards new morning."

"Inder . . . ." She held his hand.

"I have tried my best to witness change and to understand the process of change."

"You really are an owl." She said in a low tone.

"Don't feel sad because that helped me and I am doing better now." He assured.

"Then pack your bags and come back." She said in an instant.

He laughed. "I need some time. I am doing better but I am not finished. There are many more things still in my mind which I need to flush."

"Do it quick Inder, come back and just overcome everything." She paused. "Just, let's finish this."

"I can feel." He said. "We'll crush it. Believe me."

"I do."

Time kept moving so as there talks.

"How that lady from red light area looks?" She said.

"Just like the way helpless prisoned people look." He said.

"I don't find any words for these type of things." She looked embarrassed. "Don't know whom to blame; whom to abuse, if that can change anything."

"This is not a single person's fault." He said. "I see it as a drawback and a consequence of a particular society and system."

She didn't has any words.

"Even if the roots of some negative thing are way back in the time and are too deep, that doesn't mean they can't be changed or improved or vanished; whatever required." He said in a harsh tone.

"Some things are impossible."

"No, nothing is impossible. Moreover most of the times things are neither difficult nor easy instead they are just time consuming and people cannot have patience along with confidence."

"We have been brought up in this world and these things were present way before we took birth and now if we decide to change them that will take our lifetime from us."

"That's absolutely correct. No doubt about that Soma. But I want to live life with meanings and I am not going to tolerate anything like this if it comes in my path of life or in the path of my ethics." The bodies were charged up.

"I knew that. I knew this side of your behavior just after few months of our relation. It pointed towards troubles but that's the thing I admired because that's what these temples and holy books preach, isn't it." She paused. "And when we come out of these structures we get lessons to think practically."

"You know," he smiled, "I told Samar once that she can't tolerate dual behavior and that's the purity of one's self and even he agreed."

She just managed a smile as she was not in condition to think about herself. "I can't even imagine how tough for someone it must be to do . . . ." She couldn't finish the sentence.

"Leave it Soma, time will come and we'll do something about it."

"There are so many things to do." She smiled. "We have been piling up all the things which we want to do that makes me wonder if we would get time for our honeymoon after marriage." She said it jesting tone.

Both laughed.

"I don't really think that if a couple can live so much inside of each other's heart and can share a soul, they ever need a honeymoon. I don't know who invented it." He said.

"What are you talking about. I am going for it. I want to travel." She said.

"What travelling has to do with honeymoon?" He smiled.

"That's special travelling."

Both laughed.

Hours were passed but they were never enough. Time moved too quickly for both of them; too quick to become brutal. He was done with the talks, she wanted his shoulder and they wanted to sleep somewhere away from moving time. Away from all the man-made moving things. But they were in Chandigarh sitting in a restaurant . . . .

"We should go now." He said after watching time from his wrist watch.

She said nothing. They paid the bill and started moving towards bus stand. Hands didn't leave each other entire way.

"There she is." He said while pointing in Sonali's direction.

"How are you Inder?" Sonali asked.

"I am fine." Inder said.

"Just fine!" She said in jesting tone.

"Let's buy the tickets first." Inder said.

While they were getting tickets Somaya was dead silent. As if she doesn't have any life left in her body.

"Let's go." Inder said and turned towards Somaya.

Her eyes was trying its best to hide all the tears.

Inder felt everything. "I am going to come as soon as possible, ok?"

She said nothing and it became so hard for her to stand there as if there was no strength left in her legs.

Sonali left them there and went into the bus.

"Soma, look at me." He begged.

"I can't go without you." She somehow managed to say that and tears came out of her eyes.

He wiped them off right there. Stopping them to ruin her cheeks. Both of them kept standing there and none of them was able to say any word. She was trying her best to contain herself while he just wanted to end her pain and none of two were in their hands to controls. Feelings were high than their capacities to handle them.

He went towards ticket seller and bought a ticket near her seat.

She stood there in confusion.

"I'll go with you till Jallandhar, ok!" He smiled.

She smiled and held his hand and went towards bus. Inder handed over his ticket to Sonali and sat on her place with Somaya. She smiled while looking at Somaya and said intentionally, "I told you crying will work."

They all laughed.

"That was real Inder." Somaya said.

"I know dear, don't worry." Inder said.

"She is jealous." Somaya said.

They all settled down and she got his shoulder. Times were not that cruel after all as they had made it with their choices. Their hearts were delighted and eyes were pleased. They still had to get away from each other's sight but for now they can't ruin the moments which they got with this thought. They kept talking with regular intervals in time..

"This is beautiful." She exclaimed. "Travelling with you."

"I love you too Soma." There was this pleasing smile on his face, that rare smile which comes on one's face directly from one's heart. The smile which is 100 percent pure. The smile which comes unaffected from worries, complaints, struggles, rules, negativities; the smile which comes when one feels absolute contentment, when nothing else is needed. The smile with absolute freedom stored in it.

The bus kept moving but time stopped. The part of the earth which they were sharing was taking its face away from sun as it was turning orange but time stopped. The water in canals was moving at its pace but time didn't. Those moments they shared while covering the distance were frozen in time and they were going to be like that forever.

The bus stopped at Jallandhar bus stand. He placed a kiss on his palm of the hand and put it on her cheek. He took farewell from both of them. He left the bus and she kept looking him till he went out of her sight. He could stay with her for some time more but his heart had started racing. He was so near to his home but he couldn't go visit it. He just wanted to go there when he wouldn't have to go away from there. Their bus left for Amritsar and he kept staring at the window of her seat. He thought she would look for him and in that time their eyes will share the warmth for one more time but that didn't happened and he couldn't understand why. She looked out of the window but was rather lost somewhere within her own thoughts.

He had to wait there for couple of hours before he could buy the ticket to Delhi. While sitting in the bus he looked far, in the direction of his home town, to see the courtyard of his home and to see the face of his mother.

He reached Delhi on Sunday morning and he was quite exhausted. On the way back to Delhi he suddenly realized how much pain he must have given to his mother. He was ashamed of himself, he was ashamed on his decisions. He thought how weak he was. He reached at his p.g. but besides falling on bed he went into the bathroom and had a bath for long. He was exhausted but the feeling of shame filled him with some sort of frustration which burned something inside him. There was irritation which has to go out of the body. He couldn't just take a nap with this kind of thoughts. He took the bath as if fighting with some wrestler.

While taking bath he remembered that once he told Somaya that he will work day & night and asked for a chance and now he had found himself working with his thoughts and weaknesses only which haven't let him do anything. He was shocked after imagining the pain his mother must be in after witnessing Somaya.

After taking bath he went to call Somaya and told about his safe arrival and then he called his mother. Telling the excuses why he didn't call on Saturday and tried everything to show her how much he love her.

He went in his room and kept writing while Santosh and Atul were still sleeping. Then even he himself didn't know when he fell asleep. When he got up it was 9 and nobody was at p.g. He felt the weird emptiness in the room. He went on terrace with a torch and his diary and kept wandering within himself.

CHAPTER 8

8th Weekend

"It's our turn now." Atul said while waking Inder up.

"Done with packing?" Inder said while getting up.

"Packing . . . . what packing? We are not going for a month Mr. Smith." Santosh said. "We'll be back on Monday to torture you."

Inder smiled. "Yes I know."

"You are going to stay na!" Atul asked.

Inder started looking at the walls of the room. The word 'stay' got stuck in his mind. He felt like this was the first day of his in that room.

"I don't know." Inder said without thinking.

"So you'll be going Amritsar?" Santosh asked with strangeness.

"I . . . . let's see." Inder was still in confusion.

"You don't need to if you don't want to." Santosh said as if he knows that he didn't want to go.

"Yeah, Harf & Stephan are still here." Atul added.

"Ok." Inder said but with no solidness.

"So, let's go." Santosh said while looking at Atul.

Both of them went in Harf's room to say goodbye.

Inder went downstairs with them to see them off and then he went back to his room. He sat on the bed and kept thinking about what should he do now. He was not getting call from inside to go in that red light area. He wanted to meet that woman but his previous experience didn't let the idea of going there converted into decision.

"That's the character of these types of places what do you expect." He said to himself.

But he still didn't get the approval of himself to go there. May be he was not mentally ready to stand that environment for now; but tomorrow? There was no answer for that. The question at that point of time was that did he want to stay in p.g. He was that open with Harf & Stephan that he could talk with them for hours and share things comfortably. He didn't want to even make conditions for that. He grab some money and went downstairs to talk to Somaya.

"Hello dear."

"Hello Inder!"

"Such energy." He smiled.

"This week was good after seeing you at Chandigarh." She smiled.

A short sweet laugh came out of Inder's heart. "I am glad."

"I have conditioned my mind according to the demand of time." She said.

"I want to ask you something." Inder said as if suddenly something came into his mind.

"Yes. What is it?"

"How do you see this conditioning; as a compromise or as a learning which takes forward to truth?"

"Umm . . . . first of all when tough time comes I don't give a damn to what truth is." A burst of laugh came out of her. "Because that time I just needed to support myself to survive."

"Ok . . ."

"But after some time when you adapt the circumstances and with the intention to do better, you start preparing yourself for the war."

"Wow, ok."

"So this is the time when you get ready to absorb all the things; this is the time when you learn." She clarified.

"I always knew you are the right girl." He smiled.

"This is the only thing which I have been doing since you have left. I have been thinking and thinking." She said.

"Hmm . . ." He took a while. "I have been talking to myself, learning, trying to apply those in my life but I guess I am surrounded with way more things to fight with."

"Yes my owl that's why you went to Delhi."

"Yea . . ."

"Anyways how was your week?"

"It was good. A little light." He said. "Actually this week was very much neutral."

"Ok . . ."

"But now I am facing a new problem." He said.

"What is that?" She said with eagerness and less worry.

"Santosh and Atul have went back to their home and they will return on Monday now and this room is feeling very strange to me."

"Ok . . ."

"I don't want to stay here alone."

"But what about the other two."

"Yes but I don't like to be, you know. My chemistry is not that good with them." He said. "I have not spent much time with them either."

"So come back to Amritsar for the weekend." She said excitingly.

"No Soma, if I could have, I'd come last weekend with you."

"Ok . . ." She said in sad tone and then took a deep breath. "So what now?"

"I don't know but I am certainly not going to stay here for this weekend."

"But where will you go?" She said impatiently.

"Bus stand." He said.

"And then?"

"I will decide right there."

"Inder, I am worried."

"Soma please, no need to worry about anything."

"But Inder . . ."

"I'll call you after regular intervals of time, ok!" He said.

"Fine. But when you will come back, no one can save you from me."

"I love you too." He smiled.

"But this time I am loving you."

"Ok, now I am going upstairs and will call you when leave for bus stand."

"Ok, take care Inder."

"Yes Soma, I'll."

He went upstairs had bath. He got ready by taking as less time as he could. He collected all the money he had and went to Harf's room.

"Hello!" Inder said while entering the room.

"Hey!" "Hello." Harf and Stephan replied respectively.

"You are going somewhere?" Harf asked.

"Yes. I'll be back on Monday and I want you to tell this Santosh over phone." Inder said.

"No problem man." Harf said.

"Bye. Take care." Inder smiled.

"Bye." Harf & Stephan responded.

He went into the booth and called Somaya.

"Hey."

"Hello Inder." She whispered.

"Someone's near?"

"Not exactly but we can't talk for long."

"Ok no problem. I have called you to tell that I am going."

"Ok. Take care and keep updating me."

"Yeah. Sure. Bye."

"Bye dear. Love."

"I love you too."

He left for bus stand. He felt like as if he had become a gypsy but then he thought he has always liked travelling. But this was for the first time in his life that he was going for it without deciding; with some money and nothing else. He was excited yet felt emptiness. Eager yet confused about his choice. Struggling with himself he reached at the bus stand. The place seemed a little depressed to him. But soon he was overwhelmed with hawkers. He made a couple of rounds of bus stand.

Listened to the loud noises to find his destination. But got attracted to rather normal pitch of a hawker saying, "Sri Ganganagar."

"Rajasthan." He thought.

"How much time it will take to reach there?" He asked the hawker.

"We stop only on major stations." The hawker relplied.

"No I mean when I'll reach there?" He said again because it was already around 12 and he didn't want to reach anywhere in the midnight where he couldn't find any place to go.

"We'll reach there around 8." The hawker replied.

"How much for the single ticket?" He hesitated.

He moved aside from that hawker and made some calculations with the money he had at that time. After some quick estimate he bought the ticket; for Sri Ganganagar, Rajasthan.

He looked for an S.T.D. around but couldn't found any. He went back in the bus sat on his seat. He was never been to that place before nor he had ever heard about the culture of that place. He just knew that it touches the border of Punjab and hoped there must be some 'Gurduara' there where he could stay for night. He was having enough money to have a stay in a hotel but his mind was working in a way according to his comfort level.

"I don't want anything special from you." She said as a part of her try to make him realize about his responsibilities.

"Just ask you will get everything." His tongue moved under the influence of alcohol.

She was fed up from his fake promises and was completely frustrated from his habit of winning the world and place it near her feet, sort of promises. She has always controlled herself to not to talk to him about this when he is drunk. But he used to be drunk most of the time, so whenever she got filled till her throat, it becomes unbearable for her to contain anymore and she tries to convey to him that he needed to concentrate on his home more. It had never given her any solid optimism but it had certainly release the pressure built inside her. But this time she got frustrated so bad that she got up and broke the bottle of whisky.

"Aye . . . . bitch! You think it comes free." He said, completely annoyed on his loss.

"Do you understand now!" She said in complete anger.

"You don't have any manners." He shouted. "Go and call anyone, gather anyone on your side, I am not going to live with you."

She said nothing because she knew nothing is going to happen. But she had certainly got some relief by breaking that bottle. Now she was not worried of anything.

"Bitch!" He shouted while collecting the pieces of broken bottle from the floor.

"Shut up!" Inder shouted as it became unbearable for him to hear that word.

"I know that both of you are on the same side. But you don't have to tell me over and over again." His father said.

"Keep your mouth shut if you can't speak the way you should." He shouted.

"So you will tell me how to speak now! Go learn how to talk with your father first." He shouted.

"Inder you keep quite. Let him say whatever he wants to." His mother said from kitchen.

"Yes now after burning the fire . . . . Damn you! Just give me my clothes, I don't want to stay here for one more moment."

"Whatever." Inder said.

"Yes, it is not going to affect you. You two are together. What can happen in your life? All of the troubles are for the one who is alone." He said while taking his clothes out of the almirah.

His mother signaled him to stay quite.

"Have made my life hell." His father said.

"You have made our life hell." Inder shouted as he couldn't control.

"That's so."

"Yes. I don't know why parents marry their kids when they don't even know what doen it means to be married." He said in complete frustration.

"Ok, you do it better than me then. I'll see."

"Inder you stay quite." His mother said.

"Inder stay quite!" His father mimicked. "Not ashamed of what you have done. You yourself don't respect me what can I expect from this kid of yours." He said while stuffing some of his clothes in a poly bag.

"When you will get ashamed of yourself then we'll be too." Inder said.

"That day will never come because I have not done anything wrong. Go and ask anyone."

Inder laughed. "Yeah!"

"The whole world drinks. Some drink and hide it from the world and I drink in front of all and that's the only difference." He declared.

"People take care of their responsibilities also." His mother said.

"Have you ever slept hungry?" He asked in order to defend himself.

"Even that day is not far." She said.

"Ok then when that day will come then talk to me." He said and went towards main door.

"By what route we'll be going there?" Inder asked the conductor.

"Karnal, Abohar." He said quickly and moved forward while saying, "is there anyone without ticket?"

That information filled him with some certain ease. May be he got rid from the fear of the unknown by falling in the zone of his comfort. He wanted to talk with Somaya but was not possible at that moment. He didn't want to ask for phone to anyone. He smiled at his life which was going in a way like never before. "Choices do make while lot of difference." He thought.

The bus was filled with whole lot of different types of people. The journey was some minutes older now and now he was comfortably sitting in his seat, looking outside the window and sometimes his sight falls on fellow passengers.

Lost in his own thoughts he covered lot of distance. Whenever he felt tired of looking he closed his eyes and tried to relax. Faces kept coming in front of his eyes and he kept trying to empty his mind. There was nothing left in his life about which he has not given elaborated thoughts. He was clear about what was going in his life and what are the solutions but it was the time which always had made him restless because he didn't have much.

After the bus reached Karnal he went to look for a S.T.D. and he found one without struggling much.

"Hello."

"Inder!"

"Yes Soma." He smiled.

"Where are you?"

"Right now I am at Karnal and I am going to Ganganagar."

"What! Rajasthan!"

"Yes." He laughed.

"Didn't think of anything else."

"I didn't think at all. They were shouting the word and I came on board."

"Take care Inder. I don't know what are you doing?" She was worried.

"Don't worry Somaya. Look I have to go. Whenever the bus will stop for nice 5-10 minutes I'll call you and the route is via Punjab ok!"

"Ok Inder. Take care."

"You too. Bye."

"Bye."

"See Inder, the problem is that we people use our time in unnecessary things because we think that we had time. But we didn't." Samar said.

"I know. But what can I do. I can't see anything." Inder confessed.

"You need to relax and calm your mind down."

"I know but I don't get much time. I am unable to understand why we people get so eager when it comes about the marriage of our daughters." He said the later part with utter irritation.

Samar smiled. "That must not be the concern. Concentrate on your path."

Inder kept sitting there without any clue of what he should do. Sadness was occupying him more & more with every passing moment. He knew what must he do but things were not in his control and he was not getting any sign that the situation will get under control.

"As soon as you will get over this feeling you will start getting the directions and hopes. Trust me." Samar assured.

"Yes I'll anyhow." Inder said. "I can't lose. This is so simple, isn't it."

"Yes no other option."

"Yeah!."

He was feeling good at that moment but for how long he could stay like this was even unknown to him.

"See Inder just remember one thing that you have to give your best for Somaya and for your mother. They expect great things from you so you can't just consume yourself like this." Samar tried his best to take him out of his miserable condition.

"You are absolutely right. How can I stay like this. I have so many responsibilities to fulfill."

"Yes, don't waste time. Don't ever loose good things in your life just because you feel sad. If you lost them then you are going to regret every single moment you wasted in . . . ."

"No . . . ." The word came out of Inder's mind as if someone looted him. "I'll take any step needed but I'll never waste time by getting stuck in one condition."

Bus kept moving and with new stages of journey new faces kept joining and then leaving. It seemed like he was the only one to go from Delhi to Ganganagar. He spent good amount of time with his diary which he brought along with him.

"I have been waiting for so long." Somaya said.

"I have reached Bathinda." He smiled.

"Ok, now I'm feeling a little better." She said.

"Don't worry Soma. I'll be all right. It has been good so far."

"Ok. When will you come back from there?"

"Off course tomorrow."

"Yes. Off course." She smiled.

"What were you doing?"

"Waiting for your call monkey. This is what I have been doing for the last one & half month."

"Don't worry. Moreover there are no classes going on in college and I have occupied you completely."

"Monkey even if colleges were going on still I'd be thinking about you."

He laughed. "Do something Soma. Don't waste your time."

"Ok dear."

"Ok I'll call you later now."

"Ok bye-bye."

"Bye."

He thought of his mother and wanted to call her but bus was about to go. He climbed back in and things started moving again.

The views from the window were all familiar ones. Random thoughts kept coming to his mind after watching random things & people on the road and in the bus. After the bus crossed Abohar his mind started preparing him for the new place about which he didn't know anything. After entering Rajasthan the variety of people changed than that of Haryana and Punjab. But still there was nothing which may look completely different or never seen before. When he started the journey he has wondered about it but the things and people were not much different.

After reaching at his destination the strange land was not that strange at all. The typical image which he had of Rajasthan in his mind was not matching up with what he was having in front of eyes. After spending some moments with the surroundings he went to look for S.T.D. Soon after one falls within his sight, he approached there and called his mother.

"Hello Maa . . ."

"Hello my son. I have been waiting and I thought you will not call again just like the last week."

"I am sorry for the last week but don't say like this."

"I don't know why I act fool sometimes." She chuckled. "Son has called after a week and I am complaining." She said. "Tell me how are you and how was your week?"

"I am doing great Maa and week went just fine. Tell me about yourself."

"I am good too." She smiled.

"And Dad?"

"He is good too. This week he behaved like he used to be. He was better this week."

"Thank you thank you . . . ." He said. "It's good if time passes a little normal." He smiled.

"You had your dinner?"

"No . . . not yet."

"I know it's just 8:30 but I couldn't help it." She smiled.

"How is your health?"

"I am doing fine. Don't worry about me. I am doing good."

"Ok that's good."

"Tell me something new."

"There is nothing much son. You just take care and do work hard."

"Yes Maa I'll. I'll work hard."

"How are those guys at your p.g.?"

"They are good. Two of them which work with me have gone to their home."

"Ok. Why don't you come too?"

"I'll."

"Please come some weekend and I'll not ask you to come forever. You stay there if you want but do come some weekend."

"Maa . . . I am not going to stay here for long. I told you that. I'll come back soon and when I'll come back I'll stay."

"Ok. You are not an obedient son." She teased.

He laughed. "It's ok."

"Anything new . . ."

"Naa Maa. You tell me."

"Just take care and eat on time."

"Ok I'll. You too take care and now I am going to hang up and I'll call you tomorrow."

"Ok bye Inder."

"Bye Maa."

He took a deep breath. "Don't worry you are going to be there and everything will be alright. She will be happy. This will end." He said to himself and dialed another number.

"Hello Soma."

"Hey Inder." She whispered.

"Someone around?"

"No I was just about to go for dinner. Mom was calling."

"Ok I reached there and it all seems nice."

"Ok good. Now take a room at hotel."

"No I am going to a Gurduara."

"Which Gurduara?"

"I asked about any Gurduara from the fellow passenger and he told me about a famous one and I am going there and will stay for night. Then tomorrow after spending time there I'll come here and then take bus back to Delhi."

"Ok I got it. How far this Gurduara is from where you are?"

"It is a little. I have to take a taxi because local buses don't go there at this hour."

"Ok take care and bye. Mom is calling."

"Bye Soma and don't worry I'll call you tomorrow morning."

"Ok bye."

He took a taxi for that place and it took about an hour to reach there. It was dark everywhere around after they got out of the city. Roads were good and he had good chat with the driver who kept praising Ganganagar all the time. He also got to know some of the cultural aspects of the city and was amazed how fluent his Punjabi was though he was not from Punjab and nor were his parents but as many people there spoke Punjabi so he picked it from his environment and Inder felt good about it. He felt like home.

After reaching there he gave the rent and took farewell from him. He entered the premise of that Gurduara which was nicely build and had a big pond.

He went in the main central building and after paying obeisance he settled himself at one corner of the big hall and kept sitting there for long. He was little excited about the place and was attentively looking around himself. The air was fresh and he was pleased. Besides all this he was exhausted from the long journey but he was also satisfied with the result.

"It's better than staying at Delhi." He thought.

Within an hour he started feeling sleepy but his body refused to get up from there. He sat there and did his best to stay awake. There was this peace which somehow made his mind so relaxed that he felt his entire circumstances not difficult to change at all. He was at cool and realized which he already knew, that patience and hard work is the solution and he can change his life. The only difficulty for him was to keep hold on to this solution. These things were not new to him as he already know them but nothing in his life was giving him fraction of a room to implement all these things in his life. The art needed was to stay unaffected by the things which disturbs him and put unnecessary pressure so that he could do his work.

Suddenly a memory of his past life came in front of his eyes.

"Solutions sometimes seems so simple and easy to convey to ourselves or to others but when you are in a situation, then lots of other things also count. Implementation is not a short, simple and easy process." He expressed his condition to Samar.

"Yes but then what is solution?" Samar said to come to a point where he could gain the momentum.

Inder kept quiet for a while and then said, "I guess, implementation is the only solution."

"Yes exactly." Samar said. "We do things and then we come across many other things which make us change the pattern of things and we do change them." Samar stopped to get his nod. "But we don't stop."

"Yes. I know that there is a solution for everything but sometimes you feel like paralyzed in front of the conditions."

"Yes Inder I know exactly how hard it is. I mean, you know my conditions too."

"Yes I do."

"But we want to change them, isn't it."

"Yes absolutely."

"So don't think about anything else and just focus on one single thing only and that thing must be the execution of the solution found and have faith on yourself before anyone else."

"Yes. I know."

"I know that you know. But what all this knowing has brought good in life?"

"I understand."

"I'll go now and you keep your mind focused."

"Yes."

Now while sitting in that Gurduara he felt that the weakness didn't lie in the capability to understand, recognize and finding solutions of the problems but weakness lies in the level of determination. One needs to be incorrigible for the negative thought and the toughness of the situations.

"Listen to me Inder, you can cry over your condition, you can get scared about the things which are at stake but let me tell you one fact. None of these two things; what things? Crying & afraid can bring any good which you want desperately. You got me?" He said to himself.

After some time he came out of the hall and sat on the way of circumambulation. The marble was cold which gave him sheer comfort. After a while he decided to sleep right there. He put his diary beneath his head and closed his eyes. Right after he closed his eyes and tried to sleep he felt that the place was strange to him. It took a little more time for him to get comfortable and fell asleep than he imagined, even after feeling how exhausted he was.

He got up at 5 after an old man with long grey beard woke him up. He found himself in quite shrivel condition.

"It's get cold in the night." That man smiled.

Inder looked at him and replied with a smile. A smile which has a hidden thank you in it for the warmth provided by that old man's words. The way he said them was like a touch of blanket in the winter.

"It's time for morning supplication." He said.

"Yes." Inder said and got up while holding his diary.

That man took a glimpse of the diary & before looking towards the main hall he had a brief look of Inder too.

He sat right next to him after the prayer.

"So, you are travelling alone?" He said after couple of minutes.

"Yes." Inder managed to say a word only.

"So, where you from?"

"Punjab." Inder looked at him.

"Where from Punjab?"

"Amritsar." He said by bending a little towards him and then went back to his position.

"Aha!" He seemed delighted. "My wife was from Amritsar."

The way he said about his wife made Inder believe that she was dead now. He nodded in a way which conveyed that he understood the hidden message.

"I am from the Malwa region of Punjab, from a small village near Bathinda." He smiled.

"I thought of that from your accent." Inder smiled too.

He tittered.

"You, came here to visit the Gurduara?" Inder asked.

"No," he smiled, "I live here."

"In Ganganagar?"

"No in here." He pointed towards the floor.

"O! You work here?" Inder said.

"Sort of." He smiled.

Inder didn't ask about the details. "So I must address you as 'Baba Ji'." He smiled.

He laughed. "I don't know. I have never felt like one."

He gave a short laugh too.

"I am going inside the hall." He said while getting up and for the first time Inder realized that how tall he was. He was easily six feet and with well-built body. For the first time he noticed his strong fore arms and broad shoulders. He felt like as if the man who was sitting beside him was different than the one who was standing near him.

"Do you want to go inside? He asked Inder.

"What!" Inder said subconsciously.

"I said let's go inside." He took the question mark off from his expression.

"Yes why not." Inder said while getting up and grabbing his diary.

"It seems like you came straight from college." There was a hidden question in his statement.

"No," Inder smiled, "College is long gone."

"Hmmm . . ."

They went inside the hall where the entire environment was enchanted with religious recital. There were very few people inside the hall. Most of them nearby villagers. That man went to the center of the hall where holy book was placed and engaged himself in routine work.

Inder kept sitting in that hall with his back against the wall. While listening to recitals, he felt strange calm, which he didn't experienced even for once while staying in Delhi. The decision of going to Delhi from Amritsar had took him from one type of commotion to another. The only difference was that one was less disturbing than the other. The place was still strange to him but it had offered comfort right from the beginning.

"What am I doing!" He thought while smiling when he looked around himself and it seemed like a dream. His mind for the first time after a long while was not wandering. He was at ease; mentally & physically and the rhythm of recitals acted as catalyst in sending him to the doorstep of nice, sweet and deep sleep.

He woke up after someone shook his shoulder softly. He looked and it was the same old man bent in front of him.

"*Prashaad.*" He said while offering him consecrated pudding.

Inder put his both the hands, joined together, forward to receive it, along with little embarrassment.

That man smiled and moved further.

After a while Inder went out of the hall and a fresh morning welcomed him. He took deep breaths and started moving towards the same place where he slept the previous night. After some time he opened his diary and started writing. The heat of summer was different than that of Delhi but the shade was cool in which he was sitting. He looked at the pond in middle of the Gurduara and watched the moving wrinkles on its surface. The sun was enjoying the ride on top of those small wrinkles. He kept watching them for a while and felt that he should have come there instead of going Delhi but that thought didn't last long.

"Aren't you hungry?" That same man came to him and asked with a pleasing smile.

"Not really Baba ji." Inder smiled.

"Ah! Don't call me that." He said.

"But then what should I call you?" Inder smiled.

"Aa . . . . I don't know." He said.

"Then I'll call you Baba ji." Inder said.

"Ok. Seems like we don't have any other option." He smiled.

"So, where do you live in Gurduara?" Inder said just to kept conversation going.

"All of us who work here have got room at the other side of that wall." He said while pointing towards wall in front of him, on the other side of the pond.

"Ok."

"So, if you are hungry then we can go there and have our breakfast."

"Ok." Inder said hesitantly but got no reason to refuse his offer. On the other hand he felt nice.

They went in old man's room. It was small yet airy and comfortable.

"If you are feeling tired, you can have a nap." He said

"No I good." Inder said.

"Ok so wait here I'll be back with breakfast." He smiled.

That smile was a rare one. A smile which welcomes you with warmth and makes all the words unnecessary. "He is such a nice guy." He thought and for the first time he became a little curious about him.

"And I need to go to bathroom." Inder said quickly before he could left the room.

"Bathrooms are to the left, at the end of the series of these rooms." He said. "You can take my tooth paste if you want. It's right there on the shelf."

"Thank you." Inder smiled.

After some time they were back and he was holding couple of plates containing chapattis & pulses along with the glasses of water standing in each of the plate, as soldiers who protect them.

He stretched his one arm towards Inder to give him the plate and that steel band in his hand hit the plate to make a sound and it felt like bugle; bugle which told them that they can have their meal.

That man didn't spoke a single word while having their breakfast while Inder anticipated for couple of times but couldn't managed to say any word.

After their meal that old man took the utensils and went outside.

"So, young man," he said while entering the room, "for how long you have been in Rajasthan?"

"I just arrived yesterday night in Ganganagar and then I rented a taxi to reach here." Inder said.

"You came specially to visit this Gurduara!" He said.

"It seems like." Inder smiled.

"Ok! Anyways what you do for living? You told me before that college is long gone." He smiled.

"I am working in Delhi." Inder said.

"So you came from Delhi yesterday?"

"Yes."

He didn't said anything for quite some time. The silence was becoming weird for Inder. He felt like he was in some sort of cross-examination.

"How long you have been living here?" Inder said just to break the silence.

"Ah!" and the smile returned on his face. "From the last fifteen years."

"Wow!" That word just came from his mind before he could think of anything.

"So you live alone in Delhi?"

Inder was feeling the questions to be some sort of investigation process. Instead of the general questions he was asking very specific ones.

"No I live with four other guys." Inder said.

"You must have brought them too." He smiled.

"They had to go home." Inder said instantly.

"And why didn't you?" He hit right on target.

Inder felt stuck. He tried to say something but nothing came out of his mouth.

"You must be thinking why I am asking so many questions." He said before Inder could think more about what to say to him. "But, son I have been noticing you right from the moment you entered the premises. I was out there at that time." He said.

Inder felt unable to say anything.

"After I realized that you are not a local, which you didn't look like. I wondered why a young boy like you, at that late hour, was in this Gurduara, away from the main city, with a diary and nothing else." He said. "And when you stayed here for the night, it was clear to me that you come unplanned."

The word unplanned got stuck in Inder's mind. "Not exactly unplanned . . ."

"Ok, how is that?" He interrupted.

Inder took his time before saying anything. He looks at that man and felt strangely secured. His voice, his smile and the way he was asking was like as if he already knew about him and just wanted to say something.

"I . . . . have come from Delhi, may be because I didn't want to go home." He managed somehow, but just that.

"There is reason behind everything." He smiled. "If you don't want to tell me the reason then it's ok but let me tell you something from my experience."

Inder didn't say a word but his body posture conveyed that he was ready for his words of wisdom.

"Sharing always gives clarity about yourself and about the situation." He said. "And you can trust me." He smiled.

Inder took some time to absorb those words to made them affect his choice. He waited and then said, "I went to Delhi against my parents will and I know if I went back to Amritsar, it will be very difficult for me to go back to Delhi."

Before saying anything else he got up and shifted the curtain aside. The windows were already open so the greenery started peeping in from the window. That made Inder to get in a more relaxed mood. He leaned back on the chair.

"The place is nice isn't it." He said.

Inder nodded with a smile.

"I don't know where exactly you are staying in Delhi but you are going to miss this place for one or another reason." He smiled. "And this too I am telling you from my experience."

Inder gave a short but pleasing laugh.

"You looked like a troubled guy . . . . what is your name son?" He smiled. "Sorry for not asking for that before.

"Inder." He smiled. "Troubled guy."

"Everything about you, which I have observed have made me curious about you." He said.

"But I also have a question and first you have to tell me something." Inder chuckled.

"Yes, why not." He said.

"Were you in Army?" He asked.

He laughed. "Yes. But never had the opportunity to go to war." He said. "I didn't expected this."

"I don't know it just felt like so I asked." Inder smiled.

"No problem." He smiled. "So what it is in Delhi that you want to stay there badly?"

"Nothing much." He paused. "Actually, I went there just for the job."

"What type of job?"

"I work at a call center."

"Yes I know that." He said. "So why your parents were against it?"

"Actually it was not something which was not available in Amritsar." He smiled.

"So, what was the reason for Delhi?"

Inder took a long deep breath. By that time he was in a condition to share it with him, moreover he was tired of all those questions so he wanted to come on point.

"I . . . . actually ran away from my home. Because it was getting unbearable for me to stay in that disturbance." He said while controlling his irritation.

He leaned back, knowing that now he has started.

"It's ok son. I too have ran many times in my life with different burdens until I learned how not to make anything a burden."

"Not to make a burden!" Inder said. "I was thinking that you are going to say that how to handle a burden." He giggled.

He laughed. "Yes that's at your age and not in mine."

Inder nodded and there was no smile on his face. Suddenly everything got alive in his mind. Everything which was sleeping.

"So, now the question which I want to ask is that for how long you think you will stay away from your disturbance?"

"I don't know. May be few more months."

"That is good. You will solve that in that time, that means."

"I hope so. Actually disturbance can't be finished from life or from Amritsar while staying in Delhi."

"Exactly." He smiled. "That question was intentional."

Inder chuckled. "You are measuring me?"

"How can I help you, if I really want, without knowing that what exactly you need."

Inder nodded and the journey of detailing started.

"I belong to a poor family. Not extremely poor but significantly poor."

"Ok."

"But that is not the problem. Poverty can be handled, you just need good relationships, a nice loving family and poverty never hurts, as people think it does."

"Ok, an opinion. But I liked it." He smiled.

"The main problem is that there is no harmony in my family and that too in a family of three."

"Just!" He smiled.

"Yes." Inder smiled too.

"So . . ." He said.

"The problem is my alcoholic father. He never listens and never works according to the priorities."

"No, his priorities are just different."

"But he has some responsibilities. Don't you think so." Inder said in little harsh tone which he controlled at the end.

"Responsibilities are for those who think they exist."

"So you mean to say people don't think they have any responsibilities towards their families or any other institutions." Inder said a little annoyingly.

"Don't you see any mess around?"

Inder kept silent.

"Don't think much about these things." He said. "There are always reasons behind everything. Try to understand those."

"Baba ji," he said patiently, "I have tried everything and I know the reasons." He paused. "But the thing which irritated me the most that how can someone be so stuck in the past, in agony that he ruin his present. People don't value what they have now and never try to realize that how they can turn their circumstances otherwise. Which is the most important thing." He kept saying. "I don't know why I am expressing my frustration along. I know everything and I am even working on it to solve it, to change it."

"I can understand it." He said while getting up from the bed and sitting on the chair. "If you keep working in the right direction then everything will be fine because it always be." He assured. "But right direction is something tricky. It depends more on your self-belief than anything else."

"Hmmm . . ."

"Inder to get rid from your past depends upon if you really want to get rid from it, otherwise you just enjoy living with it." He paused. "What I mean to say is that it depends upon the past and your feelings about it."

"That's fine but you don't ruin your present because of it."

"Yes, I can understand your concern."

"Well, I think that explains why I am here and not in Amritsar and even why in Delhi." Inder said as if wants to end the topic.

He nodded.

"Ok son, you can rest here," he said after having a look on the clock, "I have to do some work and then I'll join you right here after some time."

"Baba ji, is there any S.T.D. nearby. I need to make some calls."

"Why S.T.D. we have a landline in here. Come with me."

"Thank you." He smiled.

He went with him and he guided him to the room where there was an old telephone set was placed on a table.

"You can make as many calls as you want." He smiled and went out of the room.

That room seemed like an office but there was no one around. He shut the door and dialed a number.

"Hello Soma!"

"Thank God. I have been waiting for so long."

"How are you dear?"

"I am fine but I was really worried."

"Don't worry I am at a very nice place." He smiled.

"Ok . . . . where are you exactly?" She said with bit of excitement.

"I am in a Gurduara away from the city of Ganganagar."

"Ok. Yeah you told me last night. So, you spent the night well."

"Yes I had nice sleep. And now I am enjoying the hospitality of a Baba ji who works here." He smiled.

"Nice." She felt relief. "At least you got someone to converse in Punjabi with." She chuckled.

"Yes." He smiled. "Anything new?"

"Naa . . . just some routine works and lots of internet and t.v."

"And cooking classes?"

"Yes off course they are going on."

"Ok, so Soma I'll leave from here in the evening. I'll call you from the same number before leaving."

"Ok, fine." She said. "There must be peace around."

"Very nice environment, trust me. I really liked it."

"Good. So weekend turned into nice adventure huh!"

"Yes, totally unexpected everything." There was clear joy in his tone.

"I am glad."

"I love you Soma." He felt thankful of everything.

"I love you too." She was pleased.

"Ok then, I'll call you before leaving from here and now I am going to call my mom."

"Ok bye dear. Smile always."

"Bye Soma. You too take care."

The words 'smile always' sunk deep inside of him.

"Don't worry Soma, I'll turn the things around." He said to himself.

He sat there for some time thinking about his process to regain himself. After coming out of his thoughts he dialed another number.

"Hello." Relatively weak voice addressed him.

"Hello Maa." He said with concern.

"Inder! My son." She said with excitement but weakness was still there.

"What happened?" He was worried.

"Nothing, dear," she said with more energy, "you get worried so quickly. I am fine just feeling sleepy."

"Ok . . ." Inder felt like as if there was no wait in her mind for his call. He felt like as if she was in some sort of tension. He knew her so well so he could easily know what must have happened. "Are you sure?"

"Yes dear, what can happen to me." She smiled. "You had your breakfast?"

"Yes I had it." He still was not satisfied.

"Maa don't hide anything please." He begged.

"Inder . . . there is nothing my son and why I had to hide anything from you?" She emphasized.

"Ok, how is dad?"

"He is good, not at home at the moment."

"It's good. You will have some moments of peace."

"Hmmm . . . he was saying last night that you don't call him and you are only my son and not his."

"I don't care." He said annoyingly.

"That's why I don't tell you anything." She said softly.

"No-no, I am fine. See I am smiling." He smiled.

"Are you having some money or have finished it?" She said.

"I am having enough."

"Ok." She said in rather low voice.

"Maa are you ok naa!" He begged again.

"Inder my son I am just feeling sleepy. I didn't have good sleep last night. That's it." She said after collecting some energy.

"Ok then have some rest and I'll call you in the evening."

"Ok Inder take care."

"You too Maa. Bye."

"Bye son."

He came out of the room with clear sadness mixed with frustration on his face. He went in the room of Baba ji and he was already in there, reading some book. Inder didn't cared to look at that.

"Everything fine?" He said after looking at Inder.

"Yes." Inder said while containing himself.

"Inder," he said, "normally we didn't get the environment nor company to just open up our heart but when we do get it, we should not try to control ourselves." He leaned a little forward. "We should let ourselves go."

"I know Baba ji. I have did that many times. I have few relations which understands me and support me every time."

"That's really nice and I am pleased to hear that but don't let this moment slip from your hands. This is just that type of moment." He said in a serious way.

With the efforts of Baba ji, for once Inder felt like the same when he was trying to help Atul & Santosh to deal with the issue of Roohi. It came to him that this man was saying all the right things.

"You are an experienced old man who knows things and is quite confident about it too." He smiled.

"Yes my beard is white." He said while running his one hand over his beard.

Both laughed.

"Baba ji," Inder started, "That lady has done things for that man which I think no one else can do for him. She has done everything for the family."

He kept listening without saying a word.

"But my father never completely recognized that. He never valued that. I think he never recognized her strength and never imagined that how with such dedicated & hard-working wife he could change his life." He paused. "Her indomitable will has made that structure of bricks a home. She is the reason behind all the good aspect in me. On the other hand my father had never made him able enough to fight with his own demons and demolish them. Some things in his personality have deepen their roots so awfully that even he can't do anything about them now. He has finished himself but that's not which makes me angry. The things which makes me angry is that he had enough chances to get back on his feet which he ridiculed. His end must have been totally different if he was not that fool." He kept saying clearly, with pace and emphasized on the last word.

"And you were about to put all this frustration bury inside of you." He said.

Inder said nothing in response to his words and resumed his expression. "He is a slave of his own demons. Helpless slave. Dangerously helpless." He looked at him while saying the last two words." He paused. "My mother used to say that if she was a man he had turned this broken home into a wonderland and I believe that. I have no doubt about that." He stopped for a while and even no word from Baba ji came out.

"He has come so forward with his irresponsible and self-willed behavior that now no one even have any sympathy for him. Almost everyone has helped him but his condition didn't changed. Because he didn't want to."

Even he has no solution for him about his father. He just could give him advices. But for the moment he decided to stay quiet and listen to him with as much attention as he could.

"Baba ji, the most foolish thing about my father which I feel is that he had tested everyone for his entire life about who really loves & cares about him. However he himself has never loved anyone because he was busy dealing with his own foolishness all the time. Everyone has cared for him once but he never was able to see that. So he never found a single person who really loves him." He smiled in scornful manner. "You have to love people around you but I guess that never happened in his life." He stopped for some time and complete silence surrounded the environment of the room.

"Even I have sympathy for him in my heart and that too is a warm feeling but I know I don't have love for him, anymore. Now before you say anything about forgiveness, I want to tell you that I know everything about it but I am not ready for that at the moment. I want him to live a better life and I am willing to give everything to both of my parents and if I tell you honestly, I do hope that may be if life gets a little easier, he may mend his behavior."

He kept silent for some time and then said, "It's not that I have not came across anything like this before or haven't witnessed these sort of conditions but every time I hear or see these kind of conditions of people something inside of me breaks down."

Inder said nothing in response. It felt like as if he had tasted something extremely bitter.

"If you want to make things better you have to save yourself from all these weak feelings." Baba ji said.

"Yes I know it very well and that's what I am doing from the last two months while staying in Delhi." He explained.

"Good. Just keep moving forward." He said. "Problems may arise but faith can overcome most of them."

"I know it all Baba ji. You can't even imagine with how many ways I have tried to implement all these things in my life." He smiled.

"I wish that you overcome all these things as soon as possible and live a better life." He paused. "Nothing in this world is richer than healthy mind and healthy body."

"Yes I know wonders can happen." Inder was lost somewhere.

"Rest one has to get rid from the past which brings no good."

"No one can get rid from the past." Inder interrupted.

He said nothing as words struggled to come out of mouth. Some pictures of his own past were dancing in front of him. "But you have to make them your friends." He said subconsciously while he was lost somewhere.

Inder saw him lost somewhere but hesitated to ask about it.

"You know Baba ji, things seems so simple but in actual they are not. Solutions seems so simple but in actual when you try to implement they start feeling like a mistake."

"Yes it happens but that's is when patience and self-belief comes into play." He said confidently.

Inder took a deep breath. "Nothing of all these talks comes into play when we find ourselves in a tough condition. He still tends to lose patience and get angry over things."

"No, son, you are wrong. These things helps. It's just about how well you have planted these inside your heart and mind."

Inder felt like he has injured his own believe by saying this. He himself believes that these things help and that's what he was doing in Delhi. "I can't believe I just said that." He said in shock. "You are right and even I strongly believe that."

He nodded.

The clock kept ticking but the pace of their conversation gradually decreased to zero. They were lost somewhere in their own lives. Moving back & forth like a pendulum between their past and present.

"It's 1." Baba ji said to Inder.

"Yes?" Inder said.

"Let's go it's time to serve the guests of the Gurduara." He smiled.

"Aha! *Langar*." Inder said and got up from the chair and went with him.

They went in *Langar* hall and served the people there. The free kitchen was operating before they went there. They served there for about couple of hours and then went back to their room.

"I have enjoyed it a lot." Inder said with a smile.

"Yes life here is simple, isn't it."

"And that's what I want to transform my life into." Inder said. "That is like my one of the main objectives of life." He said while sitting on the bed.

"Good luck Inder and if you really wanted to do that, then let me cautioned you that this is tough than earning money when you live societies like ours now. Things have changed drastically and the change has become the reality."

"Yes I can feel that." Inder said with his vision focused somewhere in the future.

And a small period of pleasing silence hosted both of them.

"Baba ji at what time bus leaves from Ganganagar to Delhi?"

"I need to ask it from someone. Why don't you wait here and I'll back with the information." He said.

"Ok." Inder smiled.

Time allowed and he started writing on his diary. He came back after some time.

"The bus leaves at 9 in the night, it's a private A.C. bus but the last bus from here to Ganganagar bus stand leaves around 6:45 in the evening." He said after sitting on the chair.

"Ok, thanks, Baba ji."

He nodded. "Inder you told me so much about your father but I believe that people are not like that from birth, they learn everything from the surroundings and from the kind of brought up they get." He said.

"That's believable but that was past and now we have present in our hands along with so many responsibilities and some lovely relations, so in that case what a grown man should do." Inder said with clarity and confidence.

"Yes that is but human weakness is not that easy to overcome." He paused. "All I want to say is that whenever you get able to, please get him chance and conditions so that he can change himself if he wanted to or if something left inside him."

"Yes no doubt about that. I want a harmonious and happy family. Even I'll get marry one day and then will grow my family and I can't do that with burden and regrets." Inder assured.

"No doubt that I have developed a kind of faith in you that you will change the life of yourself and of your dear ones." He said and a silent appreciation was there in the way he said it.

Inder nodded.

"Rest, don't get angry frequently and easily. Instead never get angry if you can." He paused. "When my wife was killed during riots in Punjab," he said with solidness, "I was filled with so much anger that I did things which I should never have done. And I think I am residing here to compensate for those but there is nothing which can erase those things."

Inder was not able to say anything at all. He just listened and stored those words inside of him.

They kept silent for some time. He didn't want to awake his memories and Inder was not able to handle those of his.

"What you write in this?" He asked him while pointing towards the diary.

"It is just another me. My friend, who talks to me whenever needed." He smiled.

"It's good." He smiled.

"I want to ask you something." Inder said with smaller eyes.

"Is it your turn to measure me?" He smiled.

Inder laughed. "No actually I want to ask that what if I am your son."

"Not bad." He laughed.

"No, listen. What if I am your son and one day I tell you that I want to marry a Hindu girl; what would be your reaction?"

He thought for some time and then said, "First of all in India, there is always a condition of push & pull between religions and money and we all are just victims of that harsh push & pull."

This provoked many thoughts in Inder's mind about the personality of that old man. He was not expecting this kind of answer from a man who seemed so religious. He didn't say a word and let him finish.

"Moreover we act as if one religion is a sin for another. We don't mix up well because we see other's rituals & traditions as taboo and others sees from the same stand point."

A burst of laugh came from Inder's heart spontaneously.

"So for me I would have seen the girl of your choice on the basis of her humane qualities irrelevant of her religion." He clarified.

"You have surprised me." Inder smiled.

"Surprises are natural in first few meetings." He smiled back. "But why did you ask me this?"

"Because there are many problems in my life other than I have explained you earlier."

"Ok . . ."

"I want to marry a Hindu girl and that's quite a challenge." He smiled.

"But if your love is worth fighting for then the result will be so pleasing that you can't even imagine." He assured.

"We feel the same." He smiled.

A smile was fixed on both of their faces and they enjoyed it for a while by staying silent.

"Your children?" Inder said hesitantly. He was curious about this but at the same time didn't want him to feel sad like he felt while telling about his wife.

"I have two boys." A pleasing smile stretched his lips to their capacity.

"Where are they?" Inder asked with fascination.

"One is settled in Germany and other is in New Zealand."

"What!" He was surprised. "And what are you doing here?"

"They have forced me many times to come with any one of them but I don't want to live anywhere else." He paused. "And now even they had stopped trying." He smiled.

Inder didn't feel like asking him the reason behind his stay there but there was unknown satisfaction in his heart.

"They come every year to visit me and I am extremely happy with that." He said.

"That's really nice." Inder said passionately.

"Anyways we were discussing something very interesting before this." He said.

"Yes you were saying some good things about people's attitude towards religions." Inder smiled.

"Yes, you are allowed to marry a girl of any religion if there are beautiful hearts involved." He smiled.

Inder smiled too. "You know these are the things which irritates me and sometimes I feel suffocating."

"I can understand son."

"I mean, I am already frustrated from homelessness, poverty, prostitution, politics, mass media, item numbers, ignorance, materialism, individualism, pollution to population, absurd social norms . . ."

"My goodness," he interrupted, "take a breath. How are you living then. With so much frustration?" He said.

"I said I feel suffocating. There are lot of things which are eating me other than my family conditions." Inder said. "I am frustrated with those who don't take risks and never think outside the traditional values." He paused. "We people are prisoners."

"Look Inder, there is a way to think outside the traditional values with offending anyone. And that is an art, not everyone knows it." He said while sitting in more attentive posture. "If everyone starts thinking like this then there will be chaos. You need to follow a way until you invent one which is better than the existing one."

"Yes I can imagine that but my concern is the rigidness of societies and religious institutions which don't offer any room for contemporary thinking."

"And I can understand that." He smiled. "But understanding is rare, isn't it." He said.

"So, that's all?" Inder said with complete disagreement.

"No, that is not all. That means, get ready for struggle." He said.

Inder stopped for a while to verify his statement and nodded.

"But I must say one thing, that you are more than your story." He paused. "Don't let finish yourself in all these unnecessary things."

"End is inevitable but I want to see my best before I finish myself. I want to win it all and honestly speaking I don't want to care of everything, whether it's social, political, religious or economic. Which even a blind can see that, are silly and needless." He cleared.

Both of them were left with so much to think off and with new perspectives and opinions. They kept silent for some time and let their minds charged up for more by organizing the heaps of thoughts.

"Have some rest." He said after having a peep on the clock. "It's already six."

"Time passed so quickly." Inder said while looking at his wrist watch.

At 6:30 both of them went towards the entrance of the Gurduara.

"It was really nice spending time with you." Inder said with a warm smile.

"It was nice having you too." He smiled too.

"Why don't we exchange phone numbers." Inder exclaimed.

"Write it on your diary." He said and gave him the landline number of Gurduara.

"I am not having my phone right now. But this is my number." Inder said while tearing a piece of paper from his diary. "If a woman picks it up then that will be my mother and if I pick up then that means I have returned to Amritsar." He smiled.

"Understood." He said and embraced him.

229

That was one warm hug, which cools down the nerves in the heat of 40 degrees.

Inder took one brief look around and said, "This place is perfect for listening classical and folk, don't you think that!"

"At my age every sound is music." He smiled.

Inder nodded with pleasure.

"I wanted to say one more thing to you." He said.

"Yes." Inder said curiously.

"May be you already know that but sometimes the most important thing is to see the situation from someone else's viewpoint."

"I'll keep that in mind." He said.

Inder wanted to say to him that he will visit him again but the words didn't came out of his mouth. He took farewell from him and went towards bus stop.

After reaching Ganganagar he called Somaya and his mother. He told some pieces about his experience there to Somaya and expressed his wish to visit him again.

His mother talked with him rather energetically but he still believed that she was hiding something inside her. He climbed in the bus for Delhi and for the entire way, other than the small naps, he kept thinking about many aspects of his life and wondered about the past of that pleasing old man. He was concerned about his mother too but there was not much control in his hands at that moment.

He felt like everything was moving to give his life a push forward. For the first time after so much time, he felt like things were in his favor; although he was not sure about how long it would stay like this.

CHAPTER 9

9th Weekend

He was eagerly waiting for Saturday. The alarm clock inside his mind didn't let him sleep for more than four hours. He was up around 11 o'clock and was happy about it. He quickly freshen himself up and left for that red light area.

He was contained all through the way. After entering the red light area he felt that no single pair of eyes were staring at him. His walk was different, the way he was looking around was different. After reaching near that building where Rajni resides he didn't find her. So he went straight to her room and the room was not closed. He went in but there was no one inside. He went out to look for her but soon returned to the room.

"I was told that someone went in my room." She said while standing on the door, placing one hand on her hip.

Inder paused for a while trying to figure out how to react. "How are you?" He said hesitantly.

"I am burning." She said while closing the door.

Inder didn't say anything.

"After seeing any young boy like you, my heart gets all wild." She said softly while moving slowly towards him.

"Just have a seat." Inder said while sitting on the bed.

"Yes why not." She whispered.

"Do you recognize me?" He said.

She froze for a while. "Shit! You are that 'not for that' guy." She said in a jesting tone and started laughing.

"I thought you would remember." Inder said.

"No I forget you right that day because I strongly felt that you will not come here again." She said while laying down sideways on the bed.

"Ok. That's alright."

"So, here for the talking again!"

"Even if I have to come at your place for thousands of times, the purpose will be the same." He said with a smile.

"If you don't know how to remove your pants I can do it for you."She laughed teasingly.

"But that's not the case." He smiled.

"What is the case then." She said in intimate voice.

"The case is that."

"The case is that no one listens to you out there and you come here to eat my head." She said annoyingly.

"Did I offend you in some way?" Inder was surprised with his reaction.

"No . . ." she smiled, "I just tried my tactic. I thought maybe that's the case." She said. "You give me money for not removing my clothes and that's fine for me." She laughed mockingly.

"Ok, whatever you think of me is fine by my side." He smiled.

"Hey kiddo, what if your mother finds you with me."

"If my mother would be here then I might not be here."

"But she is not here."

"Hmm . . ."

"Why, is she busy with your dad." She said in jesting tone.

He stared at her face for a while and then said, "This is not your fault."

"What fault. Nothing in this world is fault of anybody." She said.

"Nothing." He smiled.

"So, do you know how to do it?" She said while looking towards his lower body.

"But before that we must think about, 'do I need to tell you?'" He smiled.

"Then how will the conversation move on? You are here for that no!" She teased.

"There are so many other things to talk about."

"But I know nothing about anything else." She said while changing her posture from laying down to sitting.

"May be you are not in mood or some thought has prevented you to do so." Inder wanted to get straight on the point.

"No, I was born to talk about only one thing." She said it in an instant.

"Well that is not true." Inder didn't want to let her win with her pointless talks.

"Truth is only what you believe in." She said as if trying to break all the molds in which people pour their thinking to get the definition of truth.

Inder was struck hard with her words but soon after handling its effect he said, "And the believes are what you have seen in all your life. Maybe one has seen lies and lies only; cheapness & immorality." He knew he has hit the right spot.

She didn't said anything. Her eyes were not focusing properly on what was in front of her. They were lost somewhere.

Inder didn't do anything to wake her up from sleep.

"I want you to go from here and never come back." She said in normal pitch but the voice was determined.

For a moment he felt like as if something slipped from his hand. "If that helps to change anything then I'll go forever." He said patiently.

"Nothing can be changed." She said irritatingly.

"But I was talking about the future." He said in a clear voice but somewhere was nervous about her reaction.

"You can go now." She said while getting up from the bed.

Inder didn't get up from the bed but didn't even was able to say any word.

"Nothing good comes by burying the things in our hearts." He said it as a last try. "If you shout about it, it will lose its hold on you."

"I have other things to do." She said and opened the door. "And you can keep your money with you."

Inder got up from the bed and walk out of the door. There was nothing he could do to make her talk with him as he wants. At that time his own wish sounded stupid to him. He went downstairs and eventually went down from the glittering area made up of victims to make others its victims.

All of his enthusiasm, curiosity and will to understand her & share things from each other's past was ceased. He felt boredom which came along with a little sadness while going back to his p.g. He was getting well from his previous condition but still satisfaction would have come from the answers which he wanted to get his head clear. Answers were his main concern and all of them couldn't come from within.

While passing near from the S.T.D. booth he thought of calling Somaya but then suddenly he felt very tired. So he went upstairs and laid down on his bed. Santosh and Atul were still sleeping. He grabbed his diary and started writing in it. After writing for a while it seemed like his words ended and he got lost in his thoughts.He grabbed his wallet and went downstairs to call Somaya.

"Hello Soma!"

"Hi Inder. I was getting so restless to talk with you."

"Aren't you happy about it?"

"Absolutely."He exclaimed. "Why are you asking this?"

"Because that sex worker . . ."

"You went there again!"

"Yes, actually . . ."

"What do you want from her?" She said restlessly.

"Nothing, I just want to listen to her normal side, the side which is not a sex worker, you know." He emphasized on every word.

She kept silent for some time. "So what were you telling about her?"

"I actually tried to sneak in her past but she threw me out of her room."

She laughed silently. "How rude." She said.

"No, you laugh first." He said.

"No, just tell me more about it."

"Nothing more, what do you expect. She said get out, so I did as commanded." He smiled. "After all it was her room."

"I am happy. Say thanks to her from my side." She said with a fake anger. "You have tortured me so much."

"I have tortured everyone including myself and you should not expect anything positive and refreshing from a negative and broken person." He said it in one single breath.

"I didn't mean it." She said with a touch of apology in it.

"I am kidding don't get serious." He just wanted to feel good after the loss.

"Ok . . . . Do you have your breakfast?"

"Not yet. Santosh and Atul are still sleeping."

"Ok." She said. "You have done such hard work since you have got up, didn't you feel hungry?" She said it in jesting tone.

He smiled. "What to do. No one is here to take care of me."

"You were not told by anyone to go anywhere far from us."

"I went from there because my wife was torturing me." He chuckled.

"She is one of the best wives in the world." She laughed. "She is so nice instead you must have went because of yourself."

"Naaa . . . . who told you that! She is like a witch." He laughed.

"No need to come back now. Go and live with your . . . . I am going to hang up." She said annoyingly.

"Truth always hurts. Someone has told me that never speak truth but I didn't take him seriously." He laughed.

"Inder you are so bad."

"But you like me na!"

"What can I do, I don't have any other option." She smiled.

"That's fine." And there sweet little fight goes on for some more time before they got fed up from the inane talks. Then at the end they hung up the phone like they used to. Inder went upstairs, feeling extremely sleepy. Both of them were awake. They had there breakfast in afternoon. They all talked on random things for some time and Inder kept lying about his experience in Chandigarh last weekend. He never told them that he went Rajasthan and they kept saying that if he had to go to Chandigarh to roam like gypsies then he should have went with them to their home.

After some time he took permission from them to sleep for some time as he had woken up quite early. He slept with his tired mind more than he slept with his tired body.

He got up around 7 o'clock and went to call his mother. He was filled with some joy before he went into the booth. His weekends have been passing while revolving around that telephone booth. He dialed a number with fresh energy inside of him.

"Hello Maa."

"Hello Inder." She said as if she has requested something.

"How are you?" Inder said with sudden confusion.

"I am good son. How are you?" She said while gathering herself up.

"I am doing good. Got the salary." He said with a hope that it would bring some ease to her.

"That's good. Everything is balanced na! Expenses and timing of salary." She said.

"Yes Maa, things are getting settled."

"Good. I just wanted you to have good future." There still was not that energy in her voice nor that charm.

"Don't worry Maa, everything is going to be good." He said with excitement.

"Yes why not." She said while trying to hid her breaking belief.

"Maa there is something going inside of you which you are not telling me." He said confidently with a hint of anger.

"Nothing, what can be going on!" She said. "Everything is good."

"Is it about dad?"

"He is the same but that doesn't hurt now and you know that." She assured. "It has become a habit now to tolerate his behavior."

"Then it's me. You have not developed the habit to tolerate my behavior." He said without thinking of what he was about to say.

"I'll die before that." Tears came out of her heart, which she have blocked for almost couple of weeks somehow.

"Maa . . . ." He got so much worried.

She hung up the phone without saying a word. That shifted the very ground beneath his feet. Suddenly he got the feeling that everything which he felt that was going in right direction was merely an illusion. That it was a castle made out of sand.

He dialed the number again.

"Maa please talk to me." He begged.

"Yes Inder." She again successfully stopped her tears.

"Maa I am so sorry for everything." He just said it as he was not having any other words to say.

"There is nothing to feel sorry about. You have done everything for the good." She said while containing herself.

"Maa I am going to come back soon. Please don't say like this.I know I have made terrible mistake."

"No son, you have not. We have failed to give you everything you need." Her voice was still drenched with tears.

"No Maa please don't say like this. I have failed to be a good son."

"I know a kid has so many desires and you have killed all of them just because we were not able to fulfill that."

"No Maa, please stop it," he begged, "that's not true. You have been everything for me for always." And tears broke all the barriers and came out of his eyes all at once.

"Please don't cry Inder. I don't want you to feel bad. You have just started your new life."

"Maa . . . ." He yelled. "I have not started anything new but I'll start it after coming back to Amritsar. I have not came here to get settled down." He stopped but the tears didn't. "You know me. Why are you reacting like this!"

She kept crying uncontrollably.

"Maa please stop it. If anything happened to you I will die." He cried.

"Stop it Inder!" She said and all the sobbing became silent. "Stop it!"

"Why are you saying like this then." He tried to control himself.

"I know it is us because of whom you have gone so far."

"No Maa . . ." He kept saying the same.

"Inder this empty house comes to eat me every time I entered after coming back from work." She said.

"Maa soon I'll be back with you." There was an apology in his voice.

"I can't even talk to you." She was having no control over her emotions.

"I am so sorry Maa." He cried.

"It's so difficult to oppress the desire to hear your voice. You are the reason that I am still alive and working."

"Maa I feel so ashamed. Please stop it now." Tears once again occupied his whole cheeks.

"I can wait Inder but this hopelessness presses my throat." She confessed.

"Maa I am going to come back for always. I can't stay here for long, I promised you and I'll keep my promise. Please don't cry."

She stopped crying because the burden on her heart was all gone. She had cried and confessed her fear. Some of the hope was renovated with the words of Inder. "Inder just go now. I want to sit alone for some time." She said.

"No I can't." He said in a fearful voice.

"No son, I am fine. I'll not do this again." She said.

"Maa please wipe off your cheeks."

She smiled. "Yes I had." She said. "Inder I am so sorry."

"Maa please stop it now." He said because it was becoming unbearable for him.

"Go son. Have your dinner on time."

"Yes Maa you too take care."

"I'll, don't worry about me."

"I love you Maa."

"I love you too my son." She said. "I'll never come in your way." She promised herself.

"Ok Maa bye. I'll call you tomorrow."

"Yes. Bye."

He was torn so badly. He was hardly left with any energy to take his body upstairs. He requested Santosh and Atul to let him stay at p.g. Santosh wanted to ask what happened but his condition made him say only take care.

He kept lost in his past and kept thinking about what if he had never come to Delhi.He kept thinking about the alternatives. He kept blaming himself for everything. He didn't went to call Somaya. He just kept wandering inside his life to find a corner somewhere to sit and saw everything from a different perspective. But what he had to look upon were the immediate sights after an earthquake.

He knew nothing about when did he fell asleep and when he got up. While struggling with himself he reached at the doorstep of Rajni.

"Rajni . . . ." He called as if calling a family member to have dinner.

She emerged from somewhere. "What?" She said in a harsh tone after looking at him.

"Let's play with our bodies." He said and entered the room.

"You have been drinking?" She said after bending a little towards his mouth.

"I have a little." He said while taking out a half of whisky, which was not consumed much.

"I want to have sex with you." He said while closing the door.

"Kiddo," she said, "give me the money first and then we will talk."

He took his wallet out of his pocket and gave her exactly the same amount he has given her before. "I said sex and not talk."

"Yeah-yeah." She said in a jesting tone.

"Let's take your past with my past on each other and see what they produce." He said while signaling her to sit near him on the bed.

She sat near him. With the money she got, she decided to listen to everything he has to say before she get irritated from him.

"Ok, first I need some water to consume some of this." He said while pointing at the bottle of whisky.

She got up and grabbed a water bottle from a corner table in the room.

"Now a glass. That is mandatory. Don't you know that." He said.

She smiled inwardly and gave him a one from the almirah.

"Now, wow, this is good. What else someone could wish for." He said and drank a another peg.

"This is the second time in my life that I had consumed this thing." He said. "How many times you had?"

"I had more than you think of." She said while moving a little back on the bed and sitting with her back against the wall.

"It made me laugh when the first time I had it and even now it is doing the same. But I didn't drink it to laugh." He paused. "So tell her to shut up."

"You are really that drunk or just acting like one."

He kept silent for some time. "I really don't know." He paused. "I think I am doing this intentionally. I can keep quiet and sit on a corner but that's not why I have come here."

"So why did you came here?" She said with a smile.

"I am here to tell you something; a secret."

"About who?" She said while mimicking an attentive posture.

"About all of us." He said while sitting in more relaxed posture.

"Ok."

"You know what is one of the biggest problems of humans?"

"I guess so, but you tell me which one you have noticed."

"I am going to tell you the reason behind the sadness of most of us."

"Ok I am listening."

"We are sad because we are greedy."

"Hmmm." She said as if got some out of the world wisdom, which she never had heard of before.

"Because whenever we come to know that we can have more, that there is more available for us to grab, our minds program themselves automatically that they need more." He said. "That they need more of that which is available. And we stay sad until we get it; until we get more." He paused. "It is laughable, isn't it." He smiled.

She said nothing.

"We don't even realize that we had already enough than we need. We don't feel grateful for it, instead we get sad about it. That is why people are not happy and the rest of them thinks if others really want more then it must be good to have more, so they get sad too. One moment they were satisfied and the very next moment they become sad." He paused. "You know, your own mind can ruin your happiness."

She kept listening to him without saying any word.

"We waste time, we waste energy and make our lives a trouble." He paused. "That is one of the problem of my father. I think I have been its victim too."

She had joined herself with the things he was saying.

"We don't treat our ladies well. We think they are to use, just like we use washing machine or refrigerator." He said while looking at somewhere else. "We do take care of them but just like we service our A.C.s and other things." He paused. "We have not taken good care of the queen of our home; of our lives; our mother; my mother. She is one great lady; never gets tired. She never quits. She cries and then again get back to work; she falls ill and then again get back to work; she gets hurt but then again gets back to work. I don't think me and my father were so good to deserve this kind of lady."

She kept listening to him and his words were dissolving in her ears, giving her a nice feeling.

"You can take off your past's clothes too." He said.

Complete silence, for some time, filled the room or came to life again. She got lost somewhere and returned with eyes full of tears. But none of them came out of her eyes.

"You can do better than that." He said. "They don't need to stay inside."

But they dried up right then and there as if she drank back them. "I have a girl." She said.

"Is she charming?" He asked.

"More than anything else in this world." She paused. "I have to do so many things for her." She said. "I have a plan." She whispered.

"Never lose your grip from your plan." He said. "Execute it."

"Yes I have thought the same."

"Do the same."

"Yes I will."

He stayed silent for some time. "What to do with the rest of it." He said while pointing towards the whisky.

"Flush it." She whispered.

"Yeah!" He smiled. "Can I stay here for some more time."

She nodded.

They kept sitting at their positions. He was feeling extremely comfortable in that small dark room.

Thoughts were coming and going with every breath. There was weird yet soothing calm in his mind. He stayed there for some time and then went back to his p.g.

He bought couple of chewing gums to eliminate the odor of whisky because he knew that it could gave birth to many questions.

"Where were you?" Santosh asked when Inder entered the room.

"I went to make a phone call." He replied.

"That's what we thought but you were not there when I went to look for you."

"Actually I went to a cyber café."

"And which cyber café was open at this hour of Sunday."

"None of them and that's why I came back." He smiled.

"Come on man and we were waiting for you to have breakfast."

"I am really sorry guys. I will not go out at this time again." He was really ashamed of that.

"Have your breakfast." Atul said while pointing towards his tiffin.

"You had it." Inder said.

"Yes. We waited but then my Atul darling was starving. You know he always starve right after he comes out of the bathroom and he went to bathroom right after he wakes up." Santosh laughed loudly.

Inder gave a half hearted laugh but was feeling bad because of his poor excuses and lies.

"I should not do this to them." He thought. But then again couldn't get the courage to tell them about where he was. He felt like it would be very difficult for him to explain to them that why he went in that red light area and most importantly he didn't want them to make any judgment about him on its basis.

He had his meal and after some time grabbed one of his books to read.

"Hey Inder you didn't tell us about what you keep writing in your diary." Atul asked intentionally as he already knew that he will not get an answer.

"You know already, just some random thoughts, on daily life." Inder smiled.

"I always thought writing diary is a girl's thing." Santosh chuckled.

A quiet little laugh filled the room.

"But when and how did you start writing diary?" Atul said as an effort to fed his curiosity.

"I used to get so much time alone during my teenage as both my parents were working and there used to be no one else in the home." He said. "So I developed the habit of writing dairy."

"And I have done so much of loafing with my friends that I never got time alone." Santosh laughed and everyone followed.

"I just hope that whatever we are doing results in something better in future." Atul said. "Next month I'll be giving the exams of second semester."

"Best of senses for that!" Inder said.

"Wait a minute!" Santosh said before Atul could react. "I have heard, 'all the best' & 'best of luck.' What is this 'best of senses.'?"

Inder laughed. "All the best is fine but I don't believe in luck so I never say to anyone that best of luck." He smiled.

"So we have been living with a luck less guy and I thought you are just phone less." Santosh chuckled but there was a sincere question in his statement too.

Inder laughed. "I say best of senses because I believe that it is the most important thing if you want to succeed in anything you are doing. One needs hundred percent of one's self. On the other hand luck makes things unpredictable and gives us an option to put blame on if don't succeed."

"What are you?" Atul said with strangeness.

"I am just like you." Inder replied in the same manner.

Santosh was still trying to understand what he exactly meant.

"So you believe that luck is nothing." Santosh said as a try to get to the conclusion.

"Yes, because if it is exactly what people think then the importance and the role of choices and coincidences gets faint." Inder explained.

"Whatever we do is already decided and destiny take us towards our ultimate position." Atul said as a try to defend his beliefs.

"This is one of the most foolish things I have ever heard." Inder said in a little disrespectful manner with which he'd never talked with them. May be some of the whisky was still on his nerves.

Santosh and Atul were stunned with his words.

"Never seemed like these type of thoughts were living inside your brain." Santosh said with complete strangeness.

"Santosh may be I have lived in completely different conditions than yours or may be the reason can be anything else but these are my believes and I have and I will live my life with these beliefs." Inder said.

"It is, ok, to imagine, the perspective of yours, but to live by this belief seems difficult for me." Atul tried to solve the complication created by the clash of two perspectives.

"Please don't entrap yourself with this," Inder smiled, "I don't believe in luck because I don't want to depend on it. I want to depend on my efforts only & my choices." He cleared. "Moreover why you think like this?"

No one spoke for some time. Both of them were not sure if they were confused or in dilemma but whatever it was it has created some disturbance; making the heat of summer more intolerable. All of them went into an uncomfortable condition, trying to resume what each of them were doing before this.

Time passed and the fall in the temperature got compensated with the noise coming from the street. Inder went in the balcony to get out from the boundaries of that room. He was feeling little restless because he didn't talked with Somaya since yesterday's afternoon. So after some time he went downstairs to call her.

He entered in the booth and kept the door open because of the heat.

"Hello Soma." He said.

"Where were you Inder!" She was worried.

"Nothing, I was in p.g." He said. "I drink today." He said hesitantly.

"What! Why?" She said the later word after containing her reaction.

"I . . . . was devastated after talking with my mom last evening." He said in a tired tone.

"What happened?" She said with concern.

"She was just too sad. I don't know what she kept thinking all the time." He said. "Somewhere inside of me, pointed the finger at me so firmly, that I was not able to come out of that shock."

"Inder you have been the one who always talks about choices and consequences, so why you are reacting like this?" She was little annoyed now. "Why don't you think of a solution? I don't know what made you to go to bloody Rajasthan when you could come to Amritsar just for the weekend."

Inder was silent at the other end, unable to explain how stuck he has been feeling. He had always wanted to go back for once. But things were not going in the way he had imagined; they were but not anymore.

"What are you thinking now?" She said in a rebuking tone.

"I also went to that sex worker's place." Inder said but it was not the time for that.

"So, what should I do?" She said annoyingly. "What have you got from her?" She paused and tried to contain herself. "Inder, you know that we understand each other very well but I have no any idea at the moment that why are you not coming for just a weekend, when even you knew that it is needed."

"Somaya I'll come back soon for always. I can't come for the weekend now." He said in rather determined and decisive tone.

"Do whatever you want to." She declared in anger. "Stay depressed, drink, go to that prostitute and don't call me. This is what you want to do na!"

"Somaya please don't say like this." He begged. "I have came a long way and everybody has suffered in this journey but," he tried to hold himself, "it is not going to take any longer now, I promise."

"I believe you Inder." She said as if a warrior had lost all of his armor. "We all want the same but don't take any decision which affect our faith on you." She didn't want to talk about it anymore.

"Somaya, everything is going to be alright." He emphasized.

"Okay. I want to sit alone for some time."

"Yes. Bye-bye. Take care Soma."

"Bye Inder."

He came out of the booth with more pressure of worries but somewhere inside he knew that things were going to get better soon. He went in his room, grabbed his towel and went into the bathroom with the little mirror of his. He kept staring himself in that mirror but said nothing.

"You are going with us na!" Santosh said while Inder entered the room.

Inder nodded.

He wrapped that little mirror of his in some papers and put it at the bottom of his bag; beneath all the clothes and books of his.

Before going out Inder called his mother and tried his best to make her believe that everything would be alright and she must take good care of herself. He kept assuring her that he would come back soon.

For the rest of the night he never was entirely present with Santosh & Atul. Many thoughts kept consuming him and he had finished three water bottles already. He felt nothing new around him which could fed his curiosity about anything. His will to change his conditions felt dull to him for a while. But he knew in an instant that this feeling has to go. He has to stay passionate about the change he wanted to bring in his life.

Before they went back to p.g. he was filled with some kind of push to end his time in Delhi as soon as possible.

CHAPTER 10

10th Weekend

$\mathscr{E}$very single word was audible even in the noise produced by the standing fan. On the other side of that fan, was Inder's father sitting on a folding bed; in the courtyard; having his whisky in front of him along with couple of chapattis, which were losing their taste with every passing moment in front of that fan's reckless air. He was criticizing Inder's decision of going to Delhi from the moment he arrived home.

"Which airplane he is going to make in Delhi, huh! He is going to do the same thing na! What is giving him problems in Amritsar. He is staying in his own home, eating fresh meals what else he wants?" He was saying all in a single breath. "All he is going to do is to make calls, isn't it!"

His mother signaled him to stay quiet and to continue with his dinner.

"If he has no any plans to rob the company then he is not going to bring any money from there." He said scornfully. "What is the fun of going so far then?"

Inder kept quiet but he was filling with more & more rage to change everything around him.

"Why don't you give him some brain." He yelled from outside.

She kept silent and tried her best to ignore him. After getting no response he got busy with his whisky. Inder and his mother were lost somewhere in their thoughts. She was concerned about his future and he was worried about the decision he had made. There was no room for confidence in anyone and nor were the circumstances to let it grow. After having their meal she took the utensils to kitchen and started washing them, while Inder kept thinking about the consequences of his decision.

The night kept getting darker & darker so as the environment of the home. All the lights were off and the family of three was scattered in different parts of the it; trying to get a peaceful sleep.

The *neem* tree in the courtyard seemed unaffected from the condition of the family as its leaves were enjoying the breeze. It was not in its prime condition as leaves were still germinating. But it was the most fresh thing in the entire home. That tree was the actual treasure they were having in common.

"Hello." He whispered.

"Hello Inder."

"What were you doing?"

"Nothing, was just waiting for your call." She said while changing her side, as if was turned towards him.

"Do you have anything to say about my decision to go to Delhi?" He asked as if was tired.

"What happened?"

"Nothing, I just want to know if you had anything to say."

"Inder," she stopped to figure out what to say, "I have nothing else to say but why are you asking?"

"I am fed up of my dad's comments on my decision." He said. "Every night he repeats the same."

She didn't know what exactly to say. "I just want you to focus on what you want to do and why you have taken this decision." She took a deep breath. "I don't want you to waste your time."

"Hmmm . . ." He managed to say that only.

"We'll talk tomorrow Inder."

"Yes. Good night."

"Good night and take care."

In the middle of the night he went in front of the mirror and hid his arms behind his back.

"How are you feeling now?" He said to himself.

"Incomplete!"

"I don't think so. Because you have seen people with incomplete bodies but complete determination and belief on themselves and that was exactly what made them complete, isn't it!"

"So, even if you have your arms, you are still incomplete without your self-belief."

"You are understanding what I want to say na!"

"You have your damn body in perfect condition. You can do anything with it but not without allowing it by your weak mind."

"You are actually a handicap."

"So you think you can win in this condition?"

"Bloody get your head right." He rebuked himself. Frown had crystal clear existence on his forehead. He had placed both of his hands on the sides of the mirror and stared his face for a while.

The next morning perhaps not even a single bird sung about the beginning of the fresh new morning. It was Sunday but his father was about to leave the home for unknown reason.

"Do whatever you want to do," he said, "but always remember that you can get nothing more than your fate and before your time." He went out of the room. "It's already written you fool." He said while standing in the courtyard. "You can't run away from your reality." He stood there while saying this. "Not even a single leaf moves without the will of the God. You can suffer in as many ways as you want. After all it's your life." A short burst of laugh came out of him after the last words. He then, left the home but those words of him pinched Inder badly. They shackled his thoughts with their effect. They lit something inside of him with the motif to finish. He felt like drowning.

"Just take good care of yourself." His mother just said that as if was supporting the words of his father.

Those words of his mother gave oxygen to the fire which was lit by his father. He took the decision to go to Delhi as an effort to change the current circumstances but the attitude & beliefs of his parents put his effort in vain before he could do that.

He did rest of the packing, switched off his phone and put it in the almirah beneath his rest of the clothes. He took bath in no time and left for Samar's home.

"You are going to take something out of this diary." Santosh said in jesting tone.

Inder laughed. "I don't know."

"I feel pity on all these white pages, they are so fair." He smiled. "My notebooks were always neat & clean."

"Yes because he never wrote a single word on them." Atul chuckled.

"But I passed the exams every single time." Santosh added.

And a soothing laugh declared the weekend.

Inder had wrote on that diary for the whole week, whenever he got some time. It seemed like as if finally everything was getting an answer or the efforts were making his mind clearer.

"Where is your phone?" Samar asked.

"In the almirah." Inder said.

"Why what happened.?"

"I am not taking it with me." He declared.

"And why is that?" Samar tried to know the answer without losing his composure.

"I don't want to have anytime connection with anyone while staying there." He said. "It will ruin my motif of going there. I want to have some peace."

"But . . . . you know this can make conditions difficult for you." Samar was concerned.

"I just want to stay away from this noise and if there is love and faith, time will pass." He was determined.

"I don't know," he paused, "but you should not increase the distance by not talking your phone along."

"You are saying this!" Inder said. "Do they need to listen my voice to lessen the distance between us. What if there were no mobile phones."

"But we have become habitual of them now." Samar cleared.

"I am not going to take it with me." Inder said.

Samar smiled. "You know, circumstances are always stubborn and to change them we had to be more stubborn than them." He paused. "The more stubborn character wins, the more determined. But it also has its side effects. Just stay clear about what is more important at different times."

Inder said nothing for a while. "I need to call Somaya."

Samar gave him his phone.

"Hello!"

"It's me."

"Inder! Why are you calling from Samar's phone?"

"My phone is in my almirah and I'm at Samar's home."

"Why is that?" Her heart beat speed up.

"Because I am not taking it with me."

"Why!" She was about to break.

"Because I just don't want to. I am going there to stay away from all this madness but how can I if I took my phone with me."

"But Inder . . . ."

"Consider this as a last favor that you are giving me."

"We don't do favors in love." She sounded harsh.

"Then do whatever we do in love."

"This is not fair." She was hurt.

"What is not fair." He seemed careless and insensitive though he wasn't.

"The way you talking to me."

"This is the way I talk."

She was not able to say anything for some time.

"Soma."

"Inder just go." She said politely. "And I hope you come to know how we talk to each other."

"Soma please . . ."

"I couldn't come to see you off and now I couldn't even talk to you."

He kept silent.

"But for my sake please keep calling your mom from there."

"Soma please support me." He begged.

"Please don't say like this Inder. I can easily surrender myself to our love and expect everything to get better."

"This is all I want."

"Go Inder and take care of yourself."

"I love you Soma."

"I love you."

He stopped only to had his meal, other than that he didn't stopped even for few minutes. It was the second diary, since he had come to Delhi, which also was in its last pages.

The sweat drops fell on the pages every now & then. He had a piece of cloth in his left hand but every time forgets to wipe the sweat off from his forehead. No one disturbed him, not even he himself.

"You are going with us na!" Atul asked him hesitantly.

Inder look at the wall clock. "I have to go to make some calls." He got up from the bed. "We'll go." He said while grabbing his wallet.

"Hello Maa!"

"Hello Inder." She smiled, a weak one.

"How are you?" He said.

"I am doing good. How are you?"

"I am fine. I am . . . . I am good." He smiled.

"What is this excitement for!"

"No, nothing. What excitement!"

"You sounded like one." She smiled.

"I am just feeling good." He smiled.

"Good. Stay happy."

"Yes Maa, I'll but you tell me about your health."

"I am fine, what can happen to me."

"Good. Stay fit." He laughed.

"Yes monkey." She smiled.

"How's dad?"

"He is good."

"Ok." He said. "Tell me something new."

"Nothing is new. When you'll come back then there will be whole lot of them."

"Soon Maa; soon."

"It's ok, you take your time." She said in a soothing voice.

"Maa are you having proper meals?" He said.

"You are the one who is careless, I always eat on time." She smiled.

"No, I just . . ."

"You tell me something new." She interrupted.

"Nothing Maa; everything is revolving in a circle. All old, regular things."

"Ok. How is work?"

"Work is also smooth."

"Good."

"You sound sleepy."

"Yes I was feeling tired so I took a nap after I came from work." She said. "There were no any clothes to wash so I got all greedy."

Both laughed.

"Thanks for being greedy." He smiled.

"Ok Maa, you take care & rest. We are going out. I'll call you tomorrow."

"Bye Inder."

"Bye Maa."

He felt something missing from the way she talked with him but one side of him was satisfied after putting the receiver down.

He dialed an another number.

"Hello Soma!"

"Hello dear."

"How are you?"

"I am fine." She said. "You didn't go to that woman; what is her name!"

"She told me that her name is Rajni. I don't know if this is her real name." He smiled. "And no I didn't go to that area and I will not go tomorrow even."

"Hmm . . ." She said. "I asked because you didn't call in the noon."

"Yes I was writing something on my diary." He said. "I have been writing diary since I woke up."

"Ok! What are you writing in it?"

"Nothing special, just clearing my mind." He smiled. "Leave this. What have you been doing?"

"Nothing. Was waiting for your call. Sometimes was feeling angry and sometimes helpless and then telling myself to have patience and hope that you are all right."

He didn't say anything.

"For the first time I was feeling like he can go to that lady but can't call me on time."

"Please don't think like this Soma."

"Don't worry it's just a little frustration." She smiled.

"I am not going anywhere after this." He chuckled.

"You better not!" She cautioned.

"My goodness! At least say it with some love." He said in jesting tone.

She smiled a tired one. "Inder come back now." She sounded exhausted.

"Soon, pretty soon."

"Ok." She said as if didn't believe on what he just said. May be one side of his mind has accepted that he will not come back before long.

"Soma I'll be going out with them after some time."

"Ok Inder. Take care."

"You too. See you!" He said with energy.

"Bye. See you." She smiled.

"Tata."

"Ok then," he got up from the chair and hugged Samar, "see you."

"Take care." Samar said.

He left Samar's home and went with loads of things to think about. He just knew one thing that he had to go away from all this disturbance to get close to something helpful. Everything was done and there was no looking back. He has to move forward or he could continue with the existing routine. There were too many things which were eating him from inside and he could stop them by changing the conditions only. There were too many worries and the hope for solution and faith on the fact that things will get better were getting faint with every passing day. He has felt like everything good in his life are slipping away. He can't just sit & watch them go just because of the anxiety of the consequences his decision would bring.

"It has to be done." He assured himself.

He reached home. Sat for some time with his mother. They had little chatter about the things which a mother would say, before sending her son away. He left home a little before he actually had to; with the thought that waiting at bus stand would let him concentrate more on his path.

"Mr. Smith, get ready." Santosh said to Inder.

Inder nodded and wrapped-up his ongoing work of writing.

Sunday morning was not much different than previous days. He woke up earlier than anyone else and kept writing on his diary. And this went on for many hours, even after Santosh and Atul woke up and had their breakfast. He was very hungry but he didn't stop. He didn't felt like having his breakfast. As if he already was having his meal; the more important one.

The evening was amazingly similar to the previous one. He went downstairs to make calls at almost the same time; talked for the same duration and talked about the same things. As if it was programmed. In the night while wandering with them in a mall, he seemed to enjoy every single moment. But the happiness was coming from the satisfaction of something else. And certainly it was not the mall.

"I am anything but weak. There is no place for pity in my life. No one has to feel pity for me. I am doing good and I am richest of all. I am going to change it all forever; will not leave a single trace of this life. I'll prove. Inder, you will prove." He assured himself with his palms closed tightly before dialing the number.

"I have reached Delhi . . . ." He roared.

CHAPTER 11

11ᵗʰ Weekend

"*I* have decided Soma. We'll not meet from now on." He said while doing its best to contain himself.

"Please Inder don't say like this." She begged.

"I need time you know that." He felt helpless.

"Inder I am not doing this on my own will. They are forcing me to meet that guy. They are forcing me to get married." She was annoyed. "I am doing my best. I have not come here to hear this."

"I will ruin your life. I have already ruined it, so you should save the rest of it." He said firmly.

She kept silent for some time. "Why are you a Sikh, can't you be a Hindu."

"They are not going to accept it either with a penniless Hindu."

"So get rich and after that change your religion." She said restlessly.

"No problem but tell me how to do it overnight." He said with frustration.

"Is this the harmony in both of us about which we use to talk about." She said rudely.

He kept silent.

"Please speak." She said in the same manner.

"Soma, there is no other way. You have to prevent them to think about your marriage or just make them to postpone for some time." He started patiently but said the later part restlessly.

"This is so difficult." She cried.

"We have chosen this isn't it." He tried to divert her mind from blaming the conditions to concentrate on solution.

"Inder I am stuck badly." She emphasized.

"We are stuck." He said. "But if our motive is same then we should talk about solution."

She kept silent for some time. She was feeling suffocating. She was feeling as if something was trying to crush her; to finish her very existence.

"I love you." She said cringingly. "My emotion towards you are true. I want to live with you, what's bad in that." She got irritated at the end.

"Truth is bullshit and try to live with freedom is immaturity." He declared.

"Let's go home. I'll handle it." She said impatiently.

"I need some time Soma and I am sorry for my recent behavior." He said while holding her hand and signaled her to sit down.

"It's ok Inder. We both are scared. Let's go I don't want to sit here anymore."

He left her hand & got up from the bench. With the feel of defeat on their tongues they both went out of the park to blame the conditions separately.

Inder was writing from the moment he woke on Saturday morning. That was what he did for the whole week and a week before. There were always many things running in his mind but this week it felt like everything was just coming out as if there time was complete inside his head.

He used to get up from his bed, walked around in the room & occasionally drinks a glass of water and then gets back to writing. He didn't go anywhere that morning, not even downstairs to call Somaya.

Nothing else was important for him at that time.

"Mr. Smith *ji* . . . ." Santosh said loudly. "What are you burying in it?"

"It must be something very large." Atul said while laughing.

"It is not less than an African elephant." Inder smiled.

"My goodness!" Santosh said in a way which made everyone laughed.

The entire environment of the room was changed so Inder put his diary aside to have his breakfast.

"What are you writing?" Atul asked. "You have to tell us." He smiled.

"This is an account of my life. Nothing else." Inder said.

"I have seen this first time in my life." Atul said. "Someone writes in his diary with so much passion and energy."

"I am getting my answers." Inder didn't know what else to say to him.

"Such lengthy answers!" He smiled.

Both laughed.

"Why are you laughing?" Santosh said with smaller eyes while entering the room. "Was it about me?" He said. "I don't trust you Atul."

And a period of laugh started again.

"Yes I was telling him about your crush during school time." Atul teased.

"Oh man! She was bomb." He eyes were somewhere else but the position of hands was funny.

"Give some respect to your crush man!" Atul laughed.

"Why didn't you tell her?" Inder said.

"Who told you that I didn't proposed." Santosh laughed.

"Yes she complained to the teacher and teacher complained to principle and principle told his dad and his dad told his mother and his mother told him and he replied that he already knew." Atul said in a single breath and everyone laughed loudly. "But he didn't get beat up from anyone. Lucky bastard and I waited for that moment for so long, so eagerly."

"Someone has told the truth that your friends are your greatest enemies." Santosh said in a jesting tone while pointing towards Atul.

Everyone enjoyed a good little laugh.

"But now Santosh thinks that he can never have a girlfriend." Atul teased.

"I am compelled to think like this." Santosh said in pitiful voice. "I have stood unsuccessful at school, college and now at work too."

"Don't worry keep on trying." Inder laughed. "As this is the formula to succeed."

"Yes, I have to do more flirt." Santosh said in a determined tone.

Both of them laughed.

"Hey leave your boring tragedy and let's watch a movie on your laptop." Atul said.

"Don't worry Atul, one day you'll be jealous man." Santosh said. "And at that time don't come to me for tips." He laughed.

"Ok-ok I'll not. Now let's watch a movie." Atul said.

"If you have time diary-man." Santosh said to Inder.

"Yes we can watch that." Inder smiled while closing his diary.

"Hello Soma."

"Inder now-a-days you make me wait for so long." She said right after she picked up the phone.

"Wait-wait." He said excitingly. "I was doing some work since morning and then we all watched a movie on Santosh's laptop."

"What work! And movie! Movie was more important na!" She was trying to complain but there was no energy in her words.

"I'll tell you tomorrow morning about the work and no, movie is not important than you but they both wanted to, so didn't said no."

"Inder . . . ."

"Yes . . . ." He said in the same manner.

"I was waiting . . . ."

"I am sorry Soma. I'll call you tomorrow morning before anything else." He smiled.

"Okay . . ." She said as if she was exhausted.

"Get some energy." He smiled. "Have some energy drink." He teased.

"You are a monkey and that is proved." She said in the same manner. "Say that you are a monkey."

"Yes I am a monkey." He said just like her.

Both smiled.

"Come here." She said.

"I am right next to you." He smiled.

"Let's talk." She whispered.

. . . .

After talking with her; with the same energy, he dialed the number of his mother.

"Hello!" He said.

"Hello Inder." His father responded.

"Dad!" He paused. "How are you?"

"I am fine. How is your work?"

"Everything is fine." He said restlessly. "Where is mom?"

"She has gone to the tailor." He replied.

"Ok."

"Inder how are you?"

"I am fine. Everything is good." He said hurriedly.

"You never call me." There were no signs of complaint.

"I always come to know about you from mother." He said.

"In the same way you could have come to know about your mother from me." The words seemed like a complaint but the tone pointed towards plead.

"I'll call you from now on." He said hesitantly.

"Inder . . . ." He tried to say something while trying to gather his nerves.

"Yes dad." Inder said carelessly.

"I know you went there because of me." He stopped to get his reaction.

"Dad I don't want to talk about that." He said.

"Listen to me." He begged.

Inder kept silent.

"This decision of yours is not easy for us." He said the last word hesitantly.

"Dad I know everything well." He declared.

"But I want to say something." He took a deep breath.

"Yes."

"I am sorry." He said in a relatively low voice.

Inder got hostile for a moment but then controlled himself immediately. "It's ok, I know what I have to do and how." He said harshly.

"I know." He said to stop the topic from going further. "I just hope to see you soon."

"Don't worry. I'll there at the right time."

"Take care."

"Yes. And say this to mom too, from my side." He emphasized.

He put the receiver down and went out of the booth. He was sweating badly and decided to take a bath to wipe off his anger along with sweat.

He started writing on his diary till everyone got ready to do what weekends were meant to do in cities.

"Friends," Santosh said while standing along with Inder and Atul in a Mall, "the best of Malls or anything amusing in Delhi is nothing if we don't get to see these type of sights." He paused. "Isn't it." He said while looking at a group of girls.

Everyone laughed.

"It's not your fault." Inder said. "It's our age and moreover we are pretty much under influence of media."

"Man! You always have these type of boring things to say at extremely right times." Santosh said in jesting tone.

"Extremely right times!" Inder laughed and Atul followed.

"Come on man! We just get couple of days in a week." He said with little frustration.

Both of them kept silent for some time.

"You will get bore from these type of sights if you get to watch them daily." Inder said.

"No, he is frustrated more from call center and less from working days." Atul said as he knew him better.

"Naa . . . it's ok." Santosh said.

"You'll get the right answer for yourself; trust me." Inder said in a confident way.

"You get it for yourself!" Santosh said after a while.

"I am very close to that." Inder smiled.

"Okay let's do rest of the talking in café." Atul interrupted.

Night passed with eyes on the path which Inder covered till now. Everyone was struggling to fall asleep in the heat omitting walls of their room. They were trying to calm their minds in order to fight effectively with the heat. But neither their mind was listening to them nor summer was having any mercy for them.

The next morning seemed like emerged from somewhere; came instantly. Inder went to bathroom immediately after waking up as if had waited for the morning all night long. After taking bath he started writing on his diary. After some time he closed it and went downstairs to call Somaya with a certain vivid happiness on his face.

"Good morning dear." He said.

"Now that's like a good boy." She smiled.

"Ok I have a news for you." He said excitingly.

"You are coming back!"

"No . . . . not now." He still was quite excited.

"What then." She said in a dull way.

"I've written a novel." He was trying hard to contain his joy.

"What!" She said with extreme surprise.

"I've written a novel."

"What!"

"I am not going to repeat it again." He laughed.

"Are you," she tried to contain herself, "seriously. What. I can't believe. I mean how, when. You never told me about this."

"I expected you to be surprised but not like this." He smiled.

"Inder you are not making fool out of me?"

"No Soma, I want to be a writer. I want to write for my whole life."

She was astonished but couldn't say any word.

"I was writing diary for quiet a time and even I don't know exactly when my random thoughts on diary started converting into a novel."

"I still can't believe." She said.

"Soma, I started writing it when I was in Amritsar but most of the part I wrote in Delhi."

"Inder, really! This feels nice."

"Yes dear, it really feels nice." He smiled.

"Inder how do you do it?"

"You are just surprised that's why you are asking stupid questions." He chuckled.

She giggled.

"Inder this can take us in whole new direction." She certainly was happy.

"I know." He smiled.

"Is this promising now?" She said.

"No, writing books is not promising."

"What?" She was shocked.

"Wait Soma." He smiled. "My dedication towards it is promising."

She smiled. "This was very surprising."

"I can see that." He chuckled.

"But I need to see it as soon as possible."

"Yes, you don't have to wait long for that."

"Please come before my birthday." She requested.

"That still is a month away and don't worry I'll be back till then."

"These words are soothing." She smiled.

"I know. Ok now let me go and I'll call you in the evening."

"Ok bye Inder."

"Bye Soma, take care."

He went out of the booth and headed towards Rajni's place. Everything on the way to her was same except his attitude towards them. Nothing which he criticized and disapproved before was now acceptable for him. He just rose above than himself. He was more free now. He was more determined and more focused. When he reached in front of that building where she resides, he found her on the balcony above. They exchanged smiles and he went inside that building.

"I am here for very short time." He said while entering in her room.

"What is it?" She said while closing the door.

"Sit." He said while sitting on the bed.

"Yes." She said.

"Love is extremely powerful." He said in amazement.

She smiled.

"No, seriously. Listen to every word of mine." He paused. "Learn about love from the relation with your daughter. It is very deep and it has ultimate powers."

"Ok . . . I really love her very much."

"Yes I know but try to open yourself to new things which your relation with your daughter presents in the path of your life."

"Ok . . . . I am not understanding it completely."

"Ok." He paused. "Just remember that love has all the answers. So whenever you feel stuck, focus on your love for your daughter."

"Ok." She managed to say only one word.

He kept silent for some time. "Ok, I'll leave now. And," he paused, "take good care of your daughter and of yourself."

She nodded; trying hard to understand his emotion towards her and connecting this with the words he left, in her mind & at the doorstep of her heart.

He left from there and headed back to his p.g.

The rest of the day for him was filled with energy, joy and belief on himself. He enjoyed his time with Santosh and Atul. He talked to his mother for just one time after he took his breakfast with both of them. She sounded sleepy and he was fine with it. He didn't talked with her for long but felt an intense emotion to saw her face & to hug her. The amount of satisfaction on his newest accomplishment was overwhelming and he, in the evening isolated himself from rest of the world to concentrate on his recent future.

While going out with Santosh and Atul he called Somaya for just couple of minutes to express his love for her.

That time, life was taking a turn. He was eager to see what lies on the other side of it. Future was still not predictable but the only certain thing, which was his will, filled him with enthusiasm & energy, which made him run, run fast & with intensity, towards something beautiful and different.

CHAPTER 12

12th Weekend

"No one leaves Delhi." Santosh said with a smile.

"Take my name on top of the list." Inder replied while packing his bag.

"Will you come back to rejoin?" Atul said with a little hesitation.

"Do you really feel like!" Santosh said before Inder could.

Everyone laughed.

"It has been a nice time staying here with you." Inder smiled. "And I know I don't get mixed up so well and for some I am little weird but you have given me extreme comfort."

"O my God! I want to cry." Santosh was up with his acting.

Everyone laughed.

"No I really want to thank you for all the things." Inder said it again.

"It was nice having you." Atul said.

Inder went forward and hugged him. A tear danced in each of his eyes but he soon dissolved them in his smile. Santosh lifted him up while hugging him.

"What about the salary of this month." Atul asked as if suddenly came to his mind.

"What are you talking about." Santosh said. "Who is going to give that. He has not given any prior notice. Sometimes you talk like a kid."

They again had a good laugh.

"I don't need that Atul." Inder said.

"Why would you." Santosh said in jesting tone. "Going back after so much time to your Somaya, who the hell needed the money."

Inder laughed.

"Farewell my friend." Harf said while entering the room and hugged him.

Right after him Stephan came.

"Why are you coming in E.M.I." Santosh said. "Come together no!"

And a loud laugh filled the room with warm energy.

"Have you told them that you are coming?" Santosh said.

"No," Inder smiled like a kid, "will go straight to them."

After receiving nice warm smiles from all of them Inder took a brief look of the room. He then picked his bag and went out of the room. They all went with him downstairs to see him off. Santosh and Atul went with him to the main road. While passing near the booth, he waved it silently. They rented an auto for him and last warm hugs were presented to him by Delhi.

"I call you guys tomorrow." Inder said while sitting in the auto.

"Yeah sure. Mobile less fellow." Santosh said.

And he left from there with a loud laugh.

He knew Somaya must be waiting for his call but he didn't do it.

While sitting in bus, with his bag, going back to his home, he felt like as if dark & dense clouds have occupied the entire sky of thirsty barren land. His entire body was filled with the feeling that now was the end of one damn period of struggle. He was happy, excited and was having kid like feeling about the surprise he was about to give to Somaya and his parents. He has spent three months of no contact between his little social circle; neither with friends nor with cousins. He was completely different from the person who came to Delhi three months ago. He has suffered in many ways to get back the lost shine of his persona. Thoughts were at rest and lovely feelings were at peak. Problems were not erased but with the transformation of his, they were going to get a solution. He was having that strength now, that confidence on himself and that hope from himself which was much needed for his desires.

He didn't get restless even because of excitement. He enjoyed the every single passing moment as if the bus was going back in time; otherwise time has always seemed to running away from him. He enjoyed the every bit of that journey. Journey whose last stop was the laps of happiness, water for thirsty eyes and warmth for desperate heart.

Things were moving with time to get him home and he felt thankful of every living and non-living thing for that. He has covered a lot of distance from the time he came to Delhi and this distance from Delhi to Amritsar was nothing in front of that.

After the bus entered Punjab the entire condition of his heart and mind changed. The excitement rose, the happiness jumped inside his entire body and a soothing feeling that he is not going to hurt any of them again gave him precious satisfaction. Though he was not aware of the future but he was knowing completely in his heart that how he would react to conditions from now on and what his choices will reflect.

Finally the bus entered the city of Amritsar and the smell of it; he could never forget that for his entire life. Every building on the sides of the road seemed like welcoming him. Every tree waved at him. He felt like even the bus was excited to reach there; the ultimate destination of both of them.

He looked for a S.T.D. right after he got out of the bus. He wanted to talk to Somaya but he wanted to visit his home without letting them know. He went out of the bus stand to look for it. After wandering for some time he found one. He grabbed the receiver and his fingers danced on the dialed pad.

"Hello?" She said with strangeness.

"What hello?" He could not control his smile.

She looked again at the screen of her mobile phone to confirm that it was Amritsar dialing code. "Hello!" She said again.

"What hello!" He laughed.

She started crying and there was no control over it.

He didn't said a word and let her, until tears came in his eyes too.

"The wait is over Soma." He said while wiping the tears off before they made his cheeks their swimming pool.

She still was crying and was not able to say a word.

"You know, whenever I have called you from Delhi, from that booth, some part of me had always stayed behind in the booth." He paused. "I never came out complete once I entered it. But today I am even more than I am. I will walk away from this phone and nothing will stay back." He said.

She stopped sobbing now.

"Will you say my name now?" He said.

She started crying again.

"I should go back." He teased.

"Freeze right there goddam it." She said hurriedly.

"That's more like it." He smiled.

Tears stopped coming from her eyes. "Can't you tell before leaving from there."

"Then how one can give surprise by telling prior." He laughed.

"Wait," she said as if something came to her mind, "you are back for?"

"Yes I am not going back." He smiled.

She didn't say anything for some time. She took a deep breath closed her eyes and said something inwardly.

"Soma?" He said.

"You have almost killed me Inder."

"I love you so much Soma!" He said irrespective of what she said.

"I love you too Inder!" She said pleasingly.

"Ok, listen, I haven't told at home that I am coming. I am going there after this call and then I'll call you from my phone."

"Ok Inder. Will I get a chance to see you today?" She said.

"Soma it's late but yes." He smiled.

"Ok!" She was extremely pleased.

"See you!"

"See you tata."

"Bye Soma."

He took his bag and started moving for his home. Sat in an auto and the face of her mother stayed in front of his eyes for the entire way.

After reaching at the last turn to his home he stopped after watching his uncle and aunt coming out of his home. He wanted to see his mother only at that moment. After they went he knocked at the door. His father opened it. He couldn't believe what he just saw.

"Inder!" He said with a broad smile.

He smiled and hugged him for a moment.

He went right in her mother's room. She was laying on the bed.

"What happened?" He asked his father after realizing that she was not well.

"She was not well from three weeks."

"And you didn't tell me." He said annoyingly.

"His father signaled him to lower down his voice. "She has slept just an hour ago after having the medicine. It's typhoid."

He was so frustrated from himself. It felt like everything shattered once again. He was so ashamed once again for his decision. He remembered how his father was feeling sorry couple of weeks ago and he should have understand it then. He went back in his room and locked it. He sat on the floor and thought of holding her feet and feel sorry for everything he has done to her.

"Do she need my apology." He said to himself. "No, circumstances can't make me feel the way they want to. They will be how I wanted them to be. They will not decide my future. I'll decide it." He closed his palms tightly. "No. Not anymore. If Inder you have caused this to her then you should make her well. She don't need my apology, I know what she wanted from her son. I am the writer of my own destiny. Nothing is written you dumb, nothing is written." He said as if rebuking himself. "Stand up from here and write it. Yes I'll write it. I am the writer and this is what I do." He paused. "Nothing is ever written before you yourself write it. You listened or not! Nothing is ever written." He got up. "Prove it!"

He went out of his room and went near her. He kissed her forehead. He kissed her again and again until she opened her eyes. His father also went near her.

"Inder has come!" His father said while standing behind Inder.

She looked at him and closed her eyes again.

"Give him some water." She said in a weak voice.

"No I don't need it." Inder said while constantly looking at her.

"Maa I have come for always." He said softly near her ear.

She put her hand on his face.

"I love you Maa."

"I love you too Inder." She whispered and smiled while looking at him.

"I am not thirsty." He whispered in her ear. "I am hungry. I haven't eaten tasty food for three months. I am hungry since I have left from here." He stopped to look at her face.

"What do you want to eat?" She asked.

"I want to eat whatever you cook with your hands. I will wait for tomorrow morning."

"Eat something your father will cook for you." She said.

"I am going to wait for tomorrow morning and you better get up till then."

"I'll make everything for you." She smiled.

"And I'll never go anywhere for that long." He begged.

"Just take your phone along." She smiled.

He chuckled. "Ok do rest now. And tomorrow morning get ready to cook for me." He said energetically.

She nodded.

He laid down with her for some time till she fell asleep again.

"I am going out for some time." He said to his father while taking his mobile phone and went towards the main door before he could say anything.

He kept walking and each stride of his walk reflected determination and belief to change his circumstances. There was energy in his walk.

He called Somaya after reaching near her home.

"Hello!" She whispered.

"Can you come on terrace?" He said.

"Yes give me five minutes. I'll call you again."

"Ok."

He waited on the other side of the street, a little left of her home.

She came on the terrace after some time. He looked at her while she was still looking here & there. He dialed her number from his phone.

"I got you!" She said.

"You are looking so lovely." He said and closed his eyes.

"And you have become more skinny than before." She smiled. "We need to work on you now."

"Yeah . . ." He said effortlessly.

"Hey! How was your mom's reaction. She must be so happy." She said.

"She even smiled with difficulty." Sadness was conveyed.

"What happened! Is she not well?" She said.

"She is suffering from typhoid. And that's all because of me."

"Inder don't criticize yourself."

"And I will make it right. I'll make everything right." He said with rigid confidence.

"Hmm . . ." she paused, "Everything will be alright now." She said.

"Yes Soma it has to be no matter of what." He said in the same manner.

"My novelist!" She smiled.

He chuckled. "Yes my dear."

"I am glad."

"I am glad too." He said. "While I was coming here today, I thought if we must haven't survived the gap if we had not met at Chandigarh."

"Yes that was so important. I was . . ."

"It's ok." He said.

"You sounded a little different Inder."

"Do you like that?"

"Yes I do. We have suffered."

"Yes." He said. "After all there is nothing free."

"Hmm . . . . but the prices are so painful." She laughed.

"Yes they are."

"I should go now."

"Yes, see you tomorrow."

"Yes I will meet you tomorrow at any cost."

Smiles were exchanged. They cut the phone and she went inside. He turned to go back to his home and kept looking at the place where she was standing, after every few steps; it never went out of his sight.

. . . .